MW00940207

ESCAPE TO THE WEST
BOOK FOUR

An
UNEXPECTED
Groom

NERYS LEIGH

Prologue

January, 1870

"Door's open!" Jesse yelled at the sound of the knock, placing the lid back onto the saucepan.

"I know."

He jumped at the voice right behind him and looked round to see Adam lounging against the doorframe. "Why do you even bother knocking?"

"Common courtesy." He pushed away from the door and walked into the kitchen, reaching for the saucepan lid. "Chilli?"

Jesse batted his hand away. "Leave it, it's not ready yet."

"Smells good."

"I know."

"Want some company for supper?"

"That depends. Whose?"

"Ahaha. A letter came in for you." He pulled an envelope from his pocket and held it out. "From Boston."

Despite the delicious smell of beef and spices pervading the room, Jesse's mouth went dry. "Leave it on the table. I'll open it later."

Adam sat on one of the dining chairs. "So you can mope on your own?"

"I'm not going to mope. For all you know, she might be perfectly okay with it. She might think it makes me brave and even more loveable. Some women are like that, you know. They like to look after their men. Felicity might be one of those. It might make her even more eager to marry me." He couldn't help wondering which of them he was trying to convince.

Adam used one finger to push the letter across the table towards him. "Then why don't you open it now?"

Because, deep down, Jesse knew what was in it. The same thing that had been in all the others.

He sighed. "Fine, I'll open it now."

Picking up the envelope, he slid a finger under the flap and pulled out the single sheet of paper inside.

For a few seconds he didn't move, staring at it in silence.

"I can do it if you like," Adam said gently.

Jesse swallowed and shook his head. "It's just a letter. I can read a letter."

With a quick breath in and out, he unfolded the paper.

Dear Jesse,

Thank you for your letter.

I'm very sorry to hear about your condition and I do appreciate you being honest with me. In return, I feel I should be honest with you. I don't feel I would be able to provide you with the care you require and I don't think I would be a good wife for you.

I wish you every success in the future and hope you are able to find a wife more suited to your needs.

Yours faithfully,

Felicity

Tossing the letter onto the table, he closed his eyes. It was exactly what he'd been expecting, but it still hurt. Every time it happened, it hurt.

There was a rustle of paper as Adam picked up the letter. "The *care* you require? More suited to your *needs*? You explained, didn't you?"

Despite all his best efforts, a trace of bitterness still crept into Jesse's voice. "What do you think?"

"I think... I think you should look at this as a good thing." His voice took on an overly cheery quality. "You don't want a woman who clearly needs help tying her own shoelaces."

Jesse snorted a laugh and opened his eyes.

Adam stuffed the letter back into its envelope, squashed it into a ball, and launched it at the wastepaper basket just visible beside Jesse's desk in the parlour across the hall. It hit the doorframe and landed back in the kitchen.

"How many is that now?" He rose to fetch the crumpled ball and brought it back to the table. "What is wrong with these women? Can you imagine how many old, ugly, wrinkled men advertise for brides? You'd think they'd jump at the chance to marry someone young with a good job." He threw the paper again. This time it made it through the door, hit the desk and bounced onto the parlour floor.

"Eleven. And they do jump." Jesse held out his hand when Adam retrieved the makeshift ball for a second time. "I've had lots of responses. I'm corresponding with six different women other than Felicity right now. They're always enthused at the prospect of being an accountant's wife in an up and coming town in the west." He took aim and tossed the paper. It sailed through the air in a high arc and dropped into the basket. "Until I tell them."

Adam gaped at him. "*Six*?"

"On paper I'm irresistible," he said, shrugging.

Adam stood to fetch the paper ball from the basket. "You manage to hide your obnoxious personality then?"

Jesse fixed him with a withering stare. "Funny."

He retook his seat at the table, took careful aim, and threw. The scrunched up paper hit the edge of the desk and

3

dropped into the basket and he grinned. "You need to actually meet a girl. If they saw you in person, got to know you, they'd realise that what they see as a big drawback really isn't. Plus, I suppose *some* might think you were fairly acceptable looking. In a low light."

An idea lit up in the back of Jesse's mind. "That's brilliant! They need to meet me first."

"That's what I just said. But unless you go to them, I don't see how..."

"She could come to me."

Adam's brow furrowed. "What?"

"When I find a woman I'm sure I'd want to spend the rest of my life with, she could come to me. That's what mail order brides do anyway, for everyone else. This wouldn't be any different."

"Yeah, but the whole problem is you can't *get* any of them to come because once you tell them about your..."

"I won't tell her."

Adam was silent for a full five seconds. "That is a really, truly bad idea."

"It's a genius idea!" He sat forward, his plan taking shape. "I ask her to marry me then once she's here I can explain and ask her to give me a chance, say two weeks or so. She can stay at the hotel, or wait, maybe not the hotel, I don't think I can afford that on top of the train ticket. But I'm sure Pastor and Mrs Jones wouldn't mind her staying with them. Then I work my charm and, just like that," he snapped his fingers, "I have a wife!"

"What if she wants to leave straight away?" Adam said, sitting back. "Because you've just, you know, lied to her and got her here under false pretences."

"I won't be lying, I just won't be telling the whole truth. You think any of those old, wrinkly men tell their prospective brides about their missing teeth and the hairs sprouting from

4

their ears? And once she gets here she'll be more inclined to stay, thanks to my acceptable looks."

"In a low light."

Another inspired idea came to him. "Hey, you should take out an advertisement for a bride too."

Adam's eyes opened wide. "*Me*? I... I'm not sure I could... I mean..."

Jesse sighed. "Adam, I know you're lonely, and don't say you're not because you haven't been able to hide anything from me your entire life. You need someone, just as much as I do."

His friend was silent for a few seconds, staring at the tabletop. "I don't know if I could do that. Why would any woman come all the way across the country for me?"

"They come for all kinds of reasons. You've met some of them. What about David? That's how he found Elaine."

Adam cringed. "Elaine's a bit... you know."

"Yes, I know, but have you ever seen David happier? I'm telling you, it's the only way. How long have we been friends?"

"All our lives."

"And how often have I steered you wrong?"

"Frequently."

He frowned at the speed of Adam's answer. "Name one time."

"The time you said that pond couldn't possibly contain any leeches because the water was green."

"I was eight!"

"And I was stupid enough to think you being a year older than me made you smarter. And then there was the time when you said that bull looked friendly. And when you were convinced that bees' nest was empty. And when..."

"Okay, you've made your point. But *my* point is..." He paused, trying to recall what his point had been. "My point is

5

I'm right on this. It's been years since Daisy. You need a woman."

Adam took in a long breath and let it out slowly. "Okay, I'll think about it."

It was as good as a promise. Once Jesse got Adam to think about something, he could always get him to do it. He just needed that one tiny initial chink in his friend's armour.

He sat back and smiled. "This is going to work, you'll see. And I think I may have an idea of the woman. She's from New York and her name's Louisa. We've only exchanged a couple of letters, but she's real sweet and funny and smart. Also, she sent me a photograph and she's stunning."

Adam rolled his eyes. "You are so superficial."

"Please, like when faced with a choice between homely and pretty you wouldn't go for the pretty one."

Adam made an unsuccessful attempt to look pious. "I'd want the woman God would choose for me."

"So do I, but that doesn't mean I don't want her to be pretty." Jesse laced his fingers behind his head and stared up at the ceiling, his mind conjuring up an image of shining dark hair, almond-shaped eyes, full lips, and a tall, slender figure. "And Louisa is very, very pretty."

Chapter 1

"Can you see them?"

Lizzy bounced in excitement on the seat beside Louisa as she spoke. Louisa didn't know whether to be amused or embarrassed.

As the train slowed into the station she stared in confusion at the place that would be her new home. How could this be the growing railroad town of Green Hill Creek? There wasn't even a proper platform, just dusty, packed earth.

She glanced down at her dark green travel dress. Perhaps she should have worn something more the colour of... dirt.

In front of them, Jo hooked her elbow over the back of her seat in a most unladylike fashion. "There are so many people, how do we know..."

Lizzy leaped to her feet. "Over there! That must be them!"

Louisa grabbed her hand and tugged her back down, glancing around the carriage to see if anyone had noticed.

"Oohhhh, they're all so handsome," her exuberant friend breathed. "I can't even decide which I want to be mine."

"Calm down, Lizzy," Jo replied. "They're only men."

Hardly listening to their conversation, Louisa peered through the grime-covered window at the little group of six men and one woman gathered on what she would only loosely refer to as a platform because she could think of no suitable alternative word for it. Two of the men were too old to be among the grooms waiting for the five mail order brides arriving on the train from New York, so that left only four, none of whom fit the description Jesse had given her in his letters.

"I don't think I can see Jesse," she said, leaning forward against Lizzy to get a better look as if that would magically make him appear.

"He said he has light brown hair, didn't you say?" Lizzy said, her gaze following Louisa's to the cluster of apprehensive looking young men.

"That's right, but I don't see light brown hair. I see three with dark hair and one blond who must be your Richard. Then there are two older men, but neither of them can be him." Her worry that Jesse would be in some way disappointed in her was superseded by fear that he hadn't turned up at all. "What if Jesse's not here? What if he's changed his mind?"

What would she do then?

Jo muttered something that Louisa didn't catch, distracted as she was by the prospect of being abandoned in a town she didn't know with no way to get home.

"He absolutely wouldn't," Lizzy said, wrapping her arm around Louisa's shoulders. "He must be hidden behind the others or maybe he's been delayed or something. He'll be here, I know it. No man in possession of all his faculties would pass up the chance to marry you. You're one of the nicest people I know, and so pretty. Isn't that right, Jo?"

Despite her anxiousness, Louisa smiled. Lizzy's constant enthusiasm might sometimes be a little embarrassing, but she was a joy to be around and a wonderful friend. Louisa, Lizzy, Jo, Amy and Sara had all become close during their week long journey. If things took a turn for the worse now, at least

Louisa had four new friends she adored.

"He'd have to be an idiot all right." Jo stood as the train juddered to a complete stop. "Might as well get this over with."

Louisa watched her mingle with the other passengers heading for the door at the end of the carriage. "Anyone would think she didn't want to be here."

"She's just nervous," Lizzy said. "You know Jo, she likes to act tough." She took Louisa's hand and stood. "Come on. Let's go and get married." She touched Sara's shoulder as they passed her where she sat beside Amy in the seat in front of Jo's. "Are you coming?"

"We'll be right there," Sara replied, somewhat unnecessarily. They all knew wild horses wouldn't keep her from her intended. She'd been extolling Daniel's plentiful virtues all the way from New York.

As they joined the line of passengers slowly making their way towards the exit, Louisa took the opportunity to take her compact mirror from her reticule and check her reflection. She pulled off one glove and licked her finger, using it to smooth a wisp of hair threatening to break formation. It wouldn't do to have anything out of place when meeting her future husband for the first time, if he was indeed out there. *First impressions are absolutely crucial*, her mother's voice said inside her head.

"You look perfect," Lizzy whispered to her as they reached the door. "Especially standing next to me."

Louisa closed the mirror and returned it to her reticule. "You look perfect too. Richard will adore you."

It was true. Lizzy's dress may have been a little rumpled and her curling dark hair was always struggling to break free of whatever style she tried, but she had the cheerful, friendly disposition everyone liked, coupled with a natural, glowing beauty. Any man would be thrilled to have her as his wife.

Louisa had to work harder. She didn't have Lizzy's inherent vivaciousness and charm, nothing to draw the attention. She had to look perfect just to get noticed. And she wanted Jesse to notice her. He was her best chance.

Outside, the platform was milling with people, mostly passengers stretching their legs during the welcome stop. After a week on the train, Louisa was immeasurably glad she wouldn't be getting on it again. She'd never before appreciated how good having solid ground beneath her feet felt.

Lizzy took her hand and they made their way in the direction of the group of men waiting for their brides. They'd only gone a few steps before Louisa jerked her hand away.

"Ouch! Not so tight." She rubbed at her sore fingers. Lizzy may have been petite, but she had a grip like iron.

She gasped. "Oh! I'm sorry, I'm just so excited."

Her ever-present enthusiasm for life was well known among their little group. Louisa often found herself wondering what it was like to be as carefree and wild, without having to worry what anyone watching thought.

"I guessed that," she said, smiling and taking Lizzy's hand again. "Just try not to break any of my fingers."

"I'll do my best."

Reaching the cluster of young men, they took their place alongside Jo, Sara and Amy joining them a few seconds later. Louisa carefully studied each of the waiting grooms, hoping she'd made a mistake and one of them was Jesse. But she hadn't. He wasn't with the men and he wasn't behind the men. He simply wasn't there.

"Ladies, welcome to Green Hill Creek." The man who spoke had greying dark hair, a comfortably round belly, and a friendly smile. "I'm Pastor Simon Jones and this is my wife, Irene."

The only female in the group, a kind-looking woman,

smiled. "We're so thrilled to welcome you all. I'm sure you'll be happy in our little town."

Little seemed to be the right word. Louisa carefully kept her expression polite and friendly, not giving any indication of her nervousness. She was good at that. She'd been taught well.

"Now I'm sure you are all tired from you journey," the pastor went on, "so I'll make this quick. I will read out each of your names in turn and your intended will introduce himself, then we'll all go to the church and perform the ceremonies."

Louisa's gentle smile stayed firmly in place, but inside she began to panic. They were going to do this right here? In front of everyone? She'd be publically humiliated and there wasn't a thing she could do about it.

Moving her free hand behind her into the folds of her skirt, she made a fist and dug her nails into her palm, focusing on the pain until her heart rate began to lower.

Pastor Jones consulted a piece of paper. "First, Elizabeth Cotton."

Richard Shand, the man Louisa had identified as Lizzy's intended, stepped forward and held out his hand. "Ma'am."

Before Louisa could do anything to stop her, Lizzy released her hand, rushed forward with a squeal, and threw her arms around Mr Shand's neck.

Louisa stifled a shocked gasp. She probably shouldn't have been surprised, but she couldn't help feeling embarrassed for Lizzy.

"I'm so pleased to meet you, Richard," she said when she finally let him go. "You're very handsome."

He looked almost comically astonished. Despite Louisa's mortification at the whole situation, she had the unexpected urge to laugh.

"I'm pleased to meet you too, ma'am," he said. "And

11

thank you."

"Well, um, yes," Pastor Jones said, looking at his list. "So far so good. Louisa Wood?"

Louisa's mouth went dry and she fought the urge to swallow. *Never show your true feelings.*

At a soft tickle at her temple, she lifted a hand to push the stray hair beneath her bonnet. If indeed there was a stray hair. She couldn't tell with her gloves on. Why had she worn her gloves? Now she wouldn't be able to feel if anything was out of place.

Tamping down her growing alarm, she stepped forward and pasted on a smile.

"Louisa," Pastor Jones said, "this is Peter Johnson."

The other older man in the group moved forward and pulled off his hat. Up to now he'd been standing unobtrusively off to one side, or as unobtrusively as someone who towered above everyone around him could. "Miss Wood, I'm Jesse's father and I'll be taking you to meet him, if that's all right."

If she hadn't been standing ramrod straight she would have slumped in relief. Jesse hadn't changed his mind or forgotten her. She couldn't imagine why his father was there in his place, but at least she hadn't been abandoned.

"Of course," she said. A thought occurred to her. "I do hope he's not unwell."

"Oh no, miss. He'll explain when we get there."

She nodded and moved to stand at his side as he stepped back. For the first time in her life she felt small. For a woman, she was relatively tall, but she barely reached Mr Johnson's shoulder.

As the pastor introduced Sara to Daniel Raine, Louisa tried to think what could have prevented Jesse from coming to meet her. So he wasn't ill, but maybe he was injured somehow. Or possibly there'd been an emergency at his place of work. An emergency only an accountant could deal with. Was there such a thing as an accounting emergency? Probably not. A family emergency? But if that was the case, why didn't his father deal with it instead of coming to fetch her?

Stifling a sigh of frustration, she returned her attention to the introductions. Speculating on her own wasn't helping at all.

Sara was gazing up at Daniel adoringly, which was no surprise considering he was the most wonderful man on earth, going by what she'd told them about him. Louisa had to hand it to her, he certainly was attractive, and from his delighted expression he felt the same way about Sara.

Louisa was happy for her, but she was mystified as to why Sara would have travelled across the country to marry a farmer when she could have stayed in New York and found a suitable husband without any trouble. From what Louisa could tell, Sara's family was wealthy and, while not amongst the upper echelons of the social elite, certainly in a very respectable position in society. But she seemed happy, which was nice.

The pastor called Jo's name next and Louisa watched her meet her husband-to-be with interest.

"Pleasure to meet you, Miss Carter," Gabriel Silversmith said, holding out his hand.

All apathy from the train gone, Jo said, "The pleasure is mine, Gabriel," and then, shockingly, winked at him.

Although Louisa enjoyed Jo's company, she'd had the feeling since they met that something wasn't quite right about her. Having been raised to always present something of a facade, Louisa had a feel for when others were hiding something. Jo was definitely hiding something, although Louisa didn't think it could be anything especially bad. At least, she hoped not. She liked Jo very much.

The final couple to be introduced was Amy and Adam. Louisa remembered Jesse's excited letter telling her that Amy would be arriving on the train with her. He and Adam were close friends and Jesse had been the one to convince Adam to advertise for a bride. It seemed fitting that she and Amy should arrive together and become friends too.

To Louisa's relief, Adam didn't seem to mind that his bride was dressed most unconventionally, more like a man than a woman, with her trousers and wide-brimmed hat. Louisa had practically begged Amy to wear a dress, offering to lend her one of hers, but she'd said something vague about comfort and Louisa had eventually given up. If Adam was as nice as Jesse said he was, he'd be prepared to overlook Amy's attire this once.

If she was honest with herself, part of her was a little jealous of Amy's courage. Louisa wouldn't have ever dared to wear trousers, particularly not to meet her future husband.

"Well," Pastor Jones said, "now we're all sorted out, let's get the luggage and head to the church."

Walking towards the back end of the train surrounded by couples, Louisa suddenly felt very alone, even with Mr Johnson at her side.

"Which are yours, Miss Wood?" he said as they approached the growing pile of baggage being unloaded from the rear carriage.

"The blue ones," she said, feeling the need to add, "sorry."

He chuckled, looking from the trunks to her. "Don't worry, I'll manage. And May and June are used to pulling heavy loads so they'll be just fine."

Despite his words, she felt terribly guilty as she watched him lead a wagon pulled by two sturdy looking mares close to the mound of luggage, especially considering what was in all but three of her eight trunks. Although when he lifted the first of the heavy boxes as if it weighed no more than a valise, his bulging arm muscles stretching his shirt sleeves, she didn't feel quite so bad. Being a blacksmith, coupled with his unusual height, apparently made him exceptionally strong.

Could that have been why he'd come instead of Jesse, to fetch her luggage? No, that didn't make any sense at all.

Sara left Daniel loading her surprisingly few items of baggage into a wagon and came to stand at Louisa's side. "Are you all right?"

She stopped chewing her lower lip, a bad habit she had when nervous, and tried to smile. "Of course." She looked at Mr Johnson. "Well... maybe I'm a little worried. Oh dear, does it show?"

Sara threaded her arm through Louisa's. "Just a little bit. But it's completely understandable."

She sighed and bit her lip again. "I asked Mr Johnson why Jesse hasn't come and he just said he'd explain when we got there. Oh Sara, what if he's changed his mind? What will I do?"

Sara squeezed her arm, pulling her closer. "You showed me his letters, there is no way the man who wrote those wonderful words has changed his mind. He's besotted, that's the only word for it."

She couldn't help but smile at that. How could anyone be besotted by a letter? Yes, Jesse's letters to her had been entertaining and fascinating. And yes, she had looked forward to receiving each one with excited anticipation. But she wasn't a romantic like Sara, willing to move thousands of miles for a man she'd never met. And certainly not for love, real or otherwise. She was more practical than that.

"Besotted?" she said.

"Besotted. I might even go so far as enamoured."

She laughed softly. "I'm sorry I'm not going to be there for your wedding. Daniel's very handsome."

15

Sara nodded emphatically. "I can't stop staring at him. It's embarrassing."

Louisa nudged her shoulder, lowering her voice. "Don't worry, by the way he's been looking at you he won't mind one bit." She may not have been interested in romance, but she wasn't oblivious to it.

Mr Johnson walked towards them from the wagon, having amazingly already finished loading her trunks. "Are you ready, Miss Wood?"

"Yes, thank you." She gave Sara a quick hug. "See you Sunday."

Mr Johnson helped her up into the wagon and she looked at her new friends as he walked around to the other side, wishing she didn't have to leave them so soon. Other than as a small child, she'd never really had any close friends. Her mother and father hadn't wanted her and her two younger sisters to associate with the children her age who lived in their neighbourhood, believing such friendships would harm their chances of being socially upwardly mobile.

When she was younger she'd secretly dreamed of having friends to play with, laugh with, reveal her secrets to. She loved her sisters, but being the oldest by four years it wasn't the same. By the time she was of an age when she could have found her own friends, it was too late. Close bonds were formed in the carefree, unguarded days of childhood, and Louisa never knew how to accomplish that as an adult. But all that had changed on the train.

Away from the rules and watchful eyes of her parents, she rapidly came to realise that it didn't matter whether the women she travelled with were maids or princesses. Amy, Lizzy, Sara and Jo were just like her, travelling across the country to find new lives with men they'd never met, and it had forged a bond she'd never managed before. For the first time in Louisa's life she had true friends, and she loved each of them dearly.

The wagon started off and she waved goodbye, feeling a little teary. She at least wanted to know that her friends had good lives ahead of them.

Especially now that her own future felt so uncertain.

Chapter 2

Mr Johnson guided the wagon along a winding road lined with well kept houses.

"Is that where the weddings will take place?" Louisa said as they passed a white clapboard church.

"That's it, the Emmanuel Church." He glanced at her. "I'm sorry this isn't happening how you thought it would. I know you were expecting to arrive and get married right away, but you'll understand once you meet Jesse."

Louisa didn't know how to answer, so she simply nodded. He was obviously trying to allay her fears, but she was having a hard time feeling reassured. They turned a corner and she stared at the buildings lining the main street of Green Hill Creek as they passed. It wasn't exactly the bustling metropolis she'd been expecting of a town on the first railroad to cross the entire country, but that concern was currently vying for and losing attention to the bigger concern that Jesse hadn't come to meet her himself.

She opened her mouth to speak and then closed it again. Mr Johnson had already told her Jesse would explain when they reached his home. That should be enough. A well brought up, polite lady didn't question when she was told something. She just accepted it. Louisa was trying very, very hard to do that, but as her mouth became drier and drier and her heart beat faster and faster, her fear finally won out over her manners.

"Has he changed his mind?" she blurted out.

Mr Johnson started at the sudden outburst.

She instantly regretted it. "Forgive me, I don't mean to question you. It's just, I'm a little nervous."

A warm smile spread across his face. She had to look up to see it. Goodness, but he was tall. She wondered if Jesse was as tall as his father.

"No, Miss Wood, he hasn't changed his mind, I can promise you that. He's real excited that you've come."

She wanted to ask why, if he was so excited, he hadn't met her at the station, but she simply nodded and tried again to feel reassured. It couldn't be much further to his house.

They turned off the main street into a more residential road lined with neat wooden houses that, although of varying styles and sizes, somehow seemed to blend together. After another turn onto another street, the wagon came to a halt in front of a single storey house with white painted walls and a colour-filled yard at the front.

It was smaller than she'd been expecting, barely any larger than her own home. Jesse had a good job, being an accountant with the local bank. Surely he earned enough for more than this? Was everything in the west small?

Mr Johnson cleared his throat. It made her jump.

"Miss Wood, I, um..." He pursed his lips, appearing to consider his words. "I love my son very much and I don't want to see him hurt."

Louisa's jaw dropped briefly before she realised and rapidly closed it again. Did he know what she was thinking?

"I'm just asking that you keep an open mind," he continued, his eyes on the house. "He may not be entirely what you're expecting, but he's a good man and he'll make a fine husband. The best husband anyone could ask for."

Now she was completely confused. "I... I'll keep that in mind."

He nodded and pressed his lips together, looking like he wanted to say something more. But then he swivelled away from her, jumped down from the wagon and walked around to help her down.

The house may have been small, but it appeared very well looked after. She walked between stuffed flowerbeds along a wide paved path that sloped up to a raised porch spanning the entire front of the house. Wisteria wound around the wooden railing, swathing the porch in a stunning show of purple. Bees flitted from bloom to bloom and for a moment she envied them their single-minded, worry-free existence.

Mr Johnson moved ahead of her to open the door and she stepped into a square hallway with a polished wood floor and pale green painted walls. Four doors led from the room, two to the right, one ahead, and one to the left.

"May I take your shawl, Miss Wood?" Mr Johnson said.

"Thank you."

It was a nice hallway, she thought as she gave him her shawl and bonnet and he hooked them onto a peg at waist height by the door, next to a dark brown jacket. Clean and uncluttered.

Mr Johnson raised his voice. "Jess?"

"In here, Pa."

A shiver fluttered down Louisa's spine at the sound of the voice. It was deep but not too deep, not unlike Mr Johnson's. A smooth baritone that put her in mind of rich cream.

Rich cream? Where had that come from?

She smoothed her hair quickly as Mr Johnson opened the door on the left for her and, her heart beating double time, she walked into a parlour.

On the periphery of her vision she was vaguely aware of cream coloured walls, a large tiled fireplace, leather

20

upholstered seating, a desk in one corner with three tall bookcases behind stuffed with books. But her eyes were drawn to the man sitting on a settee facing the door.

He was astonishingly good looking, with caramel coloured hair that brushed his broad shoulders, a strong jaw line, and full lips turned up at the corners.

His smile made her already racing heart stutter. "Good afternoon, Louisa. It's so good to finally meet you."

"Well, I'll leave you two to get acquainted and take the trunks over to the Jones' house," Mr Johnson said.

It took a moment for his words to sink in. She looked back, and up, at him. "The Jones' house? I won't be..." she glanced at Jesse, "um... staying... um..."

"I know you're confused," Jesse said, "but I'll explain everything. There's nothing to worry about, I promise."

She nodded and tried, again, not to be worried as Mr Johnson smiled at her and then left the room. Preoccupied as she was, she didn't realise that she and Jesse were alone until she heard the front door close.

She spun around to look at the parlour doorway and then back at Jesse. "Uh, is there anyone else here?"

His eyebrows rose. "No. Why?"

"Don't... don't we need a chaperone?"

He gave her a smile that didn't reach his eyes. "No, believe me, we don't need a chaperone."

"Why not?"

"Would you like to sit down?" he said, ignoring her question and indicating an armchair close to where he sat.

After a moment's hesitation she walked to the chair and sank into it. She tucked her reticule beside her and folded her hands in her lap, feeling a little self-conscious under Jesse's scrutiny. She went through her mother's checklist: back straight, shoulders back, chin up, knees together, ankles crossed.

21

"You're even prettier than your photograph. I didn't think that could be possible."

It was a forward thing to say when they weren't even married yet, but the sparkle in Jesse's eyes as he smiled at her made her want to smile back. She stifled the urge. She still had no idea why he hadn't come to meet her at the station. He might turn out to be a thorough disappointment. After all, he hadn't stood to greet her when she'd arrived or even offered her something to drink.

"It's very kind of you to say, Mr Johnson," she replied in what she hoped was a noncommittal tone.

"Just the truth. And please, call me Jesse."

She gave him a small smile. "Jesse."

His eyes lowered to the floor between them and he drew in a deep breath. She couldn't help noticing how it made his already broad shoulders even broader.

Goodness, what was wrong with her today? Fatigue, that was it. The long journey must have tired her out more than she thought. It was affecting her mind.

"I'm sorry I didn't meet you at the station," he said, picking unconsciously at a loose thread on the arm of the settee. "I, well, the truth is, I haven't told you everything about me and I wanted the chance to be honest with you while we're alone. To give you time to think about what I have to say."

Now she was even more confused, and more than a little scared. "I don't understand. Were you untruthful about yourself in your letters? Are you not an accountant for a bank?"

"Oh no, that's all true. I never lied to you. There's just something I didn't tell you. Something important." The thread looked in danger of unravelling the entire settee. "Something that would have been immediately obvious if I'd come to the station."

22

She tried to imagine what he wouldn't have told her and came up empty. "And what is that?"

He took another deep breath, released the abused thread, and clasped his hands together on his lap. "I can't walk."

It took a moment for his words to register. Her eyes went to a wheelchair sitting slightly behind the settee. She'd noticed it in passing when she walked into the room but had thought it must be for an elderly relative.

"Are you injured?"

"No, it's not an injury. I have a condition called Little's Disease. I was born with it. I've never been able to walk."

For nigh on ten seconds she couldn't speak.

He couldn't walk.

How could he not *walk*?

What did that mean for her?

Her gaze flicked down to his legs. They looked normal, like anyone else's legs, if somewhat longer. He would have been tall. If he'd been able to stand.

"Is there..." Her voice cracked and she cleared her throat before trying again. "Is there a cure?"

"No. I'll be like this for the rest of my life." He said it so matter-of-factly, as if it was normal.

As if the life she'd thought she was coming to hadn't just been irrevocably crushed.

"Why did you bring me here then?" Was it rude to ask that? She didn't know. She was beginning to think she didn't know anything anymore.

"Because I want a wife, just like any other man. Because I want *you* to be my wife."

"Then why didn't you tell me?" she said, her voice rising. She *never* raised her voice.

He sighed and ran one hand over his hair. "You weren't the only woman I corresponded with, Louisa. You weren't even the first, by a long way. Before you, I exchanged letters with eleven other women and each time it went well, until I told them about my disability. Some of them wrote very polite letters back saying they were sorry but they couldn't marry me. The rest just didn't write back." He leaned forward and for a moment she thought he was going to reach out to her, but he rested his elbows on his knees and looked into her eyes. "When I decided to do this, to bring someone here without telling her the truth, you were the one I chose because I knew you were the one I'd want to spend my life with. I have one shot at this and you're it. I didn't want to risk you saying no before I'd even had a chance to try to convince you to say yes. I'm not asking you to marry me right now. I'm asking you to stay for two weeks and get to know me. Pastor and Mrs Jones have been real kind and made you a room up in their house. Then if you want to go home, I'll pay your fare back. If you really want to go back straight away, I'll still pay your fare, but I'm asking that you give me a chance. Please."

He'd clearly rehearsed the speech, his words precise and practised. Except for the *please* at the end. That was delivered with such longing it seemed to grab onto her heart. Which was ridiculous because words couldn't grab hearts.

She took a steadying breath, attempting to corral her wild thoughts. Her first instinct was to tell him he should have trusted her, but Louisa couldn't help wondering what she would have done if he'd told her about his disability in a letter like he had with all the women before her. Would she still have come? She had to admit to herself that she didn't know.

Nevertheless, she was here now and, unexpected as the situation was, she had to make the most of it. Just as her mother had taught her.

She sat up straight and tried to think clearly.

"I have some questions," she said. "Can I trust you to

answer them honestly?"

He sat back and smiled, relaxing. "Nothing but the truth from now on, I swear."

She raised her eyebrows. *"Nothing?"*

His smile faded, replaced by an awkward expression that inexplicably made her want to giggle. "Well, concerning my condition and our potential marriage. Not that I'll be lying to you about other things, but there could be times when we don't always want to tell the whole truth on certain things and I'm not helping my cause at all now am I?"

She covered her twitching lips with her fingers, but she could tell by the return of his smile that he could see her amusement.

Pursing her lips into seriousness, she lowered her hand. "If I was to stay, and I'm not saying I will, either for two weeks or forever, but if I was, what would my duties be?"

A small frown creased the space above his eyes. Which were the most dazzling shade of emerald green, she noticed.

"Duties?"

"Yes. For your..." She waved a hand at his legs. "To help you. What do you need done?"

His very green eyes opened wide. "Ohhh, you think that's why I want a wife? To take care of me?"

An uncomfortable feeling she'd got something wrong crept over her. "It isn't?"

He shook his head. "I don't need anything like that. I live here alone. I can look after myself just fine. Have done for a long time now."

She could feel her cheeks heating. "I'm sorry, I just assumed..."

"Most people do. It's okay. I'm used to it."

The dozens of marriage advertisements she and her mother had gone through came back to her. All of those men, she assumed, could walk just fine, but they mostly seemed to want a wife to do something anyway. Clean, cook, take care of the children, feed the pigs, slaughter the chickens, pan for gold.

"So why *do* you want a wife? There must be something you want."

He shrugged and one side of his mouth hitched up in a disarming half smile. "Companionship. Friendship. Love."

A shiver wobbled down her chest and exploded in her stomach. "Oh," she whispered, when she could finally get the word out.

"Why do you want a husband?" he said, his gaze holding her captive even though she wanted to look away.

Her mouth became so dry she had to swallow before replying. Of all the reasons her mother and father had for wanting her to travel clear across the country to marry, love hadn't made the list, not even at the very bottom.

"I... uh... there are so many reasons one would want to..." she drew a breath into her empty lungs "... marry. Financial concerns, security, social norms, reproduction..."

"But not love?"

She squirmed in her seat under his scrutiny. Wasn't she the one who was supposed to be asking the questions? "I... never really thought about it."

A slow, flirtatious smile slid onto his face. "Well, maybe you should."

For a few seconds she couldn't form a coherent sound. She looked away, frantically attempting to gather her thoughts. What was it about this man that flustered her so badly?

"I'll, um, consider that." She swallowed again. "Anyway, returning to my questions."

He sat back, draping one long arm along the back of the settee. "Go ahead."

"Were you telling the truth about your employment?"

26

His work. That would surely be a safe topic.

"Yes, I work for the bank. I also provide services for folks around here who find it easier to hire someone to do their accounting. I'm the only trained accountant for miles so I've cornered the market, you could say. You won't have to worry about money."

She nodded. Money was only one of her concerns, but she wasn't certain how his inability to walk impacted the others. "Are you well regarded by the town?"

He snorted a laugh. "I reckon. I've never asked. Folks who don't know me just regard someone who can't walk as harmless, if they think of me at all."

Understanding dawned. "So that's why we don't need a chaperone?"

"More often than not people who don't know me don't see me as a whole person. They wouldn't even consider that I was capable of..." he frowned and looked away, as if seeking the right words, "...any kind of intimacy. As I said, harmless."

"And are you? Harmless?"

The flirtatious smile returned, sparkling in his eyes. "That would depend on how you define harmless."

She'd walked right into that one. She could feel the blush rising again and desperately tried to quash it. The trouble was, her final question could only make it worse.

"And can you... um..." She swallowed yet again. "Would you... is everything..." Huffing out a breath, she squeezed her eyes closed and blurted out the necessary yet mortifying inquiry. "Can you father children?"

There were a few seconds of silence and when he replied there was a smile in his voice. "No reason to think not."

She didn't dare look at him. If only the floor would open up and swallow her now, it would be a kindness.

"Louisa, it's me," he said. "I'm the man you've been writing to for months, the same man you were willing to

27

cross the whole country for. That hasn't changed. Other than not being able to walk, I'm no different from any other man. I have the same needs and wants and desires, and the same ability to be a good husband. I know you're scared, but please, let me show you who I am beyond my disability. Get to know me."

She opened her eyes to see all trace of his flirtation gone.

"Will you stay?" he said. "Just for two weeks? Will you give me a chance to prove I can be the man you'd want to spend your life with?"

What on earth should she do? She wished her mother and father were there to tell her since she obviously couldn't trust her own judgement around Jesse. He made her feel strange. Discombobulated. And it had nothing to do with his inability to walk. It wasn't a feeling to which she was accustomed and it was annoying and a little frightening and she didn't understand it.

This was important. It was the rest of her life at stake. She needed to be able to think clearly, away from Jesse and his sparkling green eyes and smile that did stupid things to her heartbeat.

She took a deep breath. "If it's all right, I'd like to think about it overnight."

Shoulders slumping, he sat back. "Of course you can. I know this is a shock and I wish I could have somehow prepared you, but..." He shrugged. "Would you like something to drink? Or eat? I'm sorry I didn't offer you anything when you came in, but I wanted to get my confession out the way first. I've been pretty nervous waiting for you to arrive."

The loss of his smile made the room feel darker. She reminded herself it wasn't her fault and she had nothing to feel guilty about. If he'd told her before she came... she probably wouldn't have come.

A groan of frustration almost escaped. How was she supposed to think clearly like this?

"I understand," she said, "and it's quite all right. And thank you for the offer, but if you don't mind I think I'd like to go to the house where I'm going to be staying. It's been a long journey and I have a lot to think about."

The sadness that flitted across his features came close to making her change her mind about getting away from him as fast as possible and a desire to see him smile again gripped her.

Fortunately, he nodded before she could say anything and said, "Anything you want." He even smiled again, although no sparkle reached his eyes.

She wanted to see that sparkle again.

Stop it, Louisa. A lady of breeding is always in control. She grabbed onto her mother's frequent reminders like a lifeline.

She wasn't sure what to do as Jesse reached back to grasp the wheelchair behind him. Should she offer to help or would that seem rude? Her social upbringing hadn't included people like him and she had no idea what he'd expect of her.

As it turned out, she didn't have to do anything. She watched, impressed, as he pulled the wheelchair around to sit sideways on beside him, set the brake, and effortlessly swung himself from the settee into it.

"I'm sorry, but my father won't be back for a while," he said. "I thought you'd be... well, that you wouldn't be leaving so soon. If you don't mind walking, it's not far."

"Oh, walking will be just fine," she said, standing. "I've been sitting on a train for the past week. I'm just happy to feel stable ground beneath my feet."

His smile returned, the real one that made her insides quiver in the most frustrating manner. "Of course, if you get tired I can always give you a ride." He patted his thighs.

Her hand flew to her mouth, the idea of sitting in his lap

29

setting her cheeks flaming. Especially as she didn't hate the thought one single bit.

"I think I can manage, thank you," she said, desperately trying not to smile.

He wheeled towards the door and waited for her to go ahead of him. "Well, anytime you feel yourself weakening, just say the word."

Chapter 3

Jesse wheeled slowly along the road away from the Jones'
house, at a loss for what to do next.

He should have expected this, but he'd been sure Louisa
would stay with him for an hour or two, at least through
supper. But evidently she couldn't get away from him fast
enough. He'd thought that once she met him face to face,
spoke to him, saw that he wasn't some helpless, drooling
invalid, she'd forgive him his deception. Apparently he
wasn't as charming as he'd hoped.

Had he gone too far with the flirting? In her letters
Louisa had been very refined and polite, but he'd also
detected a sense of humour and mischievousness that had
attracted him to her over all the other women he'd written to.
So he'd decided to go all out and appeal to her fun side,
hoping she'd see the same in him. Now, he wasn't so sure.
Maybe inviting her to sit in his lap had been too much.
Although he hadn't missed her smile, even though she'd tried
to hide it.

They'd talked on the too short walk to the Jones' house,
but mostly about her journey and travelling companions. He
hadn't known what to say to convince her to give him a
chance. What if she refused? Now he'd met her, he wanted
her to stay even more.

At any other time he'd have gone to talk to Adam, but
his friend would be married by now and have better things to

do than raise Jesse's spirits. Jesse envied him, not for his ability to walk but because he didn't need to constantly explain himself. He wished he'd been there for Adam's wedding, but he couldn't take the risk that Louisa would take one look at him and get right back on the train before he had a chance to explain. He hoped his friend was happy though, and no longer as terrified as he'd been when they spoke earlier.

He wondered what Amy looked like. Clearly she couldn't be as beautiful as Louisa, that wasn't possible, but he hoped she was pretty. Despite his protestations otherwise, Adam wanted someone pretty.

His thoughts returned to Louisa. He got the feeling his thoughts would be on Louisa frequently from now on, wherever she was. He'd known from the photograph she sent that she was a handsome woman, but he hadn't been prepared for her lustrous auburn hair and pale blue eyes, or her beautiful voice, or the way she moved, practically gliding along as though she wasn't touching the ground. He'd almost lost the power of speech when she first walked into his parlour.

He shook his head. He was being ridiculous. There were plenty of beautiful women in the world and Louisa was just one. If she didn't stay, or even if she stayed and then decided to return home after two weeks, he could find another. Despite what he'd told her, she wasn't his only chance. He'd been exaggerating to persuade her to stay, for all the good that did. He would try again. And again. For as long as it took and as long as he could keep paying for train tickets.

Although he would far prefer Louisa to stay. She seemed to be perfect in every way, how could he not? But he'd done everything humanly possible. Now all he could do was pray.

Lost in his thoughts and in no hurry to get back to his empty house, it took him far longer than it normally would have to reach home. When he finally wheeled through the front door and came to a stop, his shoulders rose and fell in a deep sigh. The house seemed emptier than usual, like it remembered Louisa's presence and missed her.

Or maybe that was just him.

"Jesse?"

In his stupor of self-pity he'd left the front door open and the unexpected voice startled him. He rotated to find Mrs Goodwin standing in the doorway, a serving dish in her hands. His mood improved immediately, at least from his stomach's point of view.

"Mrs Goodwin, come in," he said, wheeling backwards to allow her room.

She frowned as she walked inside. "Are you all right?"

"Uh, yes, I'm fine." He tried for a smile.

She smiled back so he must have made it convincing.

"I brought something for you and Miss Wood," she said. "Just some of my beef stew and dumplings, nothing fancy. Is she here?" She craned her neck to peer into the parlour.

"Mrs G, your beef stew is better than the fanciest meal in the fanciest restaurant in the world. But I'm afraid it's just me." He waved through the door to Mr Goodwin seated on his wagon outside on the road then followed Mrs Goodwin into the kitchen where she set the serving dish on the table.

"What happened?" she said. "Surely she didn't refuse to stay."

"She didn't refuse, but she didn't say yes either. She wants to think it through overnight. She's with the Joneses. She seemed..." he cast about for the right word, "flustered."

"I can't imagine she'll flat out refuse to give you two weeks, not with this face." She reached out to pat his cheek and he gave her a small smile.

"I hoped she'd stay for supper, but I think she just wanted to get away from me."

"I'm certain she was just surprised, that's all, and she must be tired from her trip. You mustn't give up hope. The Lord has it in hand."

He nodded, but he wasn't sure the Lord would have approved of him not telling Louisa he couldn't walk. Jesse hadn't actually asked Him.

Mrs Goodwin's face lit up. "But there's no reason why you shouldn't give her a little gentle persuasion."

"That's what I was hoping to do, but she's there and I'm here. She didn't want to stay."

She grinned and patted the serving dish. "But now you have the perfect excuse to go back over there. You could say I brought it for the two of you and it would be too much for just you. Irene will invite you to stay to eat and that'll give you another chance to work your charm."

Jesse looked at the dish. "Mrs G, I think you're even sneakier than I am."

Her laughter filled the small room. "Never underestimate a woman's desire for a romantic, happy ending." She rose from her chair and squeezed his shoulder. "I know you can do this, Jesse. Mark my words, once Miss Wood gets to know you, she'll be begging to stay."

"Thanks, Mrs G."

A smile spread over his face as he watched her leave. He'd known Mrs Goodwin his whole life and she'd always made him feel like she was on his side. And unlike many of the people he knew, she didn't treat him like he was different. She'd even taught him a few of her recipes, a favour granted to only a few.

His gaze moved to the serving dish. The delicious aroma drifting from beneath the checked cloth covering made his mouth water. Mrs Goodwin was right, it presented the perfect opportunity to spend more time with Louisa before she made her decision.

His smile widening, he reached for the dish.

~ ~ ~

"Can I bring you anything, Louisa? Do you need any more help?" Mrs Jones' gaze swept over the mound of trunks piled into the corner of the small room.

Louisa stifled a sigh and shook her head. "No, thank you. You and Pastor Jones have already been so good to me. I know I have far too many of these."

Mrs Jones laughed. "Nonsense, it's daunting to begin a new life. It's understandable you'd want to bring everything with you. And I'm sure, if you decide to stay, that Jesse won't mind at all."

Louisa caught herself about to bite her lower lip and instead gave Mrs Jones a small smile.

"Well, I'll leave you to get settled in," Mrs Jones said, moving to the door. "There's no hurry. Just come on out whenever you're ready."

Louisa closed the door after her and slumped onto the bed. They'd had to move it from where it had jutted into the centre of the room to against one wall to fit everything in. Mr Johnson had brought all the trunks inside, but he'd been gone by the time Jesse brought her to her temporary home and Pastor and Mrs Jones had helped her pile the trunks so she could at least move around in the small space.

She'd felt awful the entire time they worked. Her mother's idea had made sense back in New York, but now she was here it was beginning to seem a bit ridiculous. No one here cared how many trunks she had. She had far more than any of the other women who arrived with her. Amy didn't even have one, somehow fitting everything into a single carpet bag. It seemed that out here in the west appearances weren't necessarily everything.

It was a new idea for Louisa and, as she considered it, a little liberating. She felt guilty just thinking about it, but maybe every tiny detail didn't have to be perfect. Maybe every person didn't have to be perfect.

She stood and walked over to open one of the three trunks she'd made sure were set where she could easily reach them. Her assertion that they contained the belongings she'd need the most was true, at least.

Her thoughts went to Jesse as she worked to unpack her few items of clothing. Not that they had strayed far from him since he'd left. She felt terrible about how she'd almost run away from him. She hoped he didn't think it was because of his condition. She wouldn't want him to think he repulsed her in any way. The exact opposite was true, if she was honest with herself. Goodness, but his eyes were incredible. She'd never seen anything like them.

Her hands stilled in the process of lifting her favourite blue skirt from the trunk and she gazed, unseeing, at the sky beyond her window. Green with gold flecks that seemed to glow when he laughed. Of course, that wasn't possible. Eyes didn't glow, even the gold parts. But she could swear Jesse's sparkled. And his voice... ohhh, his voice. It seemed to curl around her chest like a cloud, warming her insides and causing her heart to flutter in the most disturbingly pleasant fashion. And his hair, the most beautiful shade of caramel, longer than was fashionable in the east but oh so attractive on him...

A burst of birdsong from outside startled her from her reverie and she blinked, shaking her head. This was precisely why she'd left, even when she'd wanted to stay. She couldn't think straight around him.

What was wrong with her? She'd only just met the man. Yes, he was handsome, astoundingly so, but she hadn't been raised to swoon over every attractive man who looked in her direction. Unless it was on purpose, of course, to gain attention.

No, she had to consider the situation in which she found herself in a calm and rational manner. What would her parents have her do if they were here? She sighed and hung the skirt on a hook inside the small wardrobe. That was just the problem. In all the ways she'd been taught to attract the right man with the right social standing, it had never once come up that he might not be able to walk. She'd never even *seen* a young person in a wheelchair before, at least not someone who hadn't been injured in some way. Of course, she'd heard of places where people like Jesse were sent when they were children, to be looked after. For their own good. Institutions where their physical needs could be taken care of.

Although Jesse didn't seem at all like he needed taking care of.

She shook out her midnight blue evening gown, frowning at the creases. A week squashed in a trunk had not been kind to her clothing. She'd have to ask Mrs Jones for the use of her iron later.

Would a disability like Jesse's hinder his social and career advancement? She guessed that in all likelihood it would. And if her husband didn't advance, she wouldn't advance. This wasn't at all what was meant to happen. At this moment she was supposed to be spending her first evening with her new husband, an accountant for a bank in an up and coming town in the west with all the opportunities she didn't have back in New York. She wasn't supposed to be unmarried in a tiny, backwoods town whose only redeeming feature was the railroad ran through it.

All right, perhaps she was being a little harsh. It seemed like a nice enough place. But everything was still wrong. She should just go home on the next train.

Yes, that's what she would do. Jesse would be

disappointed, but it would be better for him in the end to not have her string him along for two weeks and then be let down when she left anyway. It was what her parents would have her do. It was what she would do.

She nodded her head to seal her decision and began folding her dress again. She wouldn't be needing it now. No need to iron her clothing since she'd be leaving soon.

A knock sounded on the front door along the hall from her bedroom and she listened to Mrs Jones answer it, the sounds muffled through the door.

And then she heard a voice which immediately cast doubt on her perfectly reasonable plan to leave as soon as possible. She dropped the dress into the trunk and hurried to the door, pressing her ear against the wooden surface.

"Of course you have to stay, Jesse," Mrs Jones said. "You've come all this way and there's plenty here for all of us and I wouldn't dream of depriving you of Mrs Goodwin's cooking."

"Well, if you insist," Jesse replied, a smile in his voice.

Louisa turned around and slumped against the door.

He was here. Jesse and his smooth voice and his devastating smile and his sparkling green eyes and his caramel-coloured hair and his... everything.

It was a disaster.

She almost jumped out of her skin when a knock sounded on the door at her back. Rapidly smoothing her hair, she took a breath to calm herself and opened the door.

Mrs Jones stood outside in the hallway. "Jesse came to deliver food that Harriet Goodwin prepared for the two of you so I asked him to stay. I just wanted to let you know we can eat whenever you're ready."

Louisa put on her best practised smile. "That sounds lovely. Harriet Goodwin?"

"She's a member of the church and something of a local

legend. I admit, you'll spend the rest of your time here disappointed in my cooking after tasting hers."

"Oh, I'm sure that's not true." *Prepared for the two of you.* There was a two of them. People already thought she and Jesse were a *two*.

"You'll understand once you've eaten." Mrs Jones stepped back. "Just come on through when you're ready."

Louisa closed the door as she walked away and released the forced smile which was making her face ache. She wandered to the bed and sat with a heavy sigh, raising her eyes to the ceiling. Outside of church she wasn't one for praying much, but since her parents weren't there to guide her she didn't see any other option.

"Dear Lord God," she whispered, "thank You for bringing me here safely." She remembered hearing a sermon once where the preacher said one should begin a prayer with thanks and she cast about for something else to be grateful for. "And thank You that Pastor and Mrs Jones are such nice people and didn't complain once about the trunks." That should be enough. "I suppose You know about Jesse. I'm sure You love him and You want him to be happy, but I just don't think it could be with me. Mother and Father want me to marry a man who has the right social standing and potential for advancement and..." A verse from the Bible came to her and she sat up straighter. This was surely proof of her rightness. "And You told us to honour our fathers and mothers so that means I have to do as they say, doesn't it? So if You could just make Jesse not like me and me not like him, I would be very grateful. And help me to meet a real gentleman somehow. Not that Jesse isn't a gentlemen but, well, I'm sure You know what I mean. Thank You. Amen."

The prayer made her feel somewhat better. Surely God would keep her thinking clearly and enable her to stay strong. Going right back home was obviously the right thing to do. She was glad she'd thought of the honouring her parents verse. That could only be extra proof she was right.

Nodding, she stood and went to the washstand by the window to wash her face.

Supper with Jesse wouldn't be a problem. She was a determined woman and God was on her side.

It would all be perfectly all right.

She looked down at the travel dress she was still wearing.

But first she needed to change.

~

When Louisa reached the parlour door, Jesse was facing the window that looked out onto the garden behind the house, his back to her.

There was a slight wave to his hair that made the ends of the layers cut into it crisscross over each other, creating a sense of texture and movement even though he was still. What would it feel like to feel those soft strands sliding through her fingers?

Startled by the thought, she pulled her eyes away. She would have slapped herself, if she could. It hadn't taken even five seconds in Jesse's presence for her brain to start scrambling again. She briefly considered joining Pastor and Mrs Jones in the kitchen, but that would be rude. And it wasn't like she could avoid Jesse for the entire meal.

With nothing else for it, she lifted her chin and walked into the room.

He looked round and saw her, giving her a smile that momentarily sucked all the breath from her lungs. Then he spoke and it all went downhill from there.

"I hope you don't mind seeing me again so soon," he said, turning his wheelchair from the window. "I didn't want you to miss out on Mrs Goodwin's beef stew."

She took a seat in an armchair and tried to ignore the way the sun shining in through the glass created golden highlights in his hair. "Mrs Jones said she's a good cook."

He wheeled over to her, stopping close enough that she could lean forward and touch him if she wanted to. Which she didn't. In the slightest.

"Calling Mrs Goodwin a good cook is like calling the Rocky Mountains a few hills. She taught me some of her recipes, but I still can't get mine to come out as well as hers. You'll understand when you taste it. She's a genius."

"You can cook?" She immediately regretted revealing her surprise. "I'm sorry, I didn't mean that you wouldn't be able to cook because of your..." She waved at his legs then regretted doing that too. "I just meant that it's surprising you can cook, because you're a..." What on earth was she *saying*?

His lips twitched as if he was fighting a smile. "A what?"

"A man," she finished lamely. She'd been in the room with him for barely a minute and already her poise was unravelling.

His smile won through. "I figured if I was going to live on my own it would be nice if I could eat."

"Most men seem to wait until they have a wife to cook for them." Her eyes widened in horror. "I'm sorry. That was insensitive of me." Was it too late to run back to her room and pretend to be ill? Her mother would be so disappointed.

"Most men haven't spent their lives having to prove to everyone they meet that they aren't helpless." His voice held no bitterness, it was simply a statement of fact.

Louisa suddenly felt very, very ashamed. "I don't think you're helpless."

He gave her a lopsided smile that created a perfect dimple in his left cheek. "Glad to hear it."

Mrs Jones appeared at the door. "Supper is just about

41

ready, if you'd like to come on through."

Louisa snapped her eyes from Jesse's dimple. Had she been staring?

"Thanks, Mrs Jones," he said. He smiled at Louisa and indicated the door. "After you."

They settled with Pastor and Mrs Jones at the table in the kitchen. It seemed to be the only table in the house. At home, guests who weren't either family or close friends would never have been entertained in the kitchen. Not that the house she grew up in was any larger than the Jones' home, but they did have a separate dining room which was used for breakfast and dinner. Louisa's mother insisted they always did things properly. They may not have been wealthy or lived in the best part of the city, but she was determined they would behave as if they did.

But as Louisa sat in the homely kitchen, surrounded by the delicious aroma of food and the smiling faces of Pastor and Mrs Jones and Jesse, she couldn't help thinking how pleasant it was to let go of the formality, just a bit.

If Jesse hadn't been right beside her, close enough that his elbow brushed hers as he wheeled himself into position at the table, she might even have relaxed.

"Well," Pastor Jones said, taking the seat opposite Louisa, "since Mrs Goodwin's beef stew is calling, let's not keep it waiting." He took his wife's hand. "Jesse, since you so kindly brought the food, would you say the blessing?"

Mrs Jones reached for Jesse's hand and Pastor Jones held his out to Louisa. It took her a moment to realise they were forming a circle. Taking the pastor's hand, she only realised the ramifications when Jesse held his left hand, palm up, above the table.

Bracing herself, Louisa slipped her hand into his.

Jesse's touch was warm and soft and, frustratingly, sent little tingles through her skin. And although she wasn't a

42

small woman, standing at a statuesque, as her mother called it, five feet and nine inches, his large hand easily engulfed hers. She hoped he couldn't hear her heart thudding in her chest.

Closing her eyes, she tried to concentrate on his words rather than the way the sound of his voice flowed over her like a silky, sea breeze.

"Father," he said, "I thank You for Pastor and Mrs Jones' kindness in opening their home to me and Louisa. Thank You for Mrs Goodwin's generosity and delicious beef stew. And most of all, thank You for bringing Louisa here, for keeping her safe on the journey, and for her willingness to come all this way for me. I'm feeling truly blessed tonight. In Your Name, Lord Jesus. Amen."

She opened her eyes and looked up at him. How could he still be grateful for her after she'd almost run away from him? But the small smile he gave her seemed perfectly genuine. She even found herself smiling back. And missing his touch when he released her hand.

"That was lovely, Jesse," Mrs Jones said. "Thank you. And we're very happy to have Louisa here. Now, let's not keep Harriet's stew waiting."

It was, quite simply, the most delicious thing Louisa had ever eaten. Her own cooking skills, which up to now she had thought reasonably good, suddenly seemed utterly inadequate.

"How does Mrs Goodwin do it?" she said as she laid her knife and fork onto her empty plate.

"No one knows," Jesse said. "Even the dishes she's taught me to cook haven't come out anywhere near as good as hers. She just does... something. With the exact same ingredients."

"She is truly blessed with a God-given talent," Pastor Jones said, leaning back in his chair and patting his rounded stomach with a grin. "No doubt about that. And even better, she's generous with it."

Mrs Jones stood and began gathering the plates. "As a wife I might be moved to envy, but I can admit when I'm outclassed."

Pastor Jones grasped her hand and kissed the back. "Your cooking will always be my favourite, my darling."

She leaned down to kiss his forehead, smiled sweetly, and said, "Liar," which set everyone laughing.

"Please, let me help you with the dishes, Mrs Jones," Louisa said, rising from her seat.

"Oh no, Simon will do that, won't you dear?" She threw a pointed look at her husband.

He stared at her in incomprehension.

Her eyes flicked to Jesse and Louisa.

Louisa lowered her gaze, pretending not to notice.

"Oh, um, yes," Pastor Jones said, finally catching on. "Dishes, of course."

"Why don't you show Jesse the garden?" Mrs Jones said to Louisa. "It's such a lovely evening and the flowers are outdoing themselves today."

"Of course," she said, trying to sound neutral despite her apprehension. She wasn't certain she was ready to be alone with Jesse again. The distraction of sitting so close to him all through the meal had only been mitigated by the deliciousness of the food.

There was a wooden bench a little way into the garden and Louisa sat at one end. Jesse stopped beside her and they gazed at the profusion of flowers around them.

"You've already seen the garden, haven't you?" Louisa said.

"Plenty of times," he replied. "I was here yesterday. Mrs J doesn't always do subtle so well."

She smiled a little. "I suppose she's just trying to help."

"When I was young, before my pa remarried, I spent a lot of time here when he was working. Before I was old enough to understand why sitting too near to a blazing hot furnace wasn't safe. She was almost like a mother to me."

Louisa moved her attention from a bumblebee fastidiously investigating each trumpet of a tall pink foxglove to look at him. "You never told me what happened to your mother."

He rested his elbows on the arms of his chair and linked his fingers. "She died giving birth to me."

"Oh Jesse, I'm so sorry."

He shrugged one shoulder and looked at his hands. "Doctors think that's why I'm like this. Whatever went wrong damaged something, although they don't know what."

Shame twisting her stomach, she closed her eyes and sighed. "I'm sorry for how I've been behaving. I don't think I'm doing so well with all of this."

"Actually, I was thinking how well you've taken it. I know the prospect of a disabled husband must be daunting. People like me... well, the fact is most people like me don't get to have normal lives."

"But that's not why," she said, eager that he should understand she wasn't put off by his inability to walk. She stopped, surprised at herself. She truly wasn't. That was unexpected.

"That's not why what?" he said.

"That's not why I need time to think about staying. It's not because you can't walk. Well it is, but not in the way you think."

Faint lines appeared at his brow. "I'm confused."

She huffed out a frustrated breath. How could she explain? She couldn't tell him his lack of social prospects and the town's lack of status was the true reason. He'd think she was a snob. And she wasn't a snob. Her future was at stake.

She had to be rational about it. She couldn't simply stay because Jesse was handsome and charming and kind and funny and all the other things that were of only secondary importance when choosing a husband.

"It's difficult to explain," she said, "but it's not because I don't think you would be a good husband or because I'm repulsed by you or anything like that."

One side of his mouth curled up. "It's good to know I don't repulse you, at least."

She winced. "That didn't come out right."

"Truth is, a lot of people are repulsed by me. Or at least, they don't know how to behave around me. I make them uncomfortable."

He made *her* uncomfortable, but for reasons that had nothing to do with his disability. Reasons she couldn't possibly tell him. "That must be awful for you."

"Frustrating is more the word. It was worse when I was younger and self-conscious, but it is how it is. All I can do is live my life, be the person God would have me be, with His help, and politely correct people when they say or do stupid things. Also with God's help. Lots of help."

She thought of how badly she'd reacted when they'd first met. "Like me."

"No, not like you," he said, smiling. "You didn't talk over me or treat me like a child or get angry at me. You treated me like a normal human being. That's all I want." He looked out over the garden. "Waiting for you to arrive today, all I could think about was all the ways it could go wrong. I can honestly say I've never been so scared in all my life. But you've been real good about it all. I couldn't ask for more."

For the first time since she'd arrived, Louisa properly considered what the whole situation must be like from Jesse's point of view. If she was in his position, feeling as if his only chance at the one thing he wanted was to take the risk and do the only thing he could, wouldn't she do the same? In fact, wasn't that what she had done by coming all the way across the country to marry a man she'd never met?

"I think you're very courageous," she said.

His eyes widened. "You do?"

She nodded. "You did what you had to, no matter that it was a risk. I promise I'm not taking that lightly and I will think very hard about what I'm going to do." It was all she could promise for now, until she'd had time to think through all the ramifications of her decision, but she hoped he understood.

"I appreciate that." His smile returned, the playful one that crinkled the corners of his eyes and made the gold flecks in them shine. "Is there anything I can say or do to help you make up your mind?"

She couldn't help smiling back. "Not right now."

He nodded slowly. "Well then, how about we just talk?"

"I'd like that." She found she wanted to talk to him. Maybe she'd been wrong before. In order to make an informed decision, she ought to get to know him a little.

Simply talking couldn't hurt. Could it?

Chapter 4

By the time Jesse reached home the sun had set and the sky was turning a dark purple.

He rolled up to the path towards his front door, frowning at the light glowing from the parlour window. Unlike many people, he always locked his doors, years of working in a bank having instilled in him the value of security. Was he being robbed? He briefly considered turning around and going for the marshal, but then he heard a high pitched laugh. His fears vanishing in an instant, he continued to the door. He should have guessed who was in his home. There was no way they would wait overnight for news.

The moment he wheeled through the parlour door a squealing yellow blur hurtled across the room and flew into his lap, pushing the air from his lungs and shoving his wheelchair back several inches.

"Is she nice? Is she as pretty as in her picture? Are you going to get married straight away? When can I meet her?"

He grimaced. "Nan, your knee's digging into my leg."

"Oh. Sorry." She squirmed round so she was sitting across his lap rather than kneeling on it. Her large, round eyes shone with excitement. "So? What happened?"

"Nancy, at least let your brother get in the door before you question him," Malinda said from the settee where she sat beside Jesse's father.

"He *is* in the door, Ma," Nancy pointed out. "Pa said she

had *eight* travel trunks. Does she have lots of pretty dresses?"

Luke lounged in the armchair where Louisa had sat earlier, chewing on the remains of a biscuit that looked suspiciously like one of the ones Jesse had baked that morning, with two more waiting on his plate. Jesse was surprised to see him there at all. At fourteen, his brother usually had other things to do when he wasn't in school or helping their father in the forge, mostly involving a certain other fourteen-year-old named Tabitha who lived in town.

Jesse wrapped his arms around his sister and kissed her temple. "I don't know. She didn't show me her luggage."

"But she is going to stay? Do you think if I asked her, she'd show me?"

"I don't know," he said again.

"You don't know if she'll show me her dresses or you don't know if she'll stay?"

He stifled a sigh and looked past her to his parents. "Both."

Luke looked up from his biscuit.

The excitement melted from Nancy's face. "She might not stay?"

He hated seeing his sister unhappy. Her constant childish enthusiasm for life was always such a joy to be around. Well, mostly always. "She's going to tell me tomorrow what she's going to do. She hasn't decided yet. It was kind of a shock for her, finding out I can't walk."

She rested her head on his shoulder and picked at one of the buttons on his shirt. "Yeah, but she could see you can do everything else, couldn't she? And how nice you are and everything? Why wouldn't she want to stay?"

"She likely will," Peter said. "She just needs a bit of time to think. I'm sure you'll get to meet her soon, angel."

Nancy sighed, her head remaining against Jesse's shoulder. "Yes, Pa."

49

Nothing ever happened fast enough for his ten-year-old sister. In the past week Jesse had barely seen her sit still as she helped him get his home ready for her potential future sister-in-law's arrival. There were times when she almost seemed more excited for Louisa's arrival than he was. *Almost.*

"It'll be all right, Nan. You'll see." A tight hug and a kiss to her forehead had her smiling again. He couldn't help wishing it was as easy to cheer himself up.

Although if *Louisa* gave him a hug and kissed him...

"So what's she like?" Malinda said.

He didn't even have to think about smiling, it just happened. "She's even better than her photograph. She was wearing a green dress that looked so beautiful on her. Then she changed into a blue skirt and white shirtwaist that looked even better. And she's funny and smart and interesting and real easy to talk to and... and..." He looked at the window even though outside all was in darkness. "And I really want her to stay."

Malinda stood from the settee, walked over to him and Nancy and wrapped her arms around the both of them. Even though she and Jesse weren't related by blood, she'd been married to his father since he was ten and she was as much his mother as if she'd given birth to him.

"She'll stay," she murmured. "There is no way any woman in her right mind could resist my gorgeous, wonderful son."

He smiled as she kissed the top of his head. "Thanks, Malinda."

She straightened and pushed a strand of hair away from his eyes. "You need a haircut."

"I like my hair this length." It was a little longer than most men had theirs, but he didn't want to conform. He couldn't anyway, so why even try?

"So do I," Nancy said. "And it would be even better if

you'd let me tie ribbons in it."

It had been a longstanding disagreement between them since he'd grown his hair out. One day he'd relent and let her, just once, but he was saving that for a birthday or Christmas. So he simply rolled his eyes and shook his head and she giggled.

Jesse's family stayed for another hour and he was glad for it. He'd probably have been moping for the rest of the evening and gone to bed miserable if they hadn't, but as it was, by the time they stood to leave he was feeling much better about things and much more hopeful about Louisa.

Luke handed Jesse the plate he'd used for the biscuits as he walked past. "Thanks for the food." He pushed his hands into his pockets and looked at the floor. "Even if she doesn't stay, you can find someone else. I've got some money saved up. I can help pay for another train ticket."

Jesse's mouth dropped open for a split second before he recovered and closed it again. It wasn't that he and his brother weren't close, they were, but he knew Luke was saving that money so he could marry Tabitha when they were sixteen. It was as big a gesture of sacrifice as he could imagine from the young man.

"Thank you, Luke," he said with sincerity. "That's real kind of you."

Malinda, tears in her eyes, threw her arms around her youngest son. "I'm so proud of you."

"Ma!" Luke said, batting her away. "You're embarrassing me." He rolled his eyes at Jesse and carried on into the hallway.

That was the Luke they all knew and loved.

Nancy climbed down from the chair she'd pushed to his desk and walked over to hand him the drawing she'd been working on. A white church with arched windows sat beneath a bright blue sky. Beside the church was a bride in a

51

flowing white dress and a groom in a wheelchair.

He had to clear his throat before he spoke, and even then his voice sounded a bit husky. "Thank you. I love it."

After one final hug, she followed her mother out.

Jesse's father was the last to go. "Would you like me to stay and help with your legs?"

"No, they're not bad today. I can do it."

Peter placed his hand on his shoulder. "God will work this out. I'm proud of you, son. You're going to make a fine husband and father."

Jesse looked down at Nancy's drawing of his wedding. He hoped he got the chance. "Thanks, Pa."

Once his family had left, he wheeled over to the settee and swung himself onto the cushions. The wheelchair was comfortable, thanks to his father's design and build and the padded leather seat he'd given it, but it couldn't match the softness of the settee. He pulled a footstool in front of him and lifted his right leg up, stretching it out with a sigh.

Beginning his regular massage and stretching routine to loosen his bunched muscles, he looked at his sister's drawing beside him, his thoughts turning to Louisa. Not that they'd ever strayed far from her. He wondered what she was doing, if she was thinking about him. If she was trying to decide whether to stay and give him a chance, or if she'd already made up her mind.

"Please, Father," he said. "I don't know if I did the wrong thing in not being honest with her before she came. Forgive me if I did. But please tell her to stay."

~ ~ ~

Louisa pulled the knitted blanket closer around her shoulders, staring at the blank piece of paper resting on her lap desk in front of her on the bed.

Well, it wasn't entirely blank. She'd written the Jones' address in the top right hand corner with the date beneath it. And she'd also written 'Dearest Mother and Father'. That was where her inspiration had run out.

The letter was either going to inform them that she would soon be on her way home, or tell them she was staying for two weeks and asking for their advice on whether or not she should marry Jesse if she found out that would be something she would have no objections to doing. The trouble was, she still didn't know which it was going to be.

She'd been so certain leaving straight away was the right thing to do, both for her and Jesse, until he'd arrived with the delicious meal from Mrs Goodwin and set her thoughts in a whirl again. How did he do that to her? She wasn't a flighty, silly girl with her head in the clouds. She was practical and sensible and she knew what she wanted, what her parents had raised her for - she was going to marry a well-to-do man with a good job and good prospects who could elevate her to the social status which her birth alone couldn't. She was unwaveringly sure of that, when Jesse wasn't around.

She didn't like the way he made her feel out of control and uncertain about everything. It wasn't good for her.

She picked up her pen, pulled the desk to her, and placed the nib onto the paper. It stayed there, unmoving, until the ink had leaked into a splotch. Gritting her teeth in frustration, she scrunched the paper into a ball and threw it across the room where it bounced off the wall to land on the rug. Then she punched her fist into the bed beside her with a squeak of anger.

She should go home. She knew she should go home. Right away.

Jesse's green eyes came unbidden into her mind, along with his easy smile, his infectious laughter, his smooth voice.

With a sigh of resignation, she pulled another sheet of

paper from the desk's small drawer and began to write.

Chapter 5

Louisa started at the sound of the knock on the front door, almost dropping her bonnet. She was ridiculously skittish this morning.

She placed the bonnet onto her bed and walked into the hallway. Pastor Jones had left for the church straight after breakfast and Mrs Jones had joined him not long after, so she was alone in the house. Halfway to the door she came to a halt as a frightening thought occurred to her that it could be Jesse, and she considered creeping back to her bedroom and hiding until whoever it was went away.

The knock sounded again and she almost jumped out of her skin. This was silly. She was behaving like a child. Lifting her chin, she smoothed her hands over her hair and resumed her walk to the door. She was an adult and she was going to act like one, even when she felt more like a terrified little girl.

Squaring her shoulders, she grasped the handle and pulled the front door open.

And looked down.

"Oh good, you're home." The young girl standing outside lowered the fist poised to knock again and gave Louisa a wide smile. "I'm Nancy." She held out her hand.

Louisa automatically took it and gave it a gentle shake. "It's a pleasure to meet you. I'm Louisa."

Nancy. Why did that name seem familiar?

"I know, that's why I'm here. I came to see you."

Nancy looked past her into the house and Louisa suddenly realised how rude she was being.

"I'm sorry. Would you like to come in?" She stepped aside to let her past and closed the door, wondering why a young girl she'd never met would be there to see her. "May I get you something to drink?"

"I'd like a glass of milk, thanks." She turned away and then turned back, adding, "If it's not too much trouble."

"Of course not."

Nancy followed her into the kitchen. "Mrs Jones usually has fruit scones when I'm here."

Louisa looked around. "I'll see if I can find some."

"They're in the pantry, on the third shelf up on the right," Nancy said immediately, pointing to the green striped curtain that covered the pantry doorway.

Louisa almost burst into laughter, which was surprising given her current state of mind. She liked the forthright little girl. "It's a good thing you know your way around here. I don't know where anything is yet."

Nancy slid onto a seat at the table. "I've been here a lot. I've known Pastor Jones and Mrs Jones since I was born."

Louisa found the plate of scones right where Nancy said they'd be and quickly buttered one.

"Ooh, cherry!" Nancy exclaimed when Louisa set the plate and a glass of milk in front of her and sat in the chair opposite. "Cherry's my favourite." Her eyes went to the empty space on the table in front of Louisa. "Aren't you having one? Mrs Jones makes the best scones. Apart from Mrs Goodwin."

"It's not long since I had breakfast. I'm not hungry." It was true, although she'd barely picked at her food that morning.

"Neither am I," Nancy replied, biting into her scone.

Louisa watched her chew. "So why are you here to see

56

me, Nancy?"

She swallowed her mouthful and fixed Louisa with a serious look. "I'm here to talk to you about my brother."

Brother. Realisation struck. "You're Jesse's sister."

With her dark hair and chocolate brown eyes, Nancy looked nothing like her brother. Their father's hair was light brown and he had a fairer complexion, so Louisa guessed she must favour her mother.

Nancy nodded as she took another bite. "Mm hmm."

How could Louisa have forgotten that? She must have been even more flustered than she thought. It was a terrible faux pas to forget someone's name. "I'm so sorry. He talked about you a lot in his letters, but I didn't make the connection when you told me your name. I think I'm still tired from the journey."

Nancy waved the hand not holding the scone. "That's all right. I'm glad he told you about me though. I've been looking forward to you coming. I've always wanted a sister."

Louisa's heart dropped. "Nancy, I'm not... I mean, I don't..."

"I know you're thinking of not staying," she said, "but that's why I'm here. I want to tell you all about Jesse, so you'll know how nice he is and how much you'll like him."

Not knowing what to say, Louisa simply nodded.

Nancy placed the half eaten scone onto the plate and pulled a piece of paper from a pocket in her green floral dress. Unfolding the slightly crumpled page, she smoothed it out on the table. "I wrote it all down so I wouldn't forget anything."

"That's very admirable," Louisa said. "Being prepared for things is important."

Nancy looked up from the paper. "Is that why you couldn't decide last night if you were going to stay? Because you weren't prepared?"

"I suppose so. Finding out Jesse can't walk was a big surprise." She didn't add that she also wasn't at all prepared for the effect he had on her. "I've never met someone like him before."

"But he's just like everyone else, except he can't walk. But he can do everything else." Nancy looked at the paper. "Oh wait, I have that on my list."

Louisa tried not to smile. "Then maybe you should go ahead and read me your list."

She nodded, smoothed the piece of paper again, and sat up straight as if about to give an important presentation. Louisa decided she may have been the most adorable child she'd ever met.

Not only was Jesse impossible to resist, so was his sister. He probably had a litter of fluffy kittens stashed somewhere too.

"Jesse was sixteen when I was born," Nancy read, "so when I was little he was already grown up. But he wasn't ever too busy to play with me or Luke." She looked up. "That's my other brother. He's four years older than me." When Louisa nodded she focused on the paper again. "Even when he was learning to be an accountant and I didn't really understand that he needed time for studying, he never once told me to go away or be quiet. I know when he has his own children he'll be just as nice to them too. Even though he can't walk, he can do everything else, like I said already, and he's a real good cook. He makes the best cookies apart from Mrs Goodwin and he lets me help. And he doesn't get annoyed at me when I spill things." She looked up again. "Although he does mostly make me clean it up, but he's probably right to do that. Don't tell him I said so though."

"I won't."

Nancy nodded and returned her attention to the list. "He's real strong, almost as strong as Pa, and he gives the best hugs. He's smart and funny and he makes me laugh. And he knows lots of things, like which books are the most fun to read and how to help me with my math schoolwork and lots and lots more. I think he'd make just about the best husband in the world."

She folded the paper closed and Louisa rapidly swiped at the moisture threatening to spill down her cheeks. It was just as well she'd already decided to stay for the two weeks because if she hadn't, she would have had to rewrite the letter to her parents. Jesse couldn't possibly be as perfect as his sister thought he was. Could he?

"Don't tell him I told you this," Nancy said, "but he really wants you to stay. He likes you a lot and he thinks you're real pretty, which you are, and I know he'd be sad if you went home now. So please could you stay? Because I don't want him to be sad and I know you'll love him as much as I do once you get to know him."

"Does he know you're here?"

Nancy's eyes widened. "Oh no! I don't think he'd be happy if he knew I was here. You won't tell him, will you?"

Louisa smiled. "No, I won't tell him."

"So will you stay?"

As if she had a choice after that heartfelt list of all his best qualities. "Yes, I'll stay. But that doesn't mean I'm going to marry him," she added quickly when Nancy's smile threatened to swallow her whole face. "I don't want you to get excited and then be disappointed when it doesn't work out and I leave."

"It'll work out," Nancy declared, still smiling. "You'll see." She stood and hurried around the table to hug Louisa, saying into her shoulder, "I can't wait until we're sisters." She stepped back, excitement dancing in her eyes. "Are you going to tell Jesse soon?"

Louisa briefly considered again trying to explain that it

59

was highly likely she would be leaving in two weeks, but at the expression on Nancy's face she gave up the idea. She wasn't sure anything could dampen the girl's enthusiasm.

"I was planning to walk to the post office now to mail a letter then go on to his house from there."

Nancy gasped in delight. "Could I come with you? I could show you the way. Just to the post office and Jesse's house, but I wouldn't let him see me."

She didn't need to be shown the way, with Green Hill Creek consisting of barely more than a handful of streets, but Nancy's eagerness was impossible to refuse. "Thank you, I'd like that. I'll just get my shawl."

Nancy retook her seat at the table. "I'll finish my scone."

Once in her bedroom, Louisa leaned against the door and heaved a sigh. How on earth was she going to disappoint Jesse's young sister?

By the time the two weeks was up, she was going to feel like the worst person in the world.

~ ~ ~

Louisa had hoped to see Amy at the post office, but Adam told her she was out looking for work. Which made no sense at all until he also told her the rest of what had happened after Louisa left them at the station the day before.

She was a little shocked at their situation, but it wasn't her business. Besides, she knew Amy was sensible and if she trusted Adam then he must be an honourable man. And that he was Jesse's friend also put her at ease. In fact, that alone convinced her Adam would be good to Amy. She knew she could trust Jesse. She wasn't sure how she knew, but she knew. Maybe it was because he wasn't like any other man she'd met, in a way that had nothing to do with his inability to walk.

She posted the letter to her parents explaining about him and how she was going to stay for two weeks before deciding what to do next. She wasn't sure if a reply would reach her before the two weeks was up, but she'd asked them what she should do anyway. She'd relied on their advice her entire life and being so far away from them had her feeling more than a little lost without it.

Nancy chatted more or less the entire time, a constant narrative on how wonderful Jesse was, who lived at each house they passed, where she liked to play, where Luke liked to play, how amazing Jesse was, the time she'd fallen in the creek with all her clothes on, her favourite candies at Mr Lamb's general store, the magnificence of her eldest brother...

She stopped abruptly in the middle of a story about her friend Joshua, a frog, and his terrified older sister. "I'd better not go any further or he'll see me, and Ma's expecting me home, but his house is just up there on the left. Don't forget to not mention at all that you saw me today."

"I promise I won't say a thing," Louisa said. "But you mustn't forget to act surprised when he tells you I'm staying."

"I'm going to practice in front of the mirror so I get it right."

"Good idea," Louisa replied, trying to look serious.

Nancy threw her arms around her. "I'm so pleased you're staying. We're going to have so much fun."

She let go and turned to run back the way they'd come, stopping after a few steps to wave and then taking off again. Louisa tried to remember a time when she'd had such boundless zest and energy and found she couldn't. She did remember her mother's assertion that refined young ladies didn't run. At the time she'd accepted the instruction, albeit reluctantly, but as she watched Nancy dash away she couldn't help thinking how natural it seemed that a child should run. Smiling to herself, she resumed her walk to Jesse's house.

The closer she got, the more the smile faded and her nervousness grew. By the time she reached the door she needed to pause and gather her courage before knocking.

The door opened after only a few seconds. Louisa had wondered that morning when she woke if Jesse really could have been as handsome as she'd thought the day before. Or if it had been the fatigue from the journey and the shock of what he'd told her that had scrambled her memories.

It wasn't.

And he was.

"Yes, I'll stay."

His mouth dropped open and then he smiled so wide it looked as if his face would split right in half. There was the resemblance to his sister, they had the same smile.

"But this doesn't mean I'm going to marry you," she added. "I need time to decide that."

"I know," he said, still grinning. "And good morning." He wheeled back to allow her into the house. "Have you eaten yet? Would you like breakfast?"

She had eaten, but she'd only picked at her food. She'd been too nervous at the prospect of committing herself to staying for two weeks when she would likely have to let him down at the end. And that was before she'd met his adorable sister.

What had she just *done*?

She suddenly felt as if she'd never want to eat again. "I'm not hungry, thank you."

He closed the door behind her. "Well, if it's not rude, would you mind if I finished mine? I'm going to need all my strength if we're going to spend the day together."

Her heart rate climbed. "We... we're going to spend the day together?"

"If you have no objections. I only have two weeks to charm you, and when you factor in the time I'll be working and sleeping and making myself presentable and so on, that only gives me," he paused, his eyes going to the ceiling as he worked it out, "around fifty hours. Which sounds a lot, but when you really think about it isn't so much when you're talking about falling in love. So I reckon I need to get started right away."

"Oh. Yes." She swallowed. He didn't really expect her to fall in love with him, did he? "Could I possibly have a drink of water?"

"Of course." He gestured towards the kitchen. "I'm eating out the back, since the weather's so nice."

She walked from the kitchen onto a porch at the back of the house. A ramp sloped down to the garden, just as at the front. There was no lawn or vegetable patch like in most gardens she'd seen. Instead a stone-paved courtyard encircled a magnificent walnut tree in the centre. Flowering bushes, shrubs and plants softened the edges and two raised flowerbeds, constructed from thick logs, hugged the porch either side of the ramp. Two wood and wrought iron benches sat to either side of the yard. She could see how the whole thing had been designed for ease of use by someone in a wheelchair.

There was a table on the porch and she took one of the four chairs around it as Jesse wheeled from the kitchen. He placed a glass of water in front of her then moved into a free space at the table where an empty coffee cup sat next to a plate of half eaten buttered toast and fried eggs.

"You have a lovely garden," she said, looking out over the flower-laden space.

"Thank you for saying so. I'd love to take credit for it, but as per our arrangement in that I will be almost completely honest with you from now on, I have to admit keeping plants alive is not among my skills. Mrs Jones comes every week to tend to it. I've begged her to allow me to pay her, but she won't take anything. She says she enjoys doing it. So I put extra into the church offering every week." He winced. "I hope that didn't sound like I was boasting about giving the money. I just wanted you to know I don't expect people to do things for me."

"I understand." And she was impressed. He truly was independent.

"When I first moved in here my pa laid the flagstones so I could get around in my chair, and he also built the raised beds so I could reach them easily. That was before either of us discovered my tendency to plant things and then forget about them until they're strangled by weeds."

She watched a pair of white butterflies spiral into the air and flit away. "I've always enjoyed gardening. I find it soothing. Fortunately, my mother regarded it as a suitable occupation for my time."

"Suitable occupation?"

She returned her gaze to him. "Ladylike. Providing I didn't get dirty or do any strenuous digging."

His head tilted slightly to one side as he considered her words. "I guess things are different in the city. Here, the women often work as hard as the men. Probably harder."

She remembered the many advertisements she'd read in the course of finding Jesse's. "A lot of the men who advertised for brides wanted women who were strong and had skills in farming and such. My mother was horrified. She said they needed an ox rather than a woman."

He laughed. "So I guess it's safe to say you were never going to be a farmer's wife?"

"Goodness, no," she said. "Mother would have taken to her bed and never got out again."

The smile that made his eyes shine and her insides

flutter curved his lips. "I guess I should thank your mother then, that she approved of me over all the other men you could have chosen."

She could feel the blush starting and she lowered her gaze without thinking. Too late, she realised the flirtatiousness of the move and snapped her eyes back up, horrified. She absolutely could not give Jesse false hope.

His smile faded as he watched her. "You're uncomfortable."

She sighed and looked at her hands twisted in her lap. Maybe she should be as honest with him as he was being with her. "I'm afraid of leading you on. I don't want to make you think I'll be staying beyond the two weeks. It wouldn't be fair to you."

"I'm just grateful for the two weeks. I brought you here under false pretences, remember? All I want is for us to get to know each other. Whatever happens after that I will deal with when the time comes, but I don't want you to think you have to watch your behaviour. I want you to enjoy your time here, to be able to relax and have fun." He leaned forward and ducked his head to look into her face. "I promise I won't assume from anything you do or say that you want to marry me. Okay?"

Louisa was beginning to think Nancy was right, her brother really was perfect. At that moment, she couldn't imagine there was anyone else on earth who could have soothed her nerves.

She raised her eyes and nodded, and even smiled. "Okay."

The smile he gave her in return had her heart thudding again, but this time it had nothing to do with anxiety. "Okay."

He sat back and picked up his toast and, to her mortification, her stomach rumbled loudly. She slapped a hand over it, as if that could muffle the sound.

"Sure you wouldn't like to change your mind about having some breakfast?" he said.

She gave him a sheepish smile. "I think maybe I would."

Grinning, he backed away from the table and turned towards the kitchen.

"Jesse?" she said as a thought came to her.

He looked back. "Yes?"

"You don't, by any chance, have any kittens, do you?"

"Kittens?" He looked confused. "Uh, no. Why?"

She couldn't help smiling. "Oh, no reason."

Breakfast was delicious. It was only eggs and toast, and yet Jesse added some kind of seasoning that made it burst with flavour without overwhelming the taste.

"This is incredible," she said between mouthfuls. "What have you done with it?"

"It's just herbs and a couple of spices." He pointed to one of the raised flowerbeds filled with leaves of all shapes and sizes. "Mrs Jones planted that one especially so I'd have fresh herbs to cook with."

She looked from the plants to her food. "You truly don't need anything, do you?"

"What do you mean?"

"I mean..." She pushed a piece of toast around the plate with her fork. "The only thing you brought me here for is... me."

When he didn't reply, she raised her eyes.

He looked uncertain, as if he wasn't sure how to respond. "Is that a bad thing?"

"No. It just feels like a lot of responsibility."

His smile returned. "I'm pretty sure you're up to the job."

"You don't even know me."

"I think I do, a little. We did exchange letters for almost

five months."

"Yes, but I..." She looked away, thinking how to explain without sounding as if she'd been lying to him. "I always tried to make myself sound as attractive as possible, so you'd choose me."

He spread his hands, glancing down at his legs. "Have you forgotten my own little omission?" Leaning his elbows on the table, he gazed into her face. "I figure we'll both learn a lot about each other in the next two weeks, but you want to know why I chose you and none of the other women I wrote to?"

She wasn't so sure she did, but she nodded anyway.

"I chose you because there was something about you, a kind of spark in your words. I felt like we could be friends. You have this sense of fun and adventurousness that convinced me I'd want to spend my time with you."

That didn't sound like her at all. "Are you sure you're not confusing me with someone else?"

"I'm sure," he said with a chuckle. "Maybe it's a bit hidden right now, but it's definitely there, just waiting to be set free. I can tell."

It couldn't be true. She always made sure she behaved like a lady; demure, reserved, sober. She didn't do fun and adventurous. She'd never been allowed to.

"You're just teasing me," she said, waving her fork and smiling.

He leaned back, his gaze speculative. "Well now, I think I'll take this as a challenge. I bet you two weeks from now the real Louisa will be sitting across this table from me, whoever she is. Although I think I already know."

She couldn't help laughing. "You're very sure of yourself, aren't you?"

He grinned. "Sure am."

Chapter 6

After breakfast Jesse packed up a set of saddlebags with a picnic, donned a dark brown cowboy hat, and they headed for the livery.

Parson's Livery was a large, barn-like structure on the edge of town. Louisa followed Jesse in through the open double doors at the front, immediately fighting an urge to raise her hand to her nose. Despite the doors they'd entered through and another set ahead of them being wide open, the smell was unpleasantly strong.

"George?" Jesse called into the seemingly empty building.

"Morning, Jesse."

Louisa jumped at the voice behind her, whirling round to see a man emerging from a door she hadn't noticed.

"Sorry, ma'am," the man said. "Didn't mean to startle you."

"Louisa, this is George Parsons," Jesse said. "Owner of the best livery in town, so he tells me. George, meet Louisa Wood."

Mr Parsons snorted a laugh. "Haven't heard any complaints from you or Duke." He turned to Louisa. "Pleasure to meet you, Miss Wood. I'd shake your hand, but I don't reckon you'd want me to." He held up his dirty palms.

"It's nice to meet you, Mr Parsons," she replied. "And thank you for your kind consideration."

George Parsons appeared somewhere around fifty, with sun roughened skin and dark hair sprinkled with grey. Despite his hair needing a trim and his face needing a shave, he wasn't unattractive for his age.

"Where's Zach?" Jesse said, looking around.

"Working at the hotel. Art Porter twisted his ankle pretty bad and can't walk so Zach's covering for him this morning. He said he'd be in later though. He'd better. I could use his help."

"Still haven't found anyone to replace Abner?"

"Not yet, but with this being a Saturday, I'm hoping someone will come round. Got Duke ready for you. Saddled Eagle too, like you asked." He looked at Louisa. "You know how to ride, ma'am?"

"Uh, yes, a little, although I haven't for a while."

"Don't worry, Eagle's a good, calm horse. He'll take care of you. I'll bring them in."

"You arranged all this?" she said to Jesse as Mr Parsons headed out the back.

"Yesterday, before you arrived. You said you could ride in one of your letters." He smiled. "Or were you not being entirely truthful about that?"

"Oh no, I can ride." She could, probably. Her parents had managed to get her a handful of lessons in exchange for some work for a rich family when she was eighteen, and she'd enjoyed them at the time. Admittedly, she hadn't ridden since, but she was sure she could remember how.

Almost sure.

Reasonably sure.

Mr Parsons returned through the back doors with two horses and nerves fluttered through Louisa's stomach at the sight of the big animals.

One of them, a large, muscular grey stallion, headed straight for Jesse, bending his head to nuzzle at his shoulder.

"Morning, boy," Jesse said, rubbing his neck and ruffling the mane between his ears. "Louisa, I'd like you to meet Duke, the best horse in the world."

Duke lifted his head at her cautious approach, one ear flicking back.

"Good morning, Duke," she said softly, holding out a hand.

The horse stretched his neck to sniff at her hand, blowing out a soft breath onto her knuckles then nudging her with his nose. She moved her hand to his neck, stroking down to his shoulder when he perked both ears forward and leaned into her touch.

"Looks like you've found a friend there," Mr Parsons said, taking the saddlebags from Jesse and attaching them to the back of Duke's saddle.

She stopped stroking and laughed when the horse stretched out to hook his nose beneath her hand again.

"Bit of an attention seeker," Jesse said, "especially when it comes to beautiful women."

She glanced at him out of the corner of her eye. "Are you talking about your horse?"

His eyes widened, and then he burst into laughter.

"She's got you there, kid," Mr Parsons said. He draped the reins of the second horse he'd brought in loosely over one of the stall doors and patted his neck. "This here's Eagle. He's a good horse. Had him eight months and never had any trouble with him. He'll look after you."

"Thank you, Mr Parsons." Walking slowly up to the sturdy bay, she held out her hand. "I'm sure we'll get on just fine, won't we, Eagle?" She hoped the horse believed her more than she believed herself.

He sniffed her hand and seemed happy to let her stroke his neck. Hopefully he would still be happy when she was on his back. The back that looked inordinately high off the ground.

"Can I help you up, Miss Wood?" Mr Parsons said, placing a mounting block beside Eagle.

She took his hand and stepped up onto the block. It only then occurred to her that the saddle on Eagle's back was for riding astride. She'd only ever ridden side saddle.

"Something wrong?" Mr Parsons said.

"Uh, no. No, everything's fine." Jesse didn't have to know how useless she was when it came to the practicalities of living in the west. How hard could riding astride be?

Except, what on earth was she going to do with her *skirt*?

Somehow, with a lot of quick thought and pauses to rearrange clothing, she ended up in the saddle with her legs covered demurely, although once she was up there she wasn't entirely sure how she'd managed it without becoming indecent. Or even *if* she'd managed it, which was a mortifying thought.

Thankfully, neither Jesse nor Mr Parsons looked embarrassed or awkward, so presumably she had. Or maybe they were just being polite.

Jesse wheeled in close to a stall on the other side of the livery, Duke following him. Without any instruction, the horse positioned himself side on to Jesse on the opposite side to the stall and stood still.

Grasping the top of the stall door, Jesse pulled himself to a standing position then moved one hand to the pommel of Duke's saddle. Louisa watched in amazement as, using only his arms, he raised himself into the air between the stall and the horse and at the last moment twisted to seat himself on the saddle. He pulled his leg over Duke's neck and reached down to situate his feet in the stirrups.

"You're so strong," she murmured in awe.

He looked over at her and smiled and she might have imagined it, but his chest may have puffed out a little. She couldn't help noticing, even through the fabric of his shirt, how broad a chest it was. Up on Duke with his cowboy hat and his denim trousers, he looked every inch the dashing, romantic hero.

"Anything else you need?" Mr Parsons said, wheeling Jesse's chair into an alcove by the back door.

Louisa rapidly looked away from Jesse's chest. She really needed to stop staring at him so much.

"No thanks, George. We'll be back later."

"Have a good day." Mr Parsons took a well worn brown hat hanging on one of the stall doors, nodded to Louisa, and walked out the back door.

Jesse guided Duke over to her. "You ready?"

She looked at the back of Eagle's head. To her mild surprise, she felt fairly comfortable in the saddle. Of course, so far they hadn't actually moved. "As I'll ever be."

He reached out to touch her arm. "Are you sure you're all right with riding?"

She drew a deep breath in and out. "The truth is, I haven't been on a horse for years and I'm not used to riding astride. But I'm sure I'll be okay. Mr Parsons said Eagle is a calm horse. I think I can do calm." And despite her nerves she found she was even looking forward to it.

He nodded and gave her a smile that seemed just a bit pleased with itself. "Okay then, my little adventuress. Let's go for a ride."

"Ohhh." She drew out the word as understanding struck. "You think this is the fun and adventurous real me emerging, don't you?"

He affected a wide-eyed look of innocence, laying a hand on his chest in feigned shock. "I'm sure I don't know what you're talking about."

"Of course you don't." Ignoring Jesse's grin, she rubbed the side of Eagle's neck. "Come on, Eagle. Let's show him this is simply a gentle, everyday ride with nothing at all adventurous about it."

She pressed her knees into Eagle's sides and, to her relief, he began to walk. Guiding him towards the front doors, she held herself straight and gave no indication that the sudden movement had made her stomach lurch.

She also hid her thrilled smile when she found her balance and realised she remembered how to ride a horse after all.

~ ~ ~

They rode for over an hour, Jesse taking them on a tour of the town and then out into the surrounding countryside.

After a while, with her confidence and enjoyment growing, Louisa nudged Eagle into a faster walk and was gratified when it took Jesse by surprise and he fell behind. She didn't want him to think her nerves always got the better of her. She could be brave sometimes.

She smiled at him when he caught up.

"You're doing real well with him," he said, nodding at Eagle.

"I'd forgotten how much I like riding." She gave her docile horse a pat on the side of his neck. "I'm truly enjoying myself."

"You sound surprised."

"I am, I guess. A little." She gasped, one hand going to her mouth. "Oh! I don't mean I'm surprised to be enjoying myself with you."

He chuckled, a pleasant sound that wound its way up her spine and wrapped itself around her chest in what felt like an auditory hug. She vaguely thought she should berate herself for thinking about auditory hugs, but she was having too nice a time to bother.

"That hadn't occurred to me, but I'm glad to hear it." He leaned forward and peered around the brim of her bonnet. "I'm also glad to hear you're enjoying my company."

She didn't want him to be encouraged by that, but she couldn't stop a smile from tugging at her lips.

The amusement in his eyes told her he'd noticed.

It occurred to her that she should be more careful about what she said, but then she remembered his assurance about not assuming by anything she did that she would be staying to marry him. And right now, bathed in the late morning sunshine, surrounded by stunning scenery and with a handsome, charming man at her side, she wasn't inclined to question it.

He eventually took them up a hill overlooking the town and through a stand of trees, coming to a halt where they emerged to a wildflower-drenched meadow and a vista across the valley to the mountains.

"Oh, Jesse," she breathed, "this is beautiful."

"I was hoping you'd like it. What do you say to stopping here?"

She drew in the scent of flowers and spring, releasing the air on a sigh. "I'd say it's the most perfect spot."

He walked Duke a little way out into the meadow to an ancient, stunted tree, and twisted to remove the saddlebags from behind him.

"Can I do anything to help?" Louisa said, reining Eagle in beside him.

"Are you all right getting down by yourself?"

She looked at the very, very far away ground and gave a firm nod. She'd got this far, she could get down. "I can do it. But..." she glanced up at him, "would you mind turning away? I haven't quite got the hang of what to do with my skirt when I get on and off and I might inadvertently become indecent."

His lips pressed together as he looked down at Duke's back, his shoulders quivering.

"Stop laughing at me," she said, fighting a giggle.

"I'm not laughing at you," he said, grinning. "I just think it's funny that here I am worried you might be nervous about falling and all you're concerned with is showing an ankle. I think I may be underestimating you."

She lifted her chin. "A proper lady knows that breaking a leg is one thing, but allowing anyone to see it is far, far worse."

He barked a laugh that had Duke looking back at him. Jesse patted his shoulder. "Sorry, boy."

Louisa waved her hand at him. "Just turn around. I'll tell you when I'm down."

"Yes, ma'am."

With his eyes safely in the other direction, Louisa hoisted her skirts up and dismounted, arranging her clothing again before speaking. "I'm down."

He turned back to her, his gaze briefly lowering to her feet, and she was sure she detected a hint of disappointment in his eyes. She should have been indignant that he was hoping to get an illicit glimpse of an ankle, and yet she wasn't. In the slightest.

"You can let Eagle loose, he won't go far," he said, lifting the saddlebags from Duke's back and handing them down to her. "There's a blanket in the right one, if you'd like to get it out."

She let out a yelp of surprise as he released the bags and the weight pulled her forward.

He gasped and reached down to her. "I'm sorry, I didn't think how heavy they are. Are you all right?"

She straightened, pulling the bags up with her and attempting to hide the effort it was taking. "I'm fine. I've got it."

75

She carried them a few feet away, placed them on the ground and opened the right hand one. Inside was a blue woven blanket and she pulled it out, admiring the craftsmanship as she ran her hand over the surface. The pretty material was soft yet hardwearing, with a subtle checked pattern.

"Okay, Duke," Jesse said behind her.

Duke wandered past to a juicy patch of grass in the meadow, Eagle following.

Louisa turned back to Jesse. "Where would you like..." She stopped abruptly, gasping in a breath. "You're standing!"

He was leaning against the ancient tree, his left arm wrapped around a low branch. He wasn't completely upright, but he was on his feet.

"More like holding myself up." He nodded at the arm wound around the branch. "I do have some strength in my legs, I just can't make them do anything meaningful. Could you put the blanket just there?"

He pointed with his free hand a few feet in front of him and she spread the blanket out on the grass. He lowered to the ground and shuffled himself forward onto it. She brought the saddlebags to him and lowered to the blanket, trying not to be too obvious about looking at his legs.

"I'd never even heard of Little's Disease," she said as he began unpacking a selection of food.

"Not many people have. When I was born it didn't even have a name, not until a Doctor Little started working on it about ten years ago. No one really knows what causes it and the symptoms are different for everyone. Some who have it can walk, some it affects their upper body as well, some have trouble with speaking or other movements." He placed a cloth-wrapped bundle onto the blanket and patted his thigh. "It's not exactly like being paralysed. I can feel my legs, I just can't move them properly."

The strangest urge came over her to reach out and touch his leg. She'd never had an urge to touch a man before, ever. "That must be so frustrating for you."

He shrugged and continued with his unpacking. "Sometimes, but I've had twenty-six years to get used to it." When she moved her eyes to his face, he smiled. "It's not so bad for me. To be honest, I've been blessed with good friends and a wonderful family. Other than a wife to share it all with, I really couldn't ask for anything more. And I swear I'm not saying that to put any pressure onto you," he added quickly. "It's simply the truth."

"I know." She believed him, but his mention of a wife nevertheless made her stomach shiver.

Feeling warm, she tugged at the ribbon beneath her chin and removed her bonnet, laying it beside her on the blanket. As she raised her hands to smooth any stray strands back into place, she noticed Jesse had stopped moving, his eyes fixed on her hair.

His eyes moved back to her face. "I was staring, wasn't I?"

She nodded, not knowing what to say. Especially as she didn't at all mind.

"I don't mean to make you uncomfortable, but it's such a beautiful shade." His eyes wandered back up. "The way it changes colour when the sun shines on it is so... beautiful."

There had been times back in New York when men had complimented her, even called her beautiful, but she'd always had trouble believing their sincerity. Being flattered had always felt awkward. It was different with Jesse. When he said something there was no artifice involved, no ulterior motive to garner her attention. He genuinely thought her hair beautiful, and rather than making her awkward it made her happy. Very, very happy.

"Thank you," she said, hoping she wasn't blushing. "I

get it from my mother. Father once said he fell in love with her hair from across the room, even before they'd met."

Jesse's gaze returned to her face. "I can understand that."

Now she *knew* she was blushing.

He ran one hand over his own hair. "I probably should get this trimmed..."

"Oh, no!"

At her exclamation, his eyebrows shot up.

"I mean, I like it that length." It was her turn to stare, her eyes lost in the golden caramel depths of his hair. "It suits you."

She lowered her eyes to his and for a few seconds she was caught in his gaze. Swallowing, she moved her attention to the horses. "So, why did you name him Duke?"

"Um... he's... uh... I didn't."

It was the first time she'd seen Jesse flustered and it suddenly occurred to her it was likely because of her compliment. She almost smiled. What would happen if he knew how attractive she truly thought him?

"His name isn't really Duke," he said.

"It isn't?"

"The truth is, I happened to get him on my sister's sixth birthday and she asked if she could give him a name. Since it was her birthday, I said yes. I should have known better."

She looked back at the horse. "So what's his real name?"

Jesse looked down at the blanket. "Duchess Primrose Sunshine."

There were a few seconds of silence during which she wondered if she'd heard correctly. "Could you repeat that?"

He looked sheepish. "I begged her to change her mind, I really did, but she said just because he was a boy didn't mean he couldn't have a pretty name. I kind of had to keep it after that."

She had always thought it fanciful poetic licence when people talked about a heart melting. Until that moment.

He must have seen something in her expression because he said, "You don't think it's a ridiculous name?"

"I think it's a ludicrous name for a male horse, but I also think it's the most beautiful name because it shows how much you love your sister."

The smile he gave her sent what remained of her heart trickling into her knees, which was strange since she could also feel it thumping in her chest.

This wasn't supposed to be happening. She was meant to be spending a casual, non-committal two weeks in California before returning to New York to resume the search for a suitable husband. She wasn't meant to be having feelings that might make her wish things were different.

Louisa suspected she might be in trouble.

They spent several hours there on the blanket, eating the picnic Jesse had brought and enjoying each other's company, and she loved every moment of it.

How was it possible she had never felt this way with any other man? Was it because she'd always been chaperoned and hadn't felt able to relax? Was it because she hadn't met any other men who made her feel so at ease? Or was it simply because there were no other men like Jesse?

She didn't hold to the notion that a person could only be happy with one other in the whole world. It would be entirely impractical. Besides which, as a woman she didn't need to be blissfully happy, she just needed to be secure, safe, and provided for. She could learn to enjoy another man's company, she was certain.

And yet she didn't put her bonnet back on, even on the journey back to town, and she had to admit it had nothing to do with the temperature and everything to do with the fact that Jesse liked to see her hair.

There was no denying it. She was definitely in big, big trouble.

Chapter 7

Waking early enough to ensure she had enough time to prepare for church felt like the hardest thing Louisa had ever done, still recovering as she was from a week of discomfort and infrequent sleep on the train.

She hauled herself from the wonderfully comfortable bed with a soft groan and set about getting ready. It being her first time at the church, she needed to look her best. Thank goodness she'd pressed her clothing when she got back the previous evening.

When she left her bedroom over an hour later, she found Pastor and Mrs Jones in the kitchen, Mrs Jones preparing breakfast at the stove and the pastor sitting at the table with a pencil in his hand, his large, leather bound Bible open in front of him and a few sheets of paper beside it.

"Good morning, Louisa," Mrs Jones said, smiling. "Goodness, you look like you're attending a ball."

Louisa looked down at her cream formal day dress with its lace edging and pearl buttons. It was one of the best she had, purchased from Lord & Taylor on Broadway, and her father had saved for months to afford it for her. "Is it too much? I wanted to look nice for church."

"Oh no, dear, you look absolutely lovely. Doesn't she look lovely, Simon?"

"Hmm?" Pastor Jones looked up from his Bible. "Oh, Louisa, good morning. I didn't see you there."

Mrs Jones shook her head. "Forgive my husband. He's putting the final touches to his talk for today and he forgets the rest of the world exists when he's working on his sermons."

"Sounds like it'll be a very good sermon then," Louisa said, but the pastor's attention was already back on his Bible.

Mrs Jones rolled her eyes and smiled.

Louisa walked around the table to join her at the stove. "Can I help?"

"I wouldn't want you to get anything on your beautiful dress, but you can set the table if you like."

"Of course." She turned towards the cupboard where the plates were kept then turned back again. "Do you really think the dress isn't too much? I don't want to look out of place."

Mrs Jones moved the pan of scrambled eggs from the heat and wiped her hands on her apron. "I think you will fit right in, and that has nothing to do with your clothing. And I'm sure Jesse will appreciate the dress." She sent Louisa a sideways glance and winked.

Her face heating, Louisa spun away and headed for the dresser, a smile tugging at her lips.

Following the simple but delicious breakfast of scrambled eggs and pancakes, Pastor and Mrs Jones left for church to prepare for the service.

Mrs Jones turned around at the door. "Are you sure you wouldn't like me to fetch you? I'm sorry we have to leave early, but I can come back."

"Oh no, it's only just along the road. I can make it that far on my own. But are you sure I can't do anything to help?"

Mrs Jones waved a hand. "I have more than enough ladies to help me. You'd only be sitting around with nothing to do. You take the time to pray, read your Bible, whatever you usually do on a Sunday morning before worship."

Louisa nodded and smiled and pretended that was exactly what she did before Sunday services. Back home in New York the time before church would be taken up with her mother making sure her hair was perfectly fixed and her outfit was chosen to make it look like it wasn't what she'd worn a few Sundays before. She owned more separate skirts and blouses than full dresses for just that purpose. In addition, they didn't attend the local church, instead travelling to churches in the more affluent parts of the city where her parents could socialise and discover any well-to-do bachelors, so the journey to get there invariably took longer.

Louisa wasn't sure what to do with the extra time now.

She returned to her bedroom to check her hair and clothing, but both were in order. She spent a few minutes deciding between her two bonnets, eventually settling on the blue. Then she looked around the room, wondering what to do next.

Her eyes came to rest on the Bible on the nightstand beside her bed. She kept it there for appearance's sake, in case Mrs Jones should walk in and see it and think their houseguest read God's word and said her prayers daily like any good Christian woman.

There had been a time, when Louisa was a child, when she had done just that. She'd accepted Jesus Christ as her Saviour at the age of fourteen and had truly felt that He was her friend, as the teacher at her Sunday school classes said. She'd prayed and seen answers to her prayers. She'd read her Bible every day, often more than once, and learned about her faith and her God.

Looking at that Bible now, a gift from her grandmother before she died, Louisa couldn't remember why she had stopped doing all that. Somehow, as she made the transition from childhood to womanhood, she'd become caught up in all that entailed and her closeness to God had fallen by the wayside.

She wandered to the nightstand and picked up the small Bible, feeling the soft texture of the leather against her fingertips as she rubbed her thumb over the surface. Maybe it was coming to this place where priorities were so different from at home, or perhaps it was staying with two people for whom a close relationship with God was part of everyday life, but for the first time that Louisa could remember, she wondered if she had lost something.

She carried the Bible out to the parlour, sat on the settee, and flipped through the pages. She wasn't looking for anything in particular, but on the first page she stopped at her eyes were drawn to the words *...that the God of our Lord Jesus Christ, the Father of glory, may give unto you the Spirit of wisdom and revelation in the knowledge of Him: the eyes of your understanding being enlightened; that ye may know what is the hope of His calling, and what the riches of the glory of His inheritance in the saints.*

It was the first chapter of Ephesians, one of Paul's letters if she remembered correctly.

The talk of wisdom, revelation, knowledge, understanding and enlightenment were what had caught her eye. She could use all those things, especially now in the midst of her confusion over Jesse. Paul didn't seem to be talking about life so much as he was saying the important thing was to understand what it fully meant to belong to God. Louisa had invited Jesus into her life, but did she truly know what that meant? When she really thought about it, she had to admit the answer was no.

Settling back into the settee cushions, she began to read.

She'd gone through the first three chapters of Ephesians and was about to start on the fourth when a knock on the front door startled her from her reading. She realised in horror that she had no idea how long she'd been sitting there, immersed in God's Word as she was. Was she late for church? Had Mrs Jones come to fetch her? Was church over?

Embarrassed, she leaped from the settee and ran to the door, pulling it open without even checking that her clothing was straight.

Jesse's smile melted from his face, his eyes darting down to her dress. "You... um... I came to escort you, if you have no objections. And good morning."

The way he was looking at her made her forget for a moment why she was in a hurry. And what she was meant to be doing. And what her name was.

"Uh... no. No objections." Where were they going? "Church! What time is it? Am I late?"

A smile spread across his face. "No, we have plenty of time."

She stepped back from the door and waved him in. "I was reading my Bible and lost track. Give me a moment and I'll fetch my things."

"Are you going to wear that dress?"

She came to a halt halfway along the hall and whirled back to him. "What's wrong with my dress? Is it too much? It's too much, isn't it? I wanted to make a good impression on my first Sunday at church, but I'm realising things are different here and I don't want to look like I'm putting on airs and..."

"Louisa, the dress is fine," he said, halting her in mid-panic. "In fact, it looks beautiful. Which is the problem."

Now she was confused. "Problem?"

One corner of his mouth hitched up. "How am I going to concentrate on anything Pastor Jones says with you sitting beside me looking like that?"

Her hand flew to her mouth, her heart stuttering in her chest and her cheeks heating

Jesse gave her a smile that didn't help her at all.

"I... um... I'll just... go and..." Spinning away, she fled to her room, shut the door behind her and leaned back against it as she caught her breath.

A smile crept onto her face and grew until it was stretching her cheeks. She pushed away from the door and went to her mirror to check her hair, almost laughing at the huge grin still plastered across her face. The sparkle in her eyes was unexpected. It was something she hadn't seen before, but then these feelings she had around Jesse weren't anything she'd ever felt before.

A small voice in the back of her mind that sounded very much like her father's told her she'd known him less than forty-eight hours and anything she felt was simply fanciful infatuation and not to be entertained. But right now, with warmth blossoming in her heart and a smile on her face, she wasn't inclined to pay the voice any heed. Why not enjoy herself, just for this two weeks? She'd made her position clear to Jesse and she would remind him of it if the need arose. But it felt good to have someone look at her like he did, to allow herself to have fun without having to always be judging someone's wealth and social standing and whether or not they were suitable husband material. With Jesse she could simply enjoy herself, and where was the harm in that?

Her smile grew as she made her decision. She was going experience her freedom for the next two weeks, and she was going to do it with an exceedingly attractive man who thought she was worth spending time with.

And no one could stop her.

She grabbed her reticule from where she'd left it on the bed but paused in the act of reaching for her bonnet. She knew she ought to wear it, at the very least to church, but she also wanted to leave it off and watch Jesse being captivated by her hair.

Rolling her eyes, she picked it up. It was church. She

couldn't go without a bonnet. She'd just take it off afterwards.

With one final look in the mirror, she left the room.

Jesse was in the hallway, his face lighting up in a smile when he saw her. "What did you do?"

She looked down at herself. "Um... nothing?"

"Well that can't be true because I'm sure you look even prettier than when you went in there."

Her cheeks heating yet again, she gave him a playful slap on the shoulder as she walked past him to the front door. "Stop it." Then she paused and turned back to him. "On second thoughts, don't stop it." Flashing him the kind of smile she never would have used back home, she walked outside.

He caught up with her out on the road. "What happened to you?"

"What do you mean?"

"You seem different. More... playful. Happier."

She shrugged as she pulled on her bonnet and tied the ribbons beneath her chin. "I've had an epiphany, of sorts."

"An epiphany?"

"Yes. I've come to the conclusion that since I'm going to be here for the next two weeks, I might as well enjoy myself. So that's what I'm going to do. I'm going to relax and enjoy myself."

His lips twitched. "Sounds like my kind of epiphany. So I guess I'm going to have to work on making this the most enjoyable two weeks of your life."

She wrestled the grin attempting to take over her face into submission. "I guess you are. Although this doesn't mean I'm staying."

"I know."

She had the sudden urge to perform a joyful twirl, right there in the middle of the street. She didn't, but her steps took on a bouncing quality she couldn't quite restrain.

"You know," Jesse said, looking up at her, "I'm liking this epiphany more and more. You're practically glowing."

Her grin broke through. "Am I?"

He chuckled at her expression. "Yeah."

"Hmm," she said thoughtfully, "must be the company."

She'd walked a few steps before she realised he was no longer at her side. She looked back to see him staring at her in amazement.

"Yup," he said, pushing to catch up with her, "definitely loving this epiphany."

The Jones' house being just down the road, it only took them a couple of minutes to reach the church. People were gathered outside chatting in groups, children running and playing and laughing amongst the adults, more arriving every minute on foot or horse or by wagon or buggy. It was a pleasant, welcoming scene, so unlike the churches Louisa had attended with her parents.

Her mother and father didn't hold with the types of church where people were overly sociable. Church was a serious affair, her father had once told her, to reflect the majesty and grandeur of a God who was above such frivolities as fun. It was filled with sombre music and sombre sermons and sombre congregants.

They'd moved church often after Louisa turned eighteen, staying for just enough Sundays for her mother to ascertain if there were any suitable matrimonial candidates for her and moving on when there weren't. Then returning and doing the circuit again after a while, in case any new eligible men had arrived.

The Emmanuel Church in Green Hill Creek didn't seem like any of those places. The crowd of people socialising with family and friends before they went in to worship the Lord seemed to actually want to be there.

Many of those gathered greeted Jesse and he was clearly

well liked, and he seemed eager to introduce her to everyone, as if he was proud of her. By the time they reached the door she had a sense of peace she couldn't explain, and she did something she'd rarely, if ever, done before – she offered up a spontaneous prayer of thanks.

Thank You for bringing me here, Lord.

Somehow, she knew He heard her and approved.

Just inside the door an older couple were handing out hymnals and greeting those entering.

"Louisa," Jesse said, "I'd like you to meet Mrs and Mr Goodwin. Otherwise known as the world's best cook and the world's luckiest man."

Mrs Goodwin laughed and leaned down to give him a motherly hug. "Shush, you'll make me blush. You're right about Mr Goodwin though." She gave Louisa a hug too. "It's a joy to meet you, Miss Wood. Jesse's talked about you so much the past few weeks I feel like we're good friends already."

Louisa glanced at Jesse and he smiled. Hearing he'd been talking about her shouldn't have made her as happy as it did, but she suspected she was going to have to get used to that feeling for the next two weeks.

"It's a pleasure to meet you too, Mrs Goodwin," she said. "And thank you so much for your beef stew on Friday. It was utterly delicious."

"Oh, you are a dear to say so."

She seemed to radiate joy. Louisa liked her right away.

Mr Goodwin handed a hymnal to each of them and removed his pipe just long enough to say, "Ma'am, Jesse." He was the complete opposite of his wife, her short and round and talkative and him tall and skinny and quiet. And yet they seemed to fit.

When they were inside the building, Louisa whispered to Jesse, "How does he manage to stay so thin when he has

Mrs Goodwin's cooking all the time?"

"That has been the subject of many a discussion around here," he replied. "And the answer is, no one has any idea. Not even him."

In contrast to the grand, stone-built churches Louisa was used to attending in New York, the Green Hill Creek Emmanuel Church was a homely looking place. Polished oak flooring reflected the light streaming in through tall, arched windows and the walls were painted a warm cream. Vases of flowers adorned the windowsills and dotted around the walls were cloth banners with Bible verses embroidered in bright colours. At the front, a low platform held a table, some chairs, and a simple wooden lectern. A plain, unadorned cross hung on the wall behind the platform. It was as welcoming a place of worship as any she'd been to and she felt immediately at home.

Jesse led her to the front where a wheelchair-sized space had been left open at the end of the first row, the pew ending short of those behind it.

"Did they do this for you?" she said as she took a seat.

"Just as soon as my pa made me my first wheelchair. They've always been real supportive here. I was too young to really think about it at the time, but I know it was a blessing to my pa that the people were so considerate of me."

Looking at the space that had been created just for him, she was relieved he'd had people who cared about him during his life. It didn't make sense to her that she should care so much about what had happened to him as a child, and yet she did.

"I'm glad you've had people look out for you like that."

"I'm glad you're glad," he said, a smile sauntering onto his face that made her want to laugh and blush at once. His eyes focused beyond her and the smile disappeared. "Oh no."

"Mr Johnson, I'm so glad I caught you." A diminutive,

harried looking man with greying brown hair rushed up to them, clutching a small brown ledger in his arms. His eyes flicked to Louisa.

"Mr Mead," Jesse said, "may I introduce Miss Wood?"

Mr Mead smiled faintly. "Pleasure to meet you, Miss Wood." He returned his attention to Jesse even as he spoke. "I'm sorry to bother you in the Lord's house on a Sunday, but I just can't seem to get the totals to match up and Mrs Mead says I'd better get it right or she won't know what we have left to spend on the chicken feed and..."

"Mr Mead," Jesse said, his eyes going to Louisa, "couldn't this wait until tomorrow? You could come over before work, if you like."

The man became even more flustered, if that was possible. "I would, except I can't come into town tomorrow because our Ada is about to give birth any second and Mrs Mead says if I'm not there she'll leave her to do it all by herself and I can't bear the thought of Ada out in the barn alone while it happens."

"It's all right," Louisa said to Jesse. "You go ahead."

He flashed her an apologetic smile. "I'll be right there, Mr Mead."

For just a moment, the harried expression left Mr Mead's face. "Thank you so much. I'm real grateful for this." Nodding to Louisa, he hurried off to join a tall woman seated towards the back of the church.

"Sorry," Jesse said. "I've tried to teach him, but he has probably the worst head for math I've ever come across."

Louisa laughed and touched his arm. "I'll be just fine here."

"Thanks for being so understanding. I never knew there could be accounting emergencies before I became an accountant. I'll be right back." He turned his chair then looked back at her. "By the way, Ada is a pig, in case you

91

were wondering."

Louisa donned as serious an expression as she could muster. "Thank you for telling me. I had hoped they didn't have a woman giving birth in their barn."

"I'm glad I could put your mind at ease then," he said, face perfectly straight for a good three seconds before his smile broke through.

She watched him wheel along the aisle in the direction of the Meads, vaguely aware there was a smile on her face she couldn't seem to dispel. When she'd watched him for longer than she probably should have in public, she opened her reticule, withdrew her Bible, and found her place in Ephesians.

"*Psst.*"

At the sound, Louisa looked around her, but no one else was close by.

"Psst, down here," the voice hissed.

She twisted in her seat to peer down into the row behind her.

Nancy peeked up at her from where she was crouched on the floor. "Don't look!" She stretched up to check in Jesse's direction then ducked down again.

Louisa turned away and pretended to read her Bible. "What are you doing down there?"

"We just got here and I wanted to check you remembered not to tell Jesse I came to see you yesterday."

"I remembered."

"Good. I don't know if he'll introduce you to me and Ma and Pa and Luke before or after the service, but I'm ready. I practised for half an hour and Joshua said I looked real natural when I said I'd never met you. Did you practise your expression for when you meet me?"

Louisa's stomach scrunched in on itself at the thought of meeting Jesse's stepmother for the first time. His father had been very nice, but mothers were on a whole different level when it came to being protective of their sons.

"I'm afraid I didn't, but I think I'll be okay. I've had a lot of practise pretending to be interested in people who were boring. That's kind of the same."

Nancy sighed. "I guess that will have to do. I'll be..."

"Louisa!" Sara walked right past Nancy's hiding place without seeing her and took the empty seat beside Louisa. "How is Miss Wood today? Or is it Mrs Johnson yet?"

Louisa glanced behind her, but Nancy had gone. She turned her attention to Sara and smiled. "Not yet. How is Mrs Raine?"

~ ~ ~

By the time Jesse returned the service was about to begin, which gave Louisa's nerves about being introduced to the rest of his family a good long time to get up and running.

She tried to concentrate on the service and even managed to enjoy Pastor Jones' sermon, but she couldn't help casting the occasional glance at the far side of the church where they were seated.

"My pa already likes you," he said when the service came to an end, "and Malinda, Luke and Nancy will too. You don't have to be afraid."

Her mother would have been mortified if she'd known her daughter had let her mask slip. She lowered her gaze. "And I thought I was hiding it so well."

He ducked his head to look past the bonnet into her eyes. "This may be the wrong thing to say, but I'm glad you're nervous. It means you care what they think, which means you care about me. Doesn't it? Just a bit?"

His smiling green eyes gave her stomach a whole different reason to wobble. Why did he make her so befuddled? And how could befuddlement feel so nice?

The corners of her lips curled up a little. "Maybe."

"Then is it wrong to hope you're downright terrified?" He flashed her a roguish grin.

She covered her laugh with her fingers. "I wouldn't say it's very gentlemanly, but it's not necessarily wrong."

"I'm happy to hear that." His looked beyond her. "Well, would you like to get it over with? My sister looks like she might explode if we don't go over there soon."

She turned to see Nancy saying something to her mother, pulling at her hand in an apparent attempt to get her to go to them. Seeing Louisa's eyes on her, she smiled and waved before abruptly stopping and looking at her hand in horror as if it had betrayed her.

"I suppose we could go over there now," she said, wanting to laugh despite herself.

By the time she and Jesse reached the Johnson family, all four of them were silently watching their approach. Louisa had an overwhelming urge to run and find a mirror in which to check her appearance.

"Good morning, Miss Wood," Mr Johnson said, standing. "It's good to see you again."

"Good morning." She wondered if what he really meant was it was good to see her still there rather than on a train back to New York. Either way, he appeared sincere which eased her nerves a little.

"This is my wife, Malinda."

Mrs Johnson made her way along the row and, to Louisa's surprise, wrapped her in a hug. She'd been hugged more times in the past two days since she arrived than in the last half a year back home. It was rather nice.

"We're all so glad you're here," Mrs Johnson smiling.

Jesse's stepmother was a good foot shorter than her

husband, with a face that managed to look youthful and yet worldly at the same time. Louisa had been right, Nancy did favour her mother with her dark brown hair pinned into a relaxed chignon and large, chocolate brown eyes. And she exuded a warmth that calmed Louisa's nerves further.

She breathed out in relief and smiled. "I'm glad to be here."

Mrs Johnson turned to the young man beside Peter. "This is our other son, Luke."

Luke was unmistakably Jesse's brother. Although he had brown eyes like his mother and his father's light brown hair, when he stood and said, "Pleasure to meet you, ma'am," his smile reminded her so much of Jesse she had to glance between the two of them. He had yet to reach his father's height, but at fourteen Louisa suspected he had a growth spurt coming that would change that, and his shoulders and chest were already filling out, no doubt due to the work he did with his father in the smithy.

The final member of the family was practically bouncing in her seat and when Mrs Johnson beckoned her forward Nancy leaped up and rushed to join them. "And this is our daughter, Nancy."

"It's very nice to meet you, Louisa." Her eyes widened, flicking to Jesse behind her. "I mean, Miss Wood. You look just like your photograph, except even prettier. I could have recognised you even before we met. Today. Just now. When we met for the first time."

Louisa carefully kept her face straight. "It's lovely to meet you, Nancy. Jesse wrote all about you in his letters. You're just like I imagined you. And please, call me Louisa." She looked around at the little family. "All of you."

She needn't have wasted any energy on worrying what they would think of her. Jesse's family surrounded her with smiles and warmth and a genuine friendliness she'd been unused to at home. In all the thought she'd put into preparing herself for coming here, wondering what it would be like when she did, she'd never imagined such a thing. Her concerns had been over what she would wear, how harshly she'd be judged, if she'd embarrass herself by saying or doing the wrong thing, if she'd be acceptable to Jesse and his parents. She'd never thought to be so accepted just as she was. And even if she had thought of it, she would never have imagined how good it would feel.

She glanced back at Jesse to find him smiling at her and she smiled back. Instead of being a daunting length of time, two weeks suddenly felt entirely too short.

~ ~ ~

Louisa and Jesse remained at the church for another half hour or so while she spent time with Amy, Sara and Lizzy, catching each other up on their new lives so far. It had been an eventful time for all of them since they'd arrived in Green Hill Creek and, though it wasn't even forty-eight hours since they'd stepped from the train, it felt much longer.

Jo hadn't come to church with her husband. Sara told them she'd spoken to him before the service and he'd told her Jo was ill. Louisa had noticed him leave as soon as the service was over and she assumed he'd hurried home to take care of her. She wished Jo lived closer to town so she could check on her. Now she had real friends, she wanted to make sure they were all safe and happy.

At Peter and Malinda's invitation, Louisa and Jesse spent the midday meal and much of the afternoon with the Johnsons. They were joined for dinner by a pretty girl Luke's age named Tabitha and the two young people were clearly smitten with each other. Louisa tried not to be affected by their loving looks and whispered conversations and the way they held hands whenever possible, but she found herself glancing at Jesse more than once, her thoughts wandering to what it would be like to have that kind of closeness with him.

Nancy took it upon herself to show Louisa around the house, and the smithy, and the stable, and every inch of their property. Louisa enjoyed Jesse's young sister's enthusiasm. She had two younger sisters of her own, but they were relatively close in age so she'd never appreciated them in the same way. With Malinda's help, Nancy even taught Louisa how to get on and off a horse without revealing an ankle or calf, a process that involved a lot of laughter, not to mention much patience on the part of June, one of Peter's horses.

Even though she'd only just met them, Louisa felt a sense of comfort with Jesse's family, a feeling of belonging she hadn't expected.

Surrounded as he was by love and encouragement and acceptance, it was no wonder Jesse had grown into the man he was.

~ ~ ~

"Told you they'd love you," Jesse said as they headed for his home after leaving his family.

Louisa laughed, a wonderful sound that flooded his insides with warmth. "Yes, you did."

"Did you have a good time?" Though he kept his tone casual, he was eager to know how she felt about the most important people in his life. If she liked them, he reasoned, it brought her a step closer to wanting to stay with him.

"I had a wonderful time. You have a lovely family. They made me feel very welcome. And thanks to Malinda and Nancy I will no longer be in danger of becoming immodest while mounting and dismounting Eagle."

He couldn't let that one go. "Remind me to thank them,"

he said, in a not at all thankful tone.

She laughed again and gave his shoulder a playful slap. "You are terrible."

He'd known she wouldn't take offence at his sense of humour. It was one of the reasons he'd been drawn to her letters. "I feel like I should apologise for Nancy. She's been so excited about you coming. Next time I'll tell her to let you have at least a few minutes to yourself."

"Oh no, I adore your sister. She's delightful, and so much fun."

He hadn't realised how important it was to him that they get along until this moment. He breathed out, relieved. "So what was up with her?"

Louisa kept her eyes on the road ahead of her, obviously trying to avoid his gaze. "What do you mean?" She was so adorable, even when trying to hide something from him.

"I mean the exaggerated way she greeted you in the church, and all the whispering between the two of you."

"Why are you asking me? She's your sister, you know her better than I do. I only met her today."

He watched her wince and couldn't help smiling at how bad a liar she was.

"Aha!" he exclaimed, coming to a halt. "So you have met her before."

She looked back at him, her shoulders slumping. "I can't tell you. I made a promise."

He shrugged. "That's okay, I'll just ask her."

"Oh no, please don't. She'll be mortified she didn't fool you. She was so proud of her performance."

He slowly wheeled forward and looked up at her, waiting. He didn't want her to break a promise, but he was dying to know what had happened.

She heaved a sigh. "She came to the house yesterday morning before I came to see you, to try to persuade me to

98

stay."

This was interesting. "What did she do?"

"It was the sweetest thing," she said, clasping both hands at her breast. "She'd written down everything she could think of about you and read it out to me. Like how you always played with her when she was little and never got angry with her when she interrupted your studying and how you let her bake cookies with you and all the things you can do. She said you'd be just about the best husband and father in the world." She looked down, a small smile on her face. "I thought you couldn't possibly be as wonderful as she made you sound, but if your little sister thought so much of you, you must be something special."

He needed to get Nancy something extra good for her birthday this year. "So she convinced you to stay?"

"Actually no, I'd already decided to stay. But if I hadn't she would have done a very good job of changing my mind."

Maybe he should get Nancy to speak to her again when the two weeks was up.

Louisa's expression turned serious. "You won't tell her I told you, will you?"

"No, I won't tell her. She'll tell me herself eventually anyway. She can't keep a secret for anything."

Her mouth fell open. "So I didn't have to tell you at all?"

Perhaps he should have kept that piece of information to himself. "Technically, no. But I think we're both happier this way since now I don't have to wait to find out what she did and you don't have to carry the burden of keeping her visit a secret." He flashed her what he hoped was a charming smile.

She rolled her eyes. "You are worse than terrible."

She turned away and resumed walking, but by the hint of a smile he glimpsed, he knew she didn't really mean it.

"Nancy adores you too, you know," he said, pushing at his wheels to catch up. "She was looking forward to you coming almost as much as I was, but now you're here she's just about exploding with excitement."

Her eyes stayed on the road ahead of them. "And how about you? Are you happy I'm here?"

Speeding up, he rolled round into her path, forcing her to stop and look at him.

"Do you really have to ask me that?" He studied her face as he waited for her answer. He needed to be sure she knew just how he felt about her being there.

A slow smile curved her lips. "No, I suppose I don't."

He nodded and moved out of her way. He had nothing to worry about. She knew.

"Are you tired?" he said as they started moving again. "Or would you like to go for a ride, now you can get on and off a horse while disappointingly covered up?"

She glanced down at him with a smile. "I think frustrating you with my decency sounds like a wonderful idea."

Chapter 8

Jesse wheeled through the back entrance to the bank with a smile on his face. To his mild surprise, the smile was still there after he'd hung up his jacket, deposited his lunch in his desk drawer, and gone to fetch the ledgers he'd need for his work from Mr Vernon's office.

"When Mr Emerson arrives, tell him I'd like to see him before we open," the bank's owner said from his seat behind his huge desk.

"Yes, sir."

Jesse was still smiling when he got back to his desk in the room he optimistically called his office, which also doubled, tripled and quadrupled as the file room, supplies closet, and the employee break room, as well as being the thoroughfare between the bank lobby and the rest of the building. To retain a smile for that long after getting into work was unheard of for him.

It wasn't that he didn't like his job. Considering his limited career options, accountancy wasn't bad. It paid well and he found working with the absolutes of numbers soothing, if occasionally a little monotonous. But going to the same place every day wasn't his idea of fun, so the smile was unusual. When he thought about it, however, his good mood wasn't entirely unexpected. He'd been smiling a lot since Louisa arrived.

Thinking of her made him smile even more and he

leaned back in his chair and closed his eyes, lowering the pencil he'd picked up to the desk. He wondered what she was doing at that moment. What was she wearing? Was it the green dress she'd arrived in? Or the blue skirt and white blouse she'd worn on Saturday? She probably wasn't wearing the one with the lace she'd worn the previous day, that seemed too formal for everyday wear, but he gave it some thought anyway. The way her beautiful auburn hair contrasted with the cream colour, the soft fabric skimming her figure and flowing around her as she moved.

Was she thinking about him the same way he was thinking about her? He'd noticed her watching him more than once, and he was almost sure he'd caught her staring at his chest at the livery on Saturday. He allowed himself just a touch of pride in that. He did, after all, work hard on his physical condition. It was nice to know it had benefits beyond keeping him healthy and able to take care of himself.

When he thought about it, he found it likely she was as attracted to him as he was to her. All right, maybe not *as* attracted since he thought about her practically constantly and could barely keep his eyes from her when they were together, but there was definitely some attraction there. He could work with that.

"You look cheerful."

Jesse opened his eyes to see Adam hanging his jacket on the coat rack. Engrossed in his thoughts of Louisa, he hadn't heard him come in.

He leaned back in his chair and twirled the pencil through his fingers, watching his friend with amusement. Adam was all but glowing.

"I'm not the only one." He felt the need to remind him of his impromptu short sermon during the previous day's church service. "What was all that yesterday about Miss Watts needing a friend and not a husband?"

102

"We *are* friends."

Jesse pointed the pencil at him. "That is not the face of a man who has just found a new *friend*."

"I didn't say I don't want to be more," Adam said, smirking. "So how's it going with Louisa?"

It was Jesse's turn to smile as he lowered the pencil onto the open ledger in front of him. "She's agreed to give me two weeks. That's more than any other girl has. And she's amazing. She's smart and funny and kind and she doesn't speak to me like I'm different. I have a good feeling about this." He closed his eyes and sighed. "You've seen her. Isn't she the most beautiful woman you've ever laid eyes on?"

"Don't you start," Adam said, tutting. "First Dan claims Sara is prettier than Amy, and now you're saying it about Louisa. Yes, Louisa and Sara are both pretty, but no one comes close to Amy. The two of you are obviously in need of spectacles."

Jesse burst into laughter. "I think we were all matched right. Oh, by the way, Vernon wants to see you before you open up."

He watched Adam walk through the door to the back corridor, certain he detected a spring in his friend's step. So things weren't going quite how either of them had planned, but God had brought them both wonderful women who were perfect for them. He would work it out, Jesse had no doubt.

Advertising for mail order brides was turning out to be one of the best ideas he'd ever had.

~ ~ ~

"Jesse?"

He looked up from his desk to see Adam leaning in through the doorway to the lobby. "Hmm?"

"There's a Mr Foster here, says he has questions about

the loan he took out a month ago. Can you sort it out?"

"Yeah, send him in." He did a quick tidy of his desk while Adam disappeared back through the door.

A few seconds later he walked back in with an older man wearing a crumpled blue shirt and clutching a hat in front of him like a shield. Behind Mr Foster's back Adam gave Jesse a slight shrug and returned to the lobby, closing the door behind him.

"Good afternoon, Mr Foster, I'm Mr Johnson. Please, take a seat." He waved a hand at the chair on the other side of his desk and smiled in an attempt to put Mr Foster at ease. The man looked like he was ready to bolt. "What can I do for you?"

Mr Foster set his hat in his lap. "Well, Mr Johnson..." His brow furrowed. "Wait, are you the blacksmith's boy?"

"Yes, sir, Peter Johnson is my father."

Mr Foster nodded slowly and tried to surreptitiously peer over the top of the desk to see Jesse's legs.

He stifled a sigh. Even after twenty-six years people still treated him like an oddity. "So, Mr Foster, how can I help you today? Mr Emerson said you had questions about your loan?"

Mr Foster sat back, looking slightly disappointed but decidedly more relaxed than he had when he entered. "Well, I took out a loan a month ago to build a new barn. With this weather I'm expecting a bumper crop of corn this year. Figured it was about time and my wife said she'd had enough of trying to squeeze into the other one when all the crops are in so..."

Jesse smiled and nodded and waited patiently for the tale of life on the Foster farm to get round to the point while his thoughts drifted to wondering what Louisa was doing at that moment.

"...and my oldest, Francis, he's just finishing school, real smart he is, he was taking a look at the papers Mr Ransom gave me about the loan and he said something ain't right. Now I'm not saying Mr Ransom got anything wrong, I'm sure he's an educated man and he sure does look fancy with his clothes and silver watch and everything, but I just wanted to make sure." He thrust two rumpled pieces of paper across the desk. "This is what he gave me."

Jesse dragged his thoughts from how Louisa's hair shimmered when the sun touched it and took the pages. Rotherford Ransom's precise handwriting covered the paper, setting out figures and terms and repayments. It was a standard loan agreement, the kind Ransom issued all the time when the amount of the loan was low enough and simple enough that Mr Vernon was happy to let his secretary of seventeen years deal with it.

"So what exactly is the problem, Mr Foster?" Jesse said, still reading.

"Well, Francis said the payments aren't right. He's real good at math, you see."

Jesse scanned down to the amount of the loan then on to the percentage and repayment figures. Frowning, he looked again through both pages to check if he'd missed anything then returned to the amounts.

"Would you excuse me?" He pushed back from the desk. "I need to go and double check this. I'll be right back."

He took the loan agreement, leaving Mr Foster staring after him and his wheelchair as he left the room through the door opposite the lobby and headed for his boss' office.

Mr Ransom was, as usual, at his desk outside the office door. He looked up at Jesse's approach.

"Rotherford..." Jesse began.

Ransom frowned, narrowing his eyes in disapproval. Even after four years of working together he detested the familiarity of using first names.

Every so often, Jesse used his given name on purpose, just to annoy the man.

"Sorry, *Mr Ransom*," he said. "Is Mr Vernon in?"

"He stepped out. May I help you with something?" His expression said he didn't want to help with anything and that Jesse's mere presence was disturbing his work. But then he always looked like that.

"I need to check April's ledger. I've got a Mr Foster at my desk. He took out a loan last month and he's questioning the payments. I checked and he's right, the payments are too high for the amount he borrowed at that rate. You dealt with the loan, do you remember him?"

An expression flashed across Ransom's face for a moment, barely long enough to see, but Jesse could have sworn it was fear. He dismissed the thought as soon as it came to him. What would Ransom have to be afraid about?

He put down his pen. "No, but I issue a lot of loans. Let me see." He held out his hand for the loan agreement.

Jesse handed it over and waited while Ransom pushed his narrow spectacles up onto his forehead and perused the papers.

"Ah, yes, I remember now. Mr Foster changed his mind after I'd already written the loan amount on there and asked for more. Rather than writing out a whole new agreement I wrote an addendum and filled in the new payment amount on this one. He must have forgotten to bring the addendum with him." He raised his eyes and his glasses flopped back down onto his nose. "Send him through and I'll speak with him."

"Okay. I should check the ledger anyway, make sure the correct amount is recorded in there."

Ransom gave him a smile that didn't reach his eyes. "I'll let Mr Vernon know you want it when he returns."

Jesse couldn't remember the last time he'd seen Ransom

smile, eyes or otherwise. Probably just having a particularly good day. As he headed back along the corridor, he wondered what a good day would entail for Rotherford Ransom. Maybe when he got home he was planning on alphabetising his socks by colour.

"Mr Foster," he said when he reached his office, "if you'd like to come through, Mr Ransom will help you."

With Mr Foster gone, Jesse wheeled back to his desk and picked up his pencil. Then he put it down again. Something was bothering him, but he couldn't quite put his finger on what it was. Maybe it was what had happened to Adam earlier. That was probably it.

He picked his pencil up again. Five minutes later, Mr Foster walked back into the room.

"Get everything cleared up?" Jesse said.

"Oh yes, Mr Ransom explained all about the extras. He's so helpful and kind. A credit to the bank he is. A real gentleman."

Jesse nodded slowly. "I, uh, I'm sure. Have a good day, Mr Foster."

"You too, Mr Johnson," he replied as he left. "Give my regards to your father."

"I will."

Jesse dropped his pencil again, sitting back and looking at the door to the back corridor. The bothering something had returned, nagging at the back of his mind. He wasn't by nature a suspicious person, so when it happened he took notice. Except this wasn't a suspicion, as such. More a feeling. And he was well aware feelings were often wrong.

Shaking his head to dislodge the bothering, nagging feeling that had no basis in solid fact whatsoever, he picked up the pencil. It was nothing. He'd check the ledger when Vernon got back in and reassure himself it was all fine.

Why wouldn't it be?

~ ~ ~

Mr Vernon didn't return to the bank the entire rest of the day.

That wasn't in itself unusual. He had other business concerns, being probably the richest man in Green Hill Creek, and at least once a week he would leave the running of the bank to Ransom and Jesse and whoever was manning the lobby. Usually Jesse wouldn't think twice about it. Today he thought about it much more than twice.

At two-thirty he wheeled through to Ransom's desk. "I'd really like to check that ledger before I go home."

Ransom looked up from the papers on his desk, raising one hand to lower his spectacles onto his nose. "I went to get it for you earlier, when it appeared that Mr Vernon wouldn't be returning for the day, but it seems he's taken the keys to the cupboard with him." He smiled again. That was twice in one day. "I'm sure it can wait until tomorrow."

Jesse glanced at the door to Mr Vernon's office. He could have pointed out that seeing as all there was in that cupboard was paperwork, the owner of the bank never took the keys with him, being content to leave them in his desk.

But the nagging, bothering feeling stopped him.

"Sure it can. It's not a problem. I just wanted to make sure the numbers all add up." He donned a smile that was every bit as fake as Ransom's. "That's my job, after all."

"Quite." Ransom glanced pointedly at the papers in front of him. "Is there anything else I can help you with?"

As if he'd helped him at all.

"No. That was all."

Jesse turned and wheeled away, the bothering, nagging feeling heading closer to a bothering, nagging suspicion.

Chapter 9

Mrs Jones answered the door when Jesse knocked. She didn't need to tell him where Louisa was. He'd heard the laughter from the front gate and knew exactly who was with her.

Mrs Jones disappeared into the kitchen and he wheeled to Louisa's open bedroom door, stopping outside the doorway where he could watch without being seen. Louisa was sitting on her bed, watching Nancy parade around the room in one of her dresses. Jesse's sister was swamped in the too big garment and had to lift it high to be able to move, but she was twirling in circles, head held high as if she was a princess at a ball. Her hair was piled on top of her head in an elaborate style held in place by a ribbon and, from what Jesse could tell, some kind of magic. And her face glowed with joy.

Louisa laughed and clapped as she sank into a slightly unsteady curtsy and Nancy bounced up and skipped to join her on the bed.

"When I get older I'm going to have lots of dresses just like this one," Nancy said, smoothing the skirt over her knees. "Then I'll be as pretty as you."

"You're already far prettier than me." Louisa touched her fingers to Nancy's chin and raised her face to look at her. "These big brown eyes and all this beautiful hair and this cute button nose." She lightly tapped the tip of her nose and Nancy giggled. "You are completely and utterly and absolutely adorable. That's all there is to it."

A sensation Jesse had never felt before rose in his chest as he watched Louisa with his sister, a pure joy that grew and filled his heart until it spilled over and flooded his body with warmth. To his astonishment, he even felt tears prick at the backs of his eyes. What was happening to him?

"Jesse!"

Nancy leaped from the bed and he blinked rapidly and rolled forward into the room as she rushed over to him.

She spun in a circle, the dress brushing his knees. "Do you like it? Louisa let me try on all her dresses. The ones she's unpacked, at least. And look how she did my hair! Have you ever seen anything so pretty?"

"You look beautiful," he said, holding out his arms.

She leaned over the arm of his wheelchair to give him a hug and he smiled at Louisa over her shoulder. Her answering smile made his heart skip a beat or three.

"Did you come here straight from school?" he said as Nancy straightened.

She looked down at the dress she was wearing, fidgeting with a lace ruffle. "No, I went home first to ask Ma if I could. She said I could come for an hour before I did my homework."

"And how long have you been here?"

Her hands stilled on the ruffle and she raised her eyes. "What time is it now?"

He checked his pocket watch. "Twenty-two minutes to five."

She bit her lip. "Oh."

"Get changed," he said, smiling, "and I'll take you home."

He withdrew to the kitchen to wait with Mrs Jones and Nancy and Louisa came in five minutes later, Nancy wearing her own clothing. Louisa wore a peach coloured skirt and light green blouse and Jesse placed the two new items of apparel in his 'Louisa's Clothes' mental file. He'd never paid much attention to what women wore until now, but he remembered every single thing Louisa had worn since she arrived. So far his favourite was the cream coloured dress from the previous day, but he was prepared for that to change. In fact, he was looking forward to it. With eight trunks of belongings, she surely had a lot of outfits for him to enjoy.

Louisa went with them to walk Nancy home and his sister held her hand all the way, chatting animatedly. It filled him with happiness to see the two of them getting along well. Nancy had been so excited for Louisa's arrival that he worried she might have been disappointed if Louisa didn't spend as much time with her as she wanted, but he needn't have been concerned. Louisa seemed to enjoy being with Nancy as much as Nancy enjoyed being with her. It made Jesse like her even more, but at the back of his mind he couldn't help feeling a little uneasy. Nancy would be devastated if Louisa left after the two weeks was up.

Then he would just have to do his best to persuade her to stay. Not that he needed any more motivation in that area. If she left, it wouldn't just be his sister who'd be devastated.

"I'm sorry," Louisa said after they'd left Nancy explaining to her mother why she'd arrived home forty-five minutes after she was supposed to. "I didn't realise she had a curfew."

"Oh, don't worry about that. Malinda's used to her coming home late. If Nancy was ever on time we'd think something was really wrong."

"I think it's nice Nancy can do that. Not that she's always late, but that she feels that freedom to not worry about it. I never would have dared come home late when I was young."

"Your parents are strict?"

111

"Not strict, exactly." She looked up into the sky, her gaze unfocused. "I simply would never have even thought of not obeying them. It's just how it is for my sisters and me." She lowered her gaze to him, a smile on her lips. "How about you? Were you an obedient child?"

"Oh yes," he said immediately, "I was the perfect son. Never put a foot wrong. Always did everything I was told, never got into any trouble, just a joy all round. Never gave my pa or Malinda an ounce of worry at all."

She burst into laughter. "How convincing."

He grinned and admitted nothing.

"Maybe I'll ask Malinda one day," she said. "I'm sure she has some tales to tell."

Smile vanishing, he hung his head and groaned. "Could you at least wait until after you've made a decision about marrying me? I wouldn't want my past swaying you one way or the other."

Her eyebrows rose. "That bad? Now I can't wait to hear all about your childhood."

"Just remember, in my defence I was young and determined I wouldn't miss out on anything."

"I'm glad you didn't," she said, touching his shoulder.

He gazed into her eyes, wondering if she'd object if he took her hand, but then she looked down, pulling it away.

Next time he'd have to be quicker.

"So how was your day?" she said. "Anything exciting happen at the bank?"

At the mention of his job his happiness faded. For a while there, he'd forgotten.

"What's wrong?" she said, worry creeping onto her face.

He berated himself for being so transparent. They'd only known each other three days. He had no right to lay his worries onto her. "It's nothing. Everything's fine."

She stepped in front of him, forcing him to an abrupt

112

halt. "It's not fine, I can see it in your face. If you don't want to tell me, that's okay, just say I'm being nosey and I won't ask again. But you promised you wouldn't lie to me, so don't tell me it's fine when it isn't."

Her earnest little speech took him aback. Evidently his withholding of the truth about his condition had affected her more than he'd thought. He couldn't blame her for that.

"I'm sorry, I didn't mean to lie to you. I promise I'll do my best to not do that again."

She nodded and smiled. "So am I being nosey?"

"No, not at all. I just don't want to burden you with my problems. It may not even be a problem. But if it is, it's not yours."

She moved from in front of him and started walking again. "I don't mind. Maybe talking about it could help."

He didn't reply immediately. Did he really want to involve her, for her to know that he was probably suspecting a colleague of he didn't even know what with very little reason? But then again, another point of view could help him put things into perspective.

He looked around them to check he wouldn't be overheard, but they were in a quiet street and there was no one else around.

"There's probably nothing to it, I know, but a customer came in this morning..."

Chapter 10

The following morning Jesse waited until business hours were well underway and he was sure Mr Vernon was firmly ensconced in his office before he made another attempt to see the previous month's ledger.

Mr Ransom was at his desk forming an impregnable wall outside Mr Vernon's office, as always.

Jesse took a deep breath and wheeled up to him. "Is Mr Vernon in?" He knew he was, but he didn't want to sound too eager to get in there.

Ransom paused for a moment, possibly to give him time to think up an excuse. Or maybe he simply needed to quietly clear his throat. Jesse was becoming paranoid.

"He is," Ransom said, "but he's very busy today."

Jesse pasted on his most easygoing smile. "I just want to get the ledgers so I can check them. Won't take me more than half a minute."

Another pause. "Oh, there's no need to do that. I checked Mr Foster's loan amount in the ledger and it's exactly as it should be. You can set your mind at rest."

Fat chance there was of that now. Jesse often used the previous months' ledgers when working. This was the first time Ransom had made any attempt to stop him from getting to them.

He had two choices - insist on seeing the ledger for himself thus raising suspicion and giving Ransom the chance to cover his tracks, or return to his office and wait for the opportunity to get in while Ransom was away from his desk, which would also raise suspicion but at least he'd get to see the ledger. He could also abandon all pretence and barge past and grab the ledger before anyone could stop him, but he decided to call that a last resort.

"Good," Jesse said, his smile feeling more strained by the second. "As long as it all adds up."

"It does."

He held Ransom's gaze, waiting for him to redeem himself and allow him in.

He didn't.

"Well, I'll get back to work." He turned his back on Ransom and released the smile that was now feeling more like a grimace.

He'd get the ledger later. Ransom couldn't stay at his desk forever.

~ ~ ~

Louisa moved the cake-filled basket into her left hand and knocked on the door. There was no answer.

She was a little earlier than their agreed time to meet, but she was eager to know how things had gone at the bank and if Jesse had been able to see the ledger and find out more about the loans. She felt sure he must be home from work by now.

She'd been praying for him all day, in between praying for a great many other things in her life. She hadn't truly spoken to God in a long time and it was as if He was inviting her into His presence. It felt good to be talking to Him again, as if she'd found an old friend.

No, it was more than that. She was rediscovering her place in the arms of a Saviour who loved her with a love that surpassed knowledge, as it said in Ephesians. She'd read the whole book again this morning. That was one of her favourite parts.

She tried Jesse's door and found it unlocked. Slipping inside, she called his name, but there was no reply. The parlour was empty so she walked past into the kitchen, set her basket on the table, and continued out the open back door.

And stopped dead in her tracks.

Her mouth dropped open. She automatically covered it with her hand.

Beneath the tree in the centre of the yard Jesse sat in his wheelchair. His eyes were closed and in each hand he held a strangely shaped metal object, narrow in the middle where his hand wrapped around it and bulbous on either end. He was slowly flexing his arms to raise and lower them, the movement causing the muscles in his upper arms to bulge with the effort.

Louisa could see just how much his muscles were bulging because he had taken his shirt off. It was draped over the back of one of the chairs at the table.

Somewhere in the back of her mind she knew she should look away, but her rebellious eyes refused the command as they travelled slowly over the planes of muscle sculpting his torso, lingering over the highlights and shadows rippling his smooth, taut skin.

She seemed to have forgotten how to blink.

The sound of a throat clearing snapped her gaze from a particularly arresting arrangement of ridges on his abdomen to his face. He was watching her, a smile playing on his lips.

Gasping, she whirled away to face the house.

"Good afternoon, Louisa." His rich cream voice sent a shiver down her spine.

She opened her mouth to respond, but all that emerged

was a squeak. Straightening her shoulders, she tried again. "Good afternoon, Jesse."

"Enjoy the view?"

Indignation born of mortification turned her back to him. He was smiling. And still very, very shirtless.

She spun away again. "Stop looking at me like that!"

"Like what?"

She glanced at him for a split second. "Like that. You're smirking."

"Am I?" His amusement was clear, even without looking at him.

"Yes. So stop it."

When he spoke again the smile had mostly gone from his voice. "How long were you watching me?"

"Not long. I mean I wasn't watching. I-I just happened to see... I mean... I didn't know you were... were..."

"Exercising?"

"Half naked!"

He began to chuckle, stopping abruptly when she spun round to glare at him.

"I promise I intended to be fully clothed by the time you arrived," he said, raising his hands in a gesture of surrender. The movement caused interesting things to happen to his broad shoulders. "You're early."

"Well, if I'd known you were going to be... be..." Her eyes strayed down to his chest. She'd never realised that area on a man could be so... *developed*.

"Half naked?" He was smiling again.

She rapidly turned away. "...I would have come later." To her horror, she wanted to keep looking at him. More than that, she wanted to stare at him and drink in the magnificent sight of all those muscles. She was fairly sure that was wrong, although at that moment she wasn't entirely clear on why. "Could you please put a shirt on?"

"If that's what you truly want," he said, his voice teasing.

She had to stop herself from smiling. "It is." It wasn't, but she wasn't about to admit that.

"All right then." She heard his wheelchair move and after ten seconds or so he said, "You can turn round now. It's safe."

She looked back to see him fastening the last couple of buttons on his shirt. Her eyes still managed to pick out the lines of muscle shaping the fabric so she shifted her gaze to the bulbous metal bars he'd been lifting. There were three pairs of different sizes, all lined up on the ground.

"What are they?" she said, walking over to examine them.

"They're called dumbbells. My pa made them for me so I could get strong. Makes it easier for me to do everything."

She bent to pick one of the largest up, almost falling over when it didn't leave the ground. "Oh! How heavy are they?" She tried again, using both hands this time, and managed to lift it.

"That one's the heaviest. It's about thirty pounds."

She straightened her arm, holding the dumbbell in just her right hand with her palm facing forward as she'd seen him do, and tried to raise it. It moved up a pitiful inch before she had to give up. She lowered it carefully to the ground before she hurt something.

And Jesse had been lifting it with one hand without even appearing to strain.

"You must be very strong."

"Pretty strong, I guess. My pa's stronger than me."

"But his job makes him strong. You work hard at it. It's admirable."

"I don't know if I deserve that, but thank you."

She stared down at the dumbbells. "I do admire you,

you know. The way you've overcome so many obstacles to get where you are. That you never gave up." She sighed and shifted her gaze to the far end of the garden. "I'm ashamed to admit it, but if you had told me in your letters about being unable to walk, I don't know if I would have come. I'm sorry for that."

"And now?" he said quietly. "Are you glad you came?"

She looked back at him. "Very. But..."

"That doesn't mean you're staying," he finished for her, smiling.

With the way he was looking at her, she was vaguely surprised the beating of her heart didn't scare the birds from the trees.

She glanced back at the kitchen door. "I brought lemon cake, if you're hungry after your exercise."

"I'm not particularly, but that doesn't mean I'm going to say no to lemon cake." He picked up two of the dumbbells, set them in his lap, and rolled across the flagstones to follow her inside.

"Where are your plates?" she said, looking around the kitchen at the many cupboards, none higher than he could reach.

He pointed to a cabinet as he wheeled to a wooden box by the door and placed the dumbbells inside. "Did Mrs Jones make the cake?"

She took three china plates and set them on the table. "I did. I thought since I've tasted your cooking you'd like to sample mine. You do like lemon, don't you?"

"On a cake I like more or less anything." He moved to the table and lifted the cloth on the basket.

"It's cake," she said. "How wrong could it be?"

He grinned. "Exactly."

She took the individual cakes from the basket and arranged them onto a larger plate.

"You made these for me?" He picked up a cake and drew in a deep breath of its aroma. "If this tastes as good as it smells your cooking will rival Mrs Goodwin's."

"I doubt that." She took a seat at the table. "I wanted to do something nice for you. You've been so nice to me."

"You just being here is more than enough, but I'm not discouraging the cake at all." He smiled and held his hand out to her. "Would you like to say the blessing, or shall I?"

She placed her hand in his, feeling the now familiar tingle at the contact. "You do it." In truth, her thoughts tended to flee when he touched her so she wasn't at all sure she could produce a coherent sounding prayer anyway.

When he closed his eyes her gaze was drawn to the way his long lashes grazed his cheeks and she had to remind herself to close her own eyes when he spoke.

"Father, I thank You for Your provision and that we have everything we need. Thank You for these delicious cakes Louisa has made. And thank You for her, Lord, and for bringing her into my life, for however long she's here. In Jesus' name, Amen."

He squeezed her hand gently before letting go and moved two of the cakes onto his plate. Louisa took only one. It wouldn't look quite so bad if she had another later.

"How did your day go?" she said. "Were you able to see the ledger?"

He sighed, his fingers slowly rotating one of the cakes on his plate. "No. When I asked, Mr Ransom said he'd checked it and it was fine. I didn't want him to think I was suspicious so I waited for him to leave his desk so I could get in without him seeing, but he didn't move the entire day, that I saw. Man must have a bladder of iron." He winced. "Sorry, that was crass. I'm almost sure he's trying to keep me from seeing it." His eyes widened as he took a bite of cake. "This is delicious, so light and fluffy and lemony. You'll have to teach me how to make them."

"I'd love to." She had no objections to anything that gave her more time with Jesse. "So what are you going to do? Can you talk to Mr Vernon outside the bank and tell him your suspicions?"

He stared at his plate for a few seconds before shaking his head. "I have no proof and I may be completely wrong. Right now I'm just guessing, and Ransom has worked at the bank for seventeen years. He's Vernon's right hand man. I can't go and make unfounded accusations with no proof. I need that ledger and the bank's copies of the loan agreements and I need to get them without Ransom knowing. If he is doing something and he suspects I suspect him, he could cover any evidence. If there is any." Slumping back in his chair, he rubbed one hand across his jaw. "I don't want to believe he would steal from the bank. He's a snob and has no sense of humour whatsoever, but it's hard to believe he's a thief, especially having been there for so long."

An urge to take his hand and comfort him came over her, but she wasn't sure it would be appropriate. Then he sighed and she decided she didn't care whether it was or not. Reaching across the table, she gently laid her hand over his. He seemed surprised, staring at where they touched, then he turned his hand over and wrapped his fingers around hers.

"So what are you going to do?" she said, hoping her voice wasn't trembling.

He gazed at their hands lying together on the surface of the table. Was he thinking about the bank? Or about the way her hand fit so perfectly into his?

"The only thing I can think of to do is somehow get into the bank after hours and take the ledgers, but I'm not sure how to do that. Only Mr Vernon and Ransom have keys, so the only way is for me to leave a window unlatched and go back after dark." He smiled a little. "Problem is, climbing in through windows isn't so easy for me."

"I could do it." It was only after she'd spoken that she realised what she'd said.

His eyes opened wide and he sat upright, letting go of her hand. "What? No! I wasn't suggesting that at all."

"I know. I just... I want to help. I want to do it." And, to her surprise, she truly did.

He raised his hands, shaking his head and laughing as if the mere idea was ridiculous. "Absolutely not. I am not having you breaking into banks for me! I can ask someone else. Adam would probably do it. Especially now."

"But I can do it! You'd be there with me, at the window. All I'd be doing is going in and getting the ledgers. No one will be there. I'll be safe. I can help, I know I can. Please let me help you." Why was she trying to convince him to allow her to commit a crime?

Jesse stared at her as if he was considering it, abruptly shaking his head after a few seconds. "No, this is... why am I even thinking about this? No. Absolutely not."

"Please? I really do want to help." She was hazy on why, but she did.

Huffing out a breath, he looked away and closed his eyes. She waited as he sat silently.

"What if something goes wrong?" he said after a while, opening his eyes and looking at her. "What if something happens to you?"

"What could go wrong? It'll be dark, no one will see. I'll be in and out in no time." She stood and moved around the table to sit in the chair beside him, taking his hand again and holding it in both of hers. "Something's happening to me, Jesse. A week ago I wouldn't have even considered the vaguest possibility of doing anything remotely like this, but now I want to. I feel like, for the first time in my life, I can do anything I want. And I like that feeling. Please don't take that away from me. Please let me do this. Let me help you."

Gazing into her eyes, he released a long sigh. "I'm going to regret this, aren't I?"

She grinned and bounced in her seat a little. She seemed to be turning into Lizzy. "Can we do it tonight?"

Chuckling, he shook his head. "It'll have to be tomorrow. I have to make sure the window is unlatched before I leave work so you can get in." His smile changed to a frown. "Are you really sure you want to do this?"

She wondered how long she could legitimately keep holding his hand. "Oh yes. Very much." She was excited about the prospect of doing something that would horrify her parents. What was happening to her?

"I have just one more question though," he said, his expression serious. "May I keep holding your hand while we eat?"

She raised one hand to cover her giggle. "I think that would be acceptable."

Chapter 11

Jesse wished his legs worked properly so he could pace. He needed to pace, or at least do something to work off his nervous energy.

How had he let Louisa talk him into this? It was insane. There were so many ways it could go wrong. He should never have listened to her.

But when she'd held his hand and looked into his face, pleading with those beautiful blue eyes that made his heart thump in his chest, he would have said yes to anything she asked.

And now here he was, lurking in the shadows outside the Jones' house, waiting for the woman he hoped to marry to join him in committing a crime.

He'd finally lost his mind. It was the only explanation.

Movement just visible in the light of the three-quarter moon caught his eye from the side of the house and a figure slipped into view, moving on silent feet through the garden and hurrying to him outside the fence.

Louisa was wearing a long, dark cloak and he glimpsed her smiling face beneath her hood.

"I sneaked out my bedroom window!" she whispered, her eyes shining with excitement. "I've never sneaked out before. It was so thrilling! I even used some pillows and clothes to make a shape beneath my bedcovers that looks like I'm still there sleeping, in case anyone checks. Not that anyone would check, but just in case."

He had to stop himself from laughing at her enthusiasm. "If sneaking out is exciting, how are you going to feel breaking into a bank?"

She rubbed her hands together. "Let's go find out."

It being eleven at night most of the townsfolk were at home in bed, although light still spilled from the doors of the saloon some way along the main road from the bank, accompanied by drunken laughter and a slightly out of tune piano. Jesse and Louisa kept to the shadows, staying on the back streets and hugging the sides of buildings as far as possible, only venturing into the open to cross the main street to reach the bank.

Jesse led the way around the side of the brick building to the window he'd left unlatched, hoping no one had discovered it and fastened it again after he'd left. He didn't dare pray it was still unlocked. He wasn't entirely certain God would approve of the whole breaking in thing, as good as his intentions were. If it wasn't the right thing to do, he trusted God would have guided someone to lock the window earlier.

He unlocked the barred gate covering the window with the key he'd taken from the bank that day. Slipping the knife he'd brought through the crack he'd carefully left between the window and its frame, he felt for the latch. When it flicked fully open he wasn't sure whether to be relieved or disappointed.

"All right, remember everything I told you," he whispered to Louisa. "Just go along the corridor inside and Vernon's office is the first door you'll reach on the left. There will be a lamp on his desk. The light shouldn't be seen from the road, but keep it low anyway. The ledgers..."

"I know, I know," she whispered back. "We've gone over it several times, I know what to do." She touched her fingertips to his face. "Stop worrying."

His voice fled at her touch and it was a couple of seconds before it returned. "I can't help worrying. You don't have to do this. We can just go home..."

"I'm going in and that's final," she said with a smile, unfastening her cloak. "Would you hold this for me? I don't want it to catch on anything."

She shrugged off the cloak and handed it to Jesse and his jaw dropped. Even in the low light he could see the gown she wore underneath, her shoulders bare and the shimmering fabric hugging her narrow waist and skimming over her hips.

"Why are you wearing an evening dress?" He needed to ask, even though he couldn't find a single reason to object.

"It's the only dark coloured dress I have. It's meant to have a bustle underneath so it's a bit long, but only at the back."

He swallowed. Why was his mouth so dry? "Uh, could... could I possibly see it in the light one day?" He *really* wanted to see it properly.

She gave him a smile that would have made his knees weak, if he could stand. "I'm sure I can arrange that."

For a moment he forgot why they were there, until she slid the window up and began gathering her skirt in around her. At a flash of stocking he looked away, focusing his attention on the main street along the alley and trying not to think about what else he might see if he looked back.

After a few seconds of rustling she whispered, "I'm in."

He looked round to see her standing on the other side of the window. Seeing her inside where he couldn't reach her if she needed him nudged his anxiety up to a whole new level.

"Please be careful," he begged, gripping the windowsill and fighting the urge to reach in and pull her back out.

She laid her hands over his and smiled. "I'll be just fine. I won't be long."

126

And with that she turned and hurried away from him into the darkness, leaving him silently panicking outside.

~ ~ ~

Louisa felt her way along the corridor in the darkness, brushing her left hand along the wall to guide her and fervently hoping she didn't touch any spiders.

Her heart raced and she was certain if it hadn't been so dark she would have seen her hands shaking. She hadn't wanted Jesse to know, but she was afraid. And yet the excitement of adventure also shivered through her.

She'd never done anything remotely like this before. She was always the good girl, following her parents' will in everything.

Quiet, obedient, trustworthy.

Bored.

It wasn't that she wanted to do bad things or hurt people, but deep down she'd always held a spark of adventurousness, locked away where it couldn't inspire inappropriate longings. Until she'd arrived in Green Hill Creek and met Jesse Johnson, a man who made her want to live life now rather than wait for it to happen. And somehow he'd known it, even before they met. Even before she knew herself.

The more time she spent with him, the closer all those suppressed desires came to the surface. It was both terrifying and thrilling at once and it made her do foolhardy things like breaking into a bank to help him investigate a possible crime.

But it also gave her an excitement and anticipation she couldn't ever remember feeling before. If it was only for two weeks that couldn't be bad, could it?

Her hand touched the doorframe and she felt for the handle, relieved to find the door unlocked as Jesse said it would be. She pushed the door open and slipped through the gap, closing it behind her to minimise any light escaping into the corridor.

By the small amount of light filtering in from the moon she went straight to the large desk in the centre of the room and opened the lamp, lighting it with the matches she'd brought and turning the flame down low.

She blinked in the light, waiting for her eyes to adjust as she got her first proper look at the room. She saw the cabinet Jesse had told her about in the corner, the lamplight shimmering over its polished mahogany doors. She moved around the desk and opened the top drawer, scanning the contents for the keys Jesse had said would be there. They weren't hard to find.

She found it strange that Mr Vernon would lock a cabinet and then leave the keys for it right there in the room, but Jesse said he always was overly confident about the security of his bank. Shrugging, she took them from the drawer. It was a good thing for them.

She took the ledgers Jesse wanted for the past three months from the cabinet, rearranged the rest so they didn't look like any were missing, then found the file where the loan agreements were kept. They were in date order so she took all of those from the past three months. The more Jesse had to work with, the better chance he'd be able to find out what was going on. And the more proof he'd have.

She closed and locked the cabinet, replaced the keys in the drawer, and looked around the room to check everything was as she'd found it.

"Who's back there? This is Deputy Marshal Fielding. Come out with your hands in the air."

Louisa froze at the sound of the voice outside.

Heart thudding, she rushed to turn off the lamp and hurried to the door, opening it a fraction to listen.

Jesse's wheelchair was moving away from the window. "I can either come out or put my hands in the air, Eric," he said, a jocularity to his voice she knew he wasn't feeling, "but I can't do both at the same time."

She slipped into the corridor and silently closed the door to the office. Hardly daring to breathe, she crept back to the window. Jesse had closed the bars, but the window itself was still open.

"Jesse." The deputy sounded relieved. "What were you doing back there?"

"Couldn't sleep so I came out for a walk," Jesse replied. "Or a roll, more accurately. I heard a sound and thought I should check, it being where I work and all. Can't imagine Mr Vernon would be too pleased to learn there'd been a robbery at his bank and I didn't throw myself into the line of fire to save it."

Louisa marvelled at the way he managed to sound relaxed while she was panicking.

Deputy Fielding chuckled. "I've had bosses like that. But you shouldn't be going down dark alleys on your own at night, especially unarmed. I think Mr Vernon would rather keep you than the money."

"You don't know Mr Vernon well, do you?"

The deputy laughed again.

"Anyway," Jesse said, "the dangerous outlaw turned out to be a racoon, so I think we're all safe."

"I'll go and check anyway," Deputy Fielding said, "just to make sure you didn't miss anything in the dark."

Setting the ledgers on the floor, Louisa reached up for the window and tugged it down, torn between needing to close it as quickly as possible and not wanting to make any noise.

"Oh, you don't have to do that," Jesse said. "There's nothing back there, I'm sure."

"It's no trouble."

The alley outside lightened, the sound of footsteps approaching.

Louisa pulled at the window, desperately praying for it to be silent.

The light grew.

I'm going to be seen! Please don't let me be seen.

The window finally reached the sill and she fastened the latch and threw herself into the corner beneath it. Light flared at the window above her, illuminating the corridor.

She pressed herself into the wall, holding her breath. Several excruciating seconds passed.

And then the light moved away.

Louisa breathed out.

After fifteen seconds or so, the lamp and footsteps passed the window again, not stopping this time but carrying on to the street.

"It's all clear," the deputy's muffled voice said. "Probably best if you head home though. There's only one of me and I can't cover the whole town. I love this place, but not everyone who comes through has our best interests at heart."

"Will do, Eric," Jesse said. "And thanks."

Louisa waited a full ten minutes before she dared to open the window a crack. Hearing nothing, she pushed it up just wide enough to squeeze through, pushed the bars open, and climbed outside, tugging her dress after her and closing the window. She couldn't lock it, but Jesse would take care of that in the morning when he arrived for work.

Right now, she just wanted to get back to where she was safe. She'd had enough excitement for the night.

From the mouth of the alley she saw Jesse in the shadow of a building across the street. He waved when he saw her. She peered up and down the street and, seeing no sign of Deputy Fielding or anyone else, ran across and into the darkness where Jesse waited for her. He looked immensely relieved. She was so happy to be with him again it was all she could do to not throw herself into his lap. Instead she handed him the ledgers and loan agreements.

He grasped her hand and smiled up at her, mouthing silently, "Thank you."

For reasons that had nothing to do with fear, her heart leapt.

He handed her cloak back to her and she shrugged it on, following him away from the main street. When they were a good distance from the busier part of town, he turned in the direction of the Jones' house.

"I'll walk you home and then get to work on these..."

"May I come with you?"

His eyebrows reached for his hairline.

"Just for a little while?" she said. "The truth is, I'm far too wide awake to go to bed and I really want to know what you find in those ledgers." She also wasn't ready to leave Jesse for the night.

He looked uncomfortable. "I don't know. I mean, it's so late and if anyone knew we were alone in my house during the night..."

"No one will know. I won't stay long, I promise." She felt a little like a child begging to be allowed to stay up late, but if that was what it took, she'd do it.

He sighed. "All right, just for a little while. But you have to promise to keep your hands to yourself."

She clapped her hand over her mouth to muffle her laughter. "I'll be good, I promise."

He nodded once, lips twitching with a smile, and started in the direction of his house. "See that you do. I have my reputation to think of, you know."

~ ~ ~

131

Jesse hung his jacket on a hook by the door and carried on into the parlour, pulling the curtains tightly closed before lighting the lamps.

"Would you like anything to drink?" he said, turning to face Louisa.

"A glass of water would be nice, thank you."

For a few moments all he could do was stare. She'd removed her cloak, giving him a proper view of her evening gown. He'd thought she looked beautiful in the dark. In the light, she took his breath away.

She lifted the skirt a little and twirled in a circle. "So does the dress live up to expectations? I didn't wear the bustle because I'd never have got through the window in that ridiculous thing. Mother insisted I needed the latest fashion for my only ball gown, but I hate bustles. They're so impractical, and a nightmare to sit down in. You have to perch on the edge of the chair. It's ridiculous." She gasped, her hand going to her mouth as if she'd said something she hadn't meant to, although he couldn't think what that might have been. "I mean, I have other gowns, but this was the latest."

"You look stunning," he said, sure he'd never meant anything more in his life.

She lowered her hand to reveal a shy, beautiful smile playing on her lips. "Thank you."

He had to remind himself he had work to do. "I'll just go and get you that water."

When he returned, Louisa was at his desk. "I've put all the agreements into the corresponding pages by date," she said, sliding a final piece of paper between the pages of one of the ledgers, "so you have them all in the right place. I hope that's all right."

He wheeled up to the desk and placed the glass down, amazed at how much she'd done in the short time he'd been gone. "You should come and work at the bank. I can't believe you did all this so fast."

She picked up the water and carried it to the settee, settling onto one end. "It wasn't so difficult. There are only twenty-three loans."

He flicked through one of the ledgers. "Yes it was. I was gone less than two minutes. You have an amazing eye for detail."

She shrugged one shoulder and took a sip from the glass.

He closed the ledger. "You do know how smart you are, don't you?"

She gave a small sigh and looked at her hands. "Mother always says a lady plays down her own talents in favour of a man's."

He almost laughed, until he realised she was being serious. "Well with all respect to your mother, I think that's nonsense."

Surprise swept onto her face and he hurried to continue before she got the idea he was insulting her mother, even though he couldn't understand why any parent would want to stifle their child's development in that way. Especially an amazing woman like Louisa.

"I don't think you should ever have to hide who you are or what you can do. And certainly never from me. I'm fully ready to concede you're better than me at anything that doesn't involve lifting a heavy weight."

To his relief, she laughed. "I'm sure that's not at all true, but thank you."

"So you promise to never hide from me? I want you to be able to say or do anything you want."

She nodded, smiling.

"And not to ever feel you can't be exactly who you are?"

Another nod.

"And to wear that dress as often as possible?"

To his delight, her smile turned into laughter. He would never tire of hearing her laugh.

Louisa picked out a book from Jesse's collection and read as he worked, slipping her stockinged feet from her shoes and pulling them up under her dress on the settee. He did his best to not keep glancing at her from his place at the desk, but it wasn't easy. She drew his eyes like a magnet, one elbow resting on the arm of the settee and her head leaning on her hand, the soft light from the lamps making her skin glow.

With her presence no end of a distraction, he took longer than he should have to work, comparing totals, calculating percentage rates and payments, cross checking everything with his own work books which he'd brought home with him. Not that he would have had it any other way. Every second he spent with her filled him with happiness and every second apart from her was spent wishing they were together.

He asked her a few times if she was bored and would she like to return home, but she assured him she wanted to stay. He began to consider that it wasn't just the outcome of his investigations she was there for and maybe she simply wanted to spend more time with him.

After some time she closed the book and rested her head on her arms, yawning. When he looked up again, her eyes were closed and her breathing slow and regular. He considered waking her and taking her home, but he didn't have much more to do so he decided to leave her to sleep until he was finished. Then he could tell her what he'd found and walk her back. There was no sense in disturbing her now.

He wheeled quietly to the settee and took a blanket from the back, unfolding it and draping it gently over her shoulders. She stirred a little before quieting again. Jesse reached out to move a strand of hair from across her face, resisting the urge to touch her cheek.

What would it be like to wake beside her, her beautiful face the first thing he saw every morning? To have her open her eyes and see him, her smile lighting the room more brightly than the sun? To draw her into his arms and feel her lips on his?

Sighing softly, he backed away and returned to his desk.

He'd wake her as soon as he was done.

Chapter 12

Louisa drew in a deep breath as she woke, wincing at a crick in the side of her neck. She lifted her head from her arms and looked around blearily, for a few moments unsure of where she was.

Then she remembered.

She was on the settee in Jesse's parlour. Across the room, he was still at his desk, albeit fast asleep with his head resting on his arms on top of one of the open ledgers.

The lamps had burned down, but it didn't matter because light was filtering through the curtains from outside. What time was it?

She sat up and a blanket she was certain she hadn't placed there slipped down her arm. Her eyes went to Jesse again and she smiled. He must have put it over her when she fell asleep. He was always so thoughtful.

Except now it was light outside and she was still in his house. She twisted round to look up at the clock on the wall behind her, horrified to see it was almost ten minutes past six.

What if Pastor and Mrs Jones were already awake? How would she explain being out all night?

She pushed the blanket off, slipped her feet into her shoes, and crept over to Jesse. He looked so peaceful, with his eyes closed and his lashes brushing his cheeks.

She reached out to move a lock of hair from his cheek, only realising at the last second what she was about to do and instead touching his shoulder.

"Jesse?"

He drew in a slow breath and lifted his head, blinking sleepily. "Louisa? What..." His eyes snapped open wide and darted around the room. "I fell asleep."

"Me too."

His gaze went to the window. "It's light outside."

"I noticed that."

"That's not good."

"No."

"What time is it?"

"Ten past six."

He sat up and hissed in a sharp, pain-filled breath through his teeth, looking down at his lap.

Louisa stepped towards him, alarmed. "What's wrong?"

He pushed away from the desk and rubbed at his thighs, grimacing. "If I don't sleep in the correct position my leg muscles bunch up and stiffen. Sitting at my desk is definitely not the correct position."

She had to stop herself from reaching out and touching him. "Does it hurt a lot? Can I do anything?"

"They'll be okay, they just need a good stretch and massage to loosen them up." He pushed the heels of his hands into his thighs and winced. "Just give me a minute and I'll be okay to take you back."

"Oh no, you do what you need to to get out of pain," she said, going to the chair to fetch her cloak. "I'll be fine walking back by myself. It's not far."

He frowned. "I don't know..."

"Well, I do." She walked back to Jesse and placed her hand on his shoulder. "Just take care of your legs. Will I see you this afternoon?"

The half smile she liked so much twinkled in his eyes. "Do you really have to ask? I'll pick you up with the buggy at five. I have plans for us."

"I'll look forward to it."

As she pulled her hand from his shoulder, he caught hold of it.

"Thank you," he said, looking earnestly into her eyes. "Everything you've done, the way you've helped me... I'm grateful. And I'm real happy you're here."

Her heart fluttering, she didn't even think about censoring her response so he wouldn't be encouraged. "I'm happy too."

Smiling, he brought her hand to his lips and brushed a soft kiss onto the back before releasing it.

Oh! She looked down at her hand, then back at him. "I... I'll see you at, uh, five."

Swallowing, she turned for the door and almost tripped over her own feet.

Recovering, she looked back at him, gave an embarrassed laugh, and fled.

~ ~ ~

Louisa ran back as fast as she could, hoping all the time that no one would be about. There were a couple of people out early, but she managed to hide before they saw her. She didn't recognise either of them, but better to be safe than sorry.

All the way home, she thought about Jesse's kiss. She was certain she shouldn't still be able to feel it, and yet the back of her hand tingled with the memory of his lips on her skin.

It was only a light kiss on her hand, she kept telling herself. It wasn't like that had never happened before. She'd been kissed on the hand many times, in fact, by many different men back in New York. Her reaction to each of those had largely ranged from mildly flattered to apathetic.

So why was her heart still stuttering and her skin still tingling from this one? It was just a simple kiss on the hand. That was all.

Jesse's full, warm lips on her trembling, tingling hand.

Her feet tangled in her dress and she grabbed at a wall as she tripped, only just managing to stay upright. Rolling her eyes, she lifted her skirt higher and resumed her rush for home, trying to put Jesse and his kiss from her mind. She needed to arrive in one piece.

On reaching the house, she ducked down and ran up the front path on silent feet, tiptoed up onto the porch, and flattened herself next to the parlour window. Holding her breath, she peered in. She breathed out again when she saw no one inside. She couldn't hear anything either, so hopefully that meant Pastor and Mrs Jones weren't yet awake. She might just get away with this.

Creeping around the side of the house, she rounded the back corner.

And collided with Mrs Jones.

Louisa yelped, stumbling backwards, and tripped on the hem of her overlong, bustleless dress. She landed on her backside in a bed of marigolds, gasping for breath.

"Louisa! Are you all right?" Mrs Jones dropped the basket she held and hurried forward to help her out of the dirt.

"I'm okay." She looked behind her at the flattened orange flowers, absently brushing at the back of her dress. "I've ruined your marigolds."

"Oh, don't worry, they'll spring back." She took hold of Louisa's shoulders. "What in the world are you doing out here this early?" Her eyes travelled down. "Are you wearing an evening gown? Louisa, have you been out all night?"

"I...I..." She floundered for something to say, some

excuse that would convincingly explain being out at six-thirty in the morning dressed in a ball gown. Her shoulders slumped. She had nothing. "I was at Jesse's house, for most of the time. I didn't realise how late it was. We fell asleep."

Mrs Jones released her shoulders and frowned.

Louisa's hand flew to her mouth. "Not that we were... I mean, we weren't doing anything. At least, not anything wrong. Well, maybe it was wrong, but we weren't doing *that*, I swear." Giving up, she covered her face with her hands and groaned.

There were a few seconds of silence during which she wished the ground would open up and swallow her.

"I think perhaps you should tell me what's going on," Mrs Jones said, her tone mildly disapproving.

They sat on a nearby bench and there were a good twenty seconds of silence while Louisa decided what to do. She felt compelled to tell the truth to the woman who had been so kind to her since she'd arrived, but she wasn't sure if Mrs Jones would approve of what she and Jesse had actually been doing any more than what she thought they'd been doing.

"If I tell you this, will you promise not to tell anyone else?" she said, unwilling to betray Jesse's confidence without some assurance. "Even Pastor Jones?"

Mrs Jones was quiet for a few seconds. "I'll make that promise if you promise me that if anyone needs to know, you will tell them."

She thought about that, finally nodding. "I will." She sighed and looked at her lap. "Jesse thinks that someone at the bank is stealing from the customers, but he has no proof. He needed to see the ledgers and some other papers, but whenever he tried, this person stopped him, even though he had every right to see them. So I persuaded Jesse to let me sneak into the bank through a window late last night to get the ledgers for him so he could check them without this person knowing. Afterwards I went back to his house because I wanted to know what he would find, but I fell asleep on his settee while he was working on them and then he fell asleep at his desk and we didn't wake up until fifteen minutes ago and I came straight back here. And that's all that happened, I swear."

"And did he find anything?"

Of all the questions Mrs Jones could have asked, Louisa hadn't imagined that would be the first. "I forgot to ask," she said a little sheepishly. "I wanted to get back before you noticed I was gone. I was hoping you'd still be asleep."

Mrs Jones looked out over her garden where the low, early morning sun cast long shadows across the dew-dampened ground.. "I like to come out here early, before anyone needs me, and pray while I pick out weeds and deadhead and do whatever else needs to be done. It's my time to be alone with God."

Louisa considered that. "I've never thought about needing to be alone with God. But I've been reading my Bible and praying a lot since Sunday, and it feels like He wants me to give Him my attention. I didn't very often at home. I'm beginning to think I haven't been a very good Christian."

Mrs Jones swivelled on the seat to face her. "I hope you don't mind me asking, but have you ever invited Jesus into your life?"

"Once, when I was fourteen. It was in church and the reverend was talking about the parable of the lost sheep. When he said that Jesus was searching for each one of us, waiting for us to come to Him and ask Him to come into our lives and save us, I had the strongest feeling that He was speaking right to me. So I did it then and there, quietly." It was strange that she remembered that so vividly when just about all the other Sundays she'd spent in church were

141

lumped into a vague blur of boredom and awkwardness. "I don't know if I used the right words, but I thought Jesus wouldn't mind if I didn't."

Mrs Jones was smiling. "He certainly wouldn't. All that mattered was that you heard Him calling you and you answered. And you only had to do it once. That's all you needed to do."

Louisa nodded, thinking back to that Sunday nine years before. "We never went back to that church after that. I wish we had. I would have liked to hear more of that reverend's sermons, but it wasn't the kind of church my parents approved of. A lot of the others I heard talked about judgement and sin and damnation, but he talked about love. Just like Pastor Jones did on Sunday. I much prefer that to all the doom and gloom."

Mrs Jones leaned forward and whispered, "I'll tell you a secret - I do too."

"So do you think I should have a time every day when I'm alone to talk with God too?" It seemed to be working for Mrs Jones. She was one of the happiest people Louisa had ever met.

"I think that's a very good idea."

Without warning, a huge yawn stretched Louisa's mouth and she clapped her hand over it. "Does it have to be this early?"

"No, it certainly doesn't," Mrs Jones said, laughing. "It can be any time you want. Maybe you need to get some more sleep after your adventures last night."

Louisa bit her lip. She'd almost forgotten about that. "So... you aren't angry with me for staying with Jesse all night and breaking into the bank?"

"I won't ever be angry with you, Louisa. And as far as staying with Jesse all night goes, I know the two of you weren't doing anything. I've known Jesse since he was three years old." Her smile became wistful. "Simon and I were never blessed with children so I've taken every chance I get to be around them and I've gotten to know the young people of this town well. I guess you could say I'm like a surrogate aunt to Jesse. And I know his heart. He turns on the charm and flirts, but he's one of the most honourable young men I've ever known. He's committed to following the Lord in everything and I trust him. Didn't you find it strange that Simon approved of the situation with Adam and Amy?"

"I did." The truth was, Louisa had been shocked. She knew for a fact nothing was happening between the two of them, but a pastor endorsing an unmarried man and woman living in the same house? She'd never heard of such a thing.

"The reason Simon did that was because we've also known Adam almost all his life and he's the same as Jesse. Nothing is more important to those two young men than obeying God. We trust both of them and we trust God to guide them, so when Adam told Simon he felt God was telling him to give Amy a safe place to stay, we believed him."

Louisa was quiet as she absorbed Mrs Jones' words. Coming from a life where appearance was more important than truth and a person was often judged and condemned with no recourse to the facts, finding two people like Pastor and Mrs Jones who offered only love and acceptance was a revelation. She couldn't help wishing there were more like them in the world.

Overcome by a rush of affection for the older woman, Louisa leaned forward and hugged her. "Thank you. I'm so glad to be staying with you and Pastor Jones."

"We're glad to have you here," Mrs Jones said, returning her embrace. "Just try not to have to break into anywhere again. I wouldn't want you to get into trouble."

Louisa smiled. "I'll do my best."

Mrs Jones sat back. "You must tell me what Jesse finds out. I hate to think anyone in the town is being taken advantage of."

"Jesse thinks the same. He's really worried about it all. That's why I wanted to help him however I could." She covered her mouth as another yawn erupted.

"Maybe you should go to bed," Mrs Jones said with a smile, "before you fall asleep right here."

Chapter 13

Jesse covered a yawn with one hand and leaned his head on the other, resting his elbow on the desk.

He'd only been at work for half an hour and he was already close to drifting off. How many hours' sleep had he got last night? Couldn't have been more than four, if that. His mind wandered back to watching Louisa as she slept on his settee while he worked on the ledgers and he smiled. Having her in the same room didn't exactly help him focus, but it did make the work a lot more enjoyable.

The door to the back corridor opened, startling him from his sleepy, Louisa-based reverie. Mr Ransom stepped through.

Jesse lowered his head, pretending to concentrate on the figures in front of him. He wasn't at all certain of his ability to keep a civil expression when around Mr Vernon's secretary any more. What he really wanted to do was shout at him until he admitted what he was doing.

Jesse was also nervous it would be discovered that the ledgers and loan agreements he'd been trying to see for two days were missing. Until he found out what Ransom was doing, if Jesse was suspected of taking them it would be very bad for him.

He again wondered if behind the pots in the shed behind his house was a secure enough hiding place.

"Mr Johnson?"

Jesse closed his eyes for a moment, gathering strength before looking up. "Yes?"

"I just wanted to let you know that I went out to see Mr Foster before I came in this morning, to reassure him and his son that everything is in order with his loan. They're happy that it's all been explained sufficiently, so you needn't be concerned that Mr Foster will return."

Jesse studied him carefully. Was he imagining things, or were those nerves he detected behind Ransom's eyes? "Thanks for letting me know."

Ransom gave him a short nod and then carried on to the lobby, returning a few minutes later and disappearing back into his own area without another word.

Jesse sat back, tapping the end of his pencil absently against his jaw. Since when did Ransom ever feel the need to tell anyone other than their boss what he did? Since never, that was when. That could indicate worry. Trouble was, Jesse didn't know if it should make him happy or uncomfortable that Ransom suspected he might be onto him.

Or maybe he was reading too much into the whole situation and nothing at all was going on. After all, he hadn't found anything incriminating in the ledgers, just one small thing that might be nothing. All he had to go on was what could be a completely innocent mistake on the part of a customer and his own projections of guilt onto Ransom.

Dropping his pencil onto the desk, he heaved a sigh and rubbed both hands over his face. This was getting him nowhere. He should just go back to constantly obsessing over Louisa. At least that was more fun.

"You okay?"

He looked up to see Adam standing in the doorway to the lobby.

For a moment he considered telling his friend everything, about Ransom, about Foster, about breaking into the bank and stealing the ledgers. But Adam had his own problems. The last thing Jesse wanted was to add to them.

"Just tired. I didn't get much sleep last night."

Adam raised his eyebrows. "Thoughts about Louisa keeping you up?"

Jesse smiled. "You could say that. What about you and Amy?"

Adam walked to the supply cupboard and took out a stack of deposit slips. "For the first three nights I barely closed my eyes. Then it all caught up with me and I slept like the dead. Seems to have evened out now, thankfully." He headed back to the lobby. "See you later."

Jesse watched him go then leaned his head on his hand again. If only thoughts of Louisa were the only distraction he had to contend with.

Chapter 14

Jesse arrived at precisely three minutes to five that afternoon. Louisa knew this because she was sitting by the window in the parlour, alternating her gaze between the road and the clock and barely looking at the copy of The Pilgrim's Progress on her lap Mrs Jones had suggested she read. She was learning a lot from the book, but the closer it came to the time Jesse had said he'd pick her up, the more her concentration wandered.

As soon as he pulled up in his buggy she closed the book, leapt to her feet, and grabbed her shawl from beside her.

"He's here," she called as she hurried through to the hallway.

Mrs Jones appeared in the kitchen doorway. "Should I expect you back before tomorrow morning?"

Louisa laughed and gave her a quick hug on the way to the front door. "No breaking into banks planned for tonight."

Jesse smiled as she walked along the path through the front yard towards him. "I haven't seen that dress before. That colour looks beautiful on you."

She looked down at her lilac dress with the square neckline, the one she'd always liked but her mother said washed out her colouring. "Thank you." She gave Duke a pat then climbed in beside Jesse, glancing back at the picnic basket behind her seat as they started off. "Where are we going?"

"There's a lake in the foothills about a half hour away. It's the perfect place for a picnic."

"Sounds wonderful." Anywhere she could spend time alone with Jesse sounded wonderful to her. "How are your legs? Are you still in pain?"

He guided them left onto the main street. "They're fine. I went over to my parents and my pa helped me with them. Mostly I can do the massaging myself, but he helps when they get bad."

She didn't like the idea of him suffering. "Do you get a lot of pain?"

"No, not much. Mostly at the end of the day, sometimes when I wake up. And my muscles spasm sometimes. But it's not bad. Just gets worse when I fall asleep at my desk. Last night wasn't the first time that's happened and it probably won't be the last." He stopped the buggy to let a wagon past, waving to the driver, then turned right onto a side road leading out of town. "So how did it go this morning? Did you manage to sneak back in undetected?"

She looked down at her lap. "Not exactly."

His eyes widened. "You got caught?"

"Turns out Mrs Jones likes to spend time praying and gardening early in the morning. I had no idea."

"What did you tell her?" He looked as though he was wondering if he needed to leave town.

Louisa couldn't resist. "I said we were so exhausted that we fell asleep and didn't realise what the time was."

"W-what?" he choked out.

She only managed five seconds with a straight face before her giggle escaped.

His expression of horror became a laugh and he shook his head. "You really had me scared there for a second. So you got back in all right?"

"Oh no, that part was true. She really was there when I got back."

His jaw dropped again. It was adorable. "So what *did* you tell her?"

"I told her the truth. She promised she wouldn't tell anyone about your suspicions. She was very understanding. It's okay, isn't it? I didn't know what else to do."

He looked forward, guiding Duke onto a narrow road along the side of a field of wheat. "It's okay, I don't mind her knowing." He glanced at her sideways. "I'm just relieved she doesn't think we were... you know."

"Don't worry, she trusts you," she said, smiling. "Oh, she wanted to know what you found out from the ledgers and I realised I forgot to ask you before I left. Did you find proof?"

"No, I didn't find anything." He paused. "Well, I may have found something, but I'm not sure."

"You're not sure?"

"Most of the amounts are exactly as they should be, but Mr Foster's loan, there's a place where a figure could have been changed. But it's from a one to a seven and it's possible I could have written it that way. I may just be seeing things because I want to. Not that it matters one way or the other because I can't prove anything. I don't understand it. I know something's wrong, but I don't know how to find out what it is." He stared at a barn roof just visible over the tops of the trees away to their left and heaved a sigh that broke her heart. "Most folks round here don't have that much, but they work hard and they're doing their best to provide for their families and their futures. I hate the thought that Ransom could be doing something to take that from them. Even a small amount could break some of them." He shook his head and lowered his eyes to Duke's back. "But maybe I'm wrong. Maybe Ransom isn't guilty of anything. Maybe I'm just being paranoid."

It was the first time she'd seen him doubt himself. It felt... wrong.

She touched her fingers to his jaw and turned him to face her. "Do you believe you're wrong?"

His eyes flicked between hers, as if he could find the answer there. "No."

"Then you're not wrong. You'll find it somehow, and I'll help in any way I can."

His gaze held hers and then dropped to her lips, just for a moment.

She suddenly realised she was still touching his face and that, at some point, she had leaned towards him. She quickly lowered her hand to her lap and sat back.

He gave her a small smile. "Thank you. It means a lot that you believe me."

She nodded and looked forward, willing her heart to slow.

She was fairly sure she'd wanted to kiss him just then, with her fingertips touching the smooth skin of his cheek and his eyes gazing into hers. There hadn't been a conscious thought, but deep down the desire was there, prodding her closer.

She'd never been kissed by a man before. On the lips, anyway. The several times on the hand didn't count. At least, with most men it didn't count. She thought back to how Jesse had kissed her hand that morning. That had felt entirely different and most certainly like it counted. But then Jesse wasn't most men.

What would it be like to be kissed, properly kissed, by him? Would his lips be soft? They looked soft. Would he wrap his arms around her? Would her lips tingle just as her hand had? Would she know what to do? Would he be able to tell she'd never been kissed before? Would he mind?

"What are you thinking about?"

Louisa started at the question, eyes whipping to Jesse. He couldn't possibly know she'd been thinking about kissing him. Could he?

"Uh, I was just thinking about..." she frantically cast about for something to say, "apples." *Apples?*

He looked confused. "Apples?"

"Yes. I was just wondering if you'd brought any. I find I have a sudden desire for an apple."

"I did bring a couple. You must really love apples."

Now *she* was confused. "I, um, they're nice. Why do you say that?"

"Because from the look on your face, you were thinking about something you enjoy a lot."

Don't blush. Do not blush. "I... yes, apples are a favourite of mine. Very much so."

She feigned interest in a tree they were passing so she could turn her face away from him. In case her desperate efforts to not blush failed her.

They reached the lake twenty minutes later. Twenty minutes of enjoying Jesse's company while trying to not think about kissing him. Or at least, trying not to *look* like she was thinking about kissing him.

"There's a real nice place down there," he said, pointing to a track leading into the trees separating the road from the lake's shore. "You can see all the way up the lake to the mountains."

She twisted in her seat to peer along the track as they passed. "We aren't going there?"

"Not right now. That's Adam's favourite spot and I don't want to risk him showing up to our picnic. Today I want you all to myself."

She couldn't help smiling as she turned her attention to the road ahead of them. When she first arrived, his forwardness had shocked her. Now she knew it was just part of who he was. And she couldn't deny she loved it.

He took them further along the lake, eventually pulling into a stand of trees and bringing the buggy to a halt by an outcrop of rock that overhung the water and sloped down to meet the shore. The trees filtered the sunlight, dappling the ground in a latticework of gold and shadow and casting shimmering green patterns on the gently undulating water. Birds sang amongst the leaves overhead and insects buzzed between the wildflowers dotting the ground.

"It's beautiful," Louisa breathed, climbing from the buggy the moment Jesse set the brake and turning in a circle to take everything in. "Even Solomon in all his glory was not arrayed like one of these."

She surprised herself. She'd read the verse in Matthew that morning, but she didn't expect to remember it.

"The Lord certainly didn't hold back when He designed this place," Jesse said.

He pulled the lever on the ingenious contraption his father had built into the buggy that held his wheelchair while travelling and lowered it to the ground beside him when he needed it.

She could be happy in a place like this, Louisa had no doubt. She looked over at Jesse where he was moving onto his chair. She could be happy with a man like him.

Would remaining in the same social circle really be so bad if it meant she could feel this way for the rest of her life?

Jesse unhitched Duke while she stepped up onto the rocky outcrop and wandered to the edge of the overhang, leaning over to peer into the water. Even though the surface was only three feet or so below her, the rippling reflections made it impossible to see the bottom.

She watched a small fish swim past close to the surface, its scales shimmering silver. "How deep is it?"

"Hmm?" he said, lifting the picnic basket and blanket from the buggy.

"The lake, how deep is it?"

"I'm not sure. Further out it's deep enough to not be able to touch the bottom. I swim here a lot."

She looked back at him. "You can swim?" Just a few days ago she would have been embarrassed asking such a question, but now there wasn't even a hint of awkwardness. It felt good being so comfortable around him.

"My pa took me into the water from when I was young. He figured it would give me confidence and help my muscles and he was right. I enjoy swimming. Being in the water makes me feel almost normal."

She looked back at the lake. In the heat of the day it looked cool and inviting. "I'd love to be able to swim."

"Maybe I could teach you one day."

He said it matter-of-factly, as if he was suggesting they take a stroll around the town, but Louisa knew the implication. There was no way they'd be able to get into the water together without being husband and wife. She didn't reply, even though the thought of Jesse teaching her to swim was far from unpleasant.

"The food is ready," he said, "whenever you are."

A flash of colour in the water caught her attention and she moved closer to the edge to get a better look.

"Be careful up there," he called. "The rocks can get slippery."

"I see the most wonderful coloured fish." She took another step forward, her eyes on the water.

Something crumbled under her feet and she cried out as her footing slipped from beneath her and she plummeted forward.

The last thing she heard was Jesse screaming her name. And then she hit the lake.

Cold water rushed in around her body and face. Her dress billowed on the surface, entangling her in its suddenly sodden folds. Panicking, she flailed against the fabric, struggling to free herself. Water rushed into her mouth, her nose.

Hands grabbed her, pulling her to the surface. The material of her dress was tugged from around her face and shoulders. She opened her eyes to see Jesse's face inches from hers.

A fit of coughing seized her and she clutched at his shoulders, gasping in air and frantically trying to stay above the water.

"Just relax and breathe," he said, sounding calm despite the fear in his voice. "You're safe."

"Can't... swim," she spluttered.

"It's not deep here. Just put your feet down."

She shook her head and threw her arms around his neck, clutching onto him. He sank under her weight, his head dipping beneath the surface. She let go, horrified, and immediately began to sink herself.

Jesse bobbed back up and shook wet tendrils of hair from his eyes. "Louisa, listen to me. Put your feet down."

His commanding tone penetrated her frenzied panic and, heart pounding, she obeyed. Her feet touched more or less solid ground. The water still came to her chest, but she could easily stand.

"Oh," she said, her fear slipping away. Embarrassment replaced it.

"Are you all right?"

She nodded. "Thank you for saving me."

"Are you hurt at all?"

She shook her head and tried to smile. "Only my pride."

He blew out a breath. "You scared me half to death there. I thought you were drowning."

"So did I." She shifted her feet on the bottom of the lake. "Drowned in four feet of water. How humiliating would that have been?"

"Don't worry, I would have told everyone you were hauled in by a huge monster and fought valiantly before finally succumbing."

"How noble of you." She looked at the water around them. "Wait, there aren't any...?"

"No, no monsters that I know of. Still, I've only been swimming here for twenty-five years so you never know."

Smiling, she gave his shoulder a small push.

He was gazing into her face, his eyes dancing with warmth, and she found she couldn't look away. Or maybe she simply didn't want to look away. Even soaking wet he was beautiful, droplets of water adorning his skin like diamonds.

Realisation hit her. "You're standing!"

"Not really," he said, smiling. "My feet are on the bottom, but the water is supporting most of my weight. If I was truly standing, I'd be taller."

He was using one hand to stabilise himself on the rock at the side of the lake and his face was more or less on the same level as hers.

She looked down, trying to see the rest of him through the water. "How tall are you?"

He shrugged one shoulder. "I'm not completely sure. From when I was about five, every year on my birthday my pa would get me to lie on the floor and then he'd lie next to me to compare our heights. I finally caught up with him when I was fifteen. Think I grew maybe another inch or two after that before I stopped."

"How tall is he?"

"Six feet and four inches."

Her mouth dropped open. "You're really tall."

156

"Not that anyone notices, but yes."

She looked at the rock beside them. "I noticed. I mean, I didn't know how tall, but I noticed you have long legs and arms so I thought you must be taller than most men."

She didn't have to be looking directly at him to see the smile slide onto his face.

"You noticed that, did you?"

She tried to sound casual. "I might have, in passing."

"In passing," he repeated, drifting a little closer.

"Just in passing." Her gaze moved to his hair, darkened by the water and curling in gentle waves to his wide shoulders.

His hair.

She raised a hand to her head and felt the sodden mess of the remains of her chignon. Gasping, she spun away from him as fast as the water and her floating clothing would allow.

"Louisa, what's wrong?"

"Don't look at me, I must be an absolute fright." She ran her fingers over her hair, trying in vain to push the drenched strands into some semblance of order.

He touched her shoulder and gently rotated her back round to face him.

"Oh my goodness," he exclaimed, his smile changing to a comically overwrought expression of horror, "you're right! You are utterly hideous. I can barely stand to look at you!"

Suppressing the urge to smile, she donned her best hurt look, complete with trembling lower lip, and turned away again.

From the corner of her eye she saw the teasing smile melt from his face. "I didn't mean that. Louisa please, I swear, you are the most beautiful woman I've ever seen, even soaking wet. *Especially* soaking wet."

Ignoring the surge of joy that rose at his words, she

157

produced a sad sniff.

"Please don't cry," he begged, drifting closer. "It was just a stupid joke. Please..."

Spinning back, she used both hands to push a big splash into him, leaving water dripping down his face and his mouth hanging open in surprise.

"And now we're even," she said, smiling.

He stared at her for a moment and then burst into laughter. Laughing with him, she couldn't remember ever feeling so perfectly happy.

He shook his head slowly as his laughter faded. "You... you are..." He breathed out a sigh. "Incredible."

Her heart leapt as he raised one hand to her face, his fingertips tracing a feather-light touch down her cheek. She watched his eyes flick to her mouth and back up again. She'd never before been in such an intimate situation with a man and she knew she should back away, stop this before it started. But instead, she found herself moving closer.

He closed the distance between them. His hand moved to cradle her head. He leaned forward.

And his mouth captured hers.

Her eyes fluttered closed as all the things she'd wondered about her first kiss slipped from her mind in an instant, swallowed in a flurry of sensation that ebbed and flowed with the movement of his lips.

His right hand was still holding onto the rock wall beside him, but his left was all hers, beginning at her neck and sliding down her back to pull her against him.

She might have been shocked at their lack of propriety if she'd had any ideas in her head at all, but every thought fled at his touch. The experience was unlike anything she could have imagined, a whirlwind of sensation and emotion that left her breathless and feeling like she was floating on air.

When they finally, slowly parted, she opened her eyes to

find Jesse staring at her, his chest rising and falling in rapid breaths.

He moved his hand from her back and brushed his thumb over her cheek, whispering her name.

She would have expected him to be smiling in that way he had when he knew he'd elicited some kind of response from her, but instead his expression was serious. The kiss had been important to him, she could tell.

"That was my first kiss."

Her eyes widened at her sudden, blurted confession. Why on earth had she said that? She'd wanted to convey to him that it had meant something to her too, but that?

A slow smile touched his lips. "I'm glad. I don't want to share your kisses with any other man."

His reply swept away all her embarrassment and her eyes lowered to his mouth. "Of course, this doesn't mean I'm staying," she murmured, leaning forward.

"I know," he replied as their lips met again.

Louisa wasn't sure how long she spent in the lake, blissfully exploring the new experience of being thoroughly kissed, but it was her shivering that finally prompted Jesse to suggest they get out of the water. She hadn't even noticed. She felt wonderfully warm and tingly from head to toe.

He climbed out first, hauling himself into his chair which he'd left at the edge of the lake when he plunged in to save her. She followed his every movement, captivated by the way his drenched shirt clung to his torso. He was like a statue, carved from marble, every facet sculpted to perfection.

A sigh escaped her lips. She'd never imagined she would develop such an appreciation for wet clothing.

Wet clothing.

Her eyes widened.

"Here, take my hand," Jesse said, leaning forward and stretching out his arm.

"I-I can't."

She looked down at herself. Most of her was underwater, but as soon as she got out of the lake her calico dress would be clinging to her as much as Jesse's shirt was to him. She'd be positively indecent.

"I beg your pardon?"

"My clothes will stick to me." She pointed at his shirt. "You'll see everything."

That wasn't entirely accurate, her dress was far thicker than his shirt and naturally she was wearing undergarments, but it would still be far too revealing.

His mischievous grin wasn't entirely unexpected. "Your point being?"

She flicked a handful of water up at him with a smile. "You're shameless. You'll have to turn around. I can get out by myself."

He shrugged and wheeled back from the lake, turning to face away from her. "Am I supposed to not look at you for the rest of the afternoon? Because I'm going to say now, that's going to be very hard for me to do."

She grabbed onto the rock and pulled herself from the water, struggling to her feet as a torrent streamed around her legs and back into the lake. Her dress felt like it weighed a hundred pounds.

"What would you suggest we do?" she said, gathering the front of her skirt and wringing it out.

He was silent for a while as he thought. "What about over there?" He pointed through the trees into the open. "It's warm out today. We could lie in the sun until we dry off."

She straightened and followed his gaze to the grassy rise. "What if someone sees us?"

"No one's come past in the entire time we've been here. At least, I think no one has. I was a bit distracted for a while back there in the lake."

She couldn't help smiling at that.

"But it's always quiet around here," he went on. "And if anyone does come, we'll just tell them the truth – you fell in the lake and I went in after you. It's either that or go back to town soaking wet, and then everyone will see you." His voice hardened. "I think I would have serious objections to that."

Her smile grew at the possessiveness in his tone. "All right then. You go first and lie down and close your eyes."

"Anything you want."

She moved behind a tree and waited for him to get out into the sun and choose a place in the grass before joining him. She took off her shoes and stretched out beside him, arranging her skirt out wide to catch as much of the warmth as possible. She wished she could remove her petticoat as well, but she didn't dare. At least if the outer layer dried she'd be halfway presentable, if not entirely comfortable.

"You can open your eyes now," she said.

He did, turning his head to glance at her.

"Eyes front."

He obeyed with a chuckle, moving his gaze to the azure sky above them.

After a few seconds, she looked over at him.

"Eyes front," he said immediately.

Laughing, she looked up again.

A few moments later, she felt his hand wrap around hers, entwining their fingers.

And her heart soared into the sky above.

Chapter 15

"This is all your fault."

Adam paused halfway across the office. "What's all my fault?"

"You didn't warn me." Leaning his elbows on his desk, Jesse dropped his head into his hands. "You've been in love before. Why didn't you warn me?"

Adam hung his jacket on the coat stand in the corner and turned to him with an unnecessarily smug smile. "I warned you that bringing her here without telling her first was a bad idea. As usual, you didn't listen to me."

Jesse heaved a sigh. "What if she leaves? I thought it wouldn't be so much of a gamble. I mean yes, I'd lose the money for the train tickets, but I can save that up again. I just thought if it didn't work out and she left that I could find someone else. But now..." He raised his head and fixed his friend with an accusatory stare. "Confound it, Adam, why didn't you *warn* me? I feel like I'm losing my mind! She's all I think about, all the time. I can't concentrate on anything." He rolled his right sleeve up to reveal three red marks of varying sizes on his forearm. "I've burned myself three times in the past two days because I can't keep my mind on what I'm doing. And if she leaves..." He slumped back in his wheelchair and stared at the desk. "I don't want anyone else. A thousand women could line up to marry me and I wouldn't want any one of them. Louisa is the only one for me. I can't imagine my life without her. I don't want to."

Adam walked over and sat on the edge of Jesse's desk. "If it's any consolation, I know exactly how you feel. And I mean *exactly*."

It dawned on him what Adam meant. "You too, huh?"

"Yep."

Guilt prodded at him. He was the one who'd persuaded Adam to advertise for a bride. If Amy left, his friend's broken heart would be his fault. "Why are women so... so..."

"Frustrating?" Adam suggested.

"No. If they were just frustrating we could simply ignore them. Why do they have to be so *amazing*?"

Adam gave him a resigned smile. "Would you want it any other way?"

Jesse groaned and dropped his head back into his hands. "Ask me again in two weeks."

~ ~ ~

Louisa placed her Bible onto her nightstand and wondered what to do next.

She'd spent most of the morning at the church with Mrs Jones, giving the wooden floors a polish while thinking about Jesse. Mostly kissing Jesse.

After lunch, Mrs Jones had left to visit Mrs Knapp, an elderly member of the congregation who was unwell, and Louisa took the opportunity to spend some time praying and reading her Bible. After just managing to drag her thoughts away from Jesse and the whole kissing thing.

Though this was only the second day on which she'd set aside time to concentrate on God, she undoubtedly felt closer to Him for it. She wished she'd done it earlier in her life. She felt as if He'd been waiting for her all this time and it was exciting to think of all He might have to teach her. Even if she returned to New York when her two weeks here was up, she would definitely continue.

As it turned out, most of that afternoon's time with the Lord had involved asking Him to guide Jesse concerning the situation at the bank. When she was around him, Jesse was almost always cheerful, but she could tell the situation was worrying him and she desperately wanted to help.

"What can I do, Lord?" she whispered. "There must be something." She rose and began to pace back and forth across her bedroom, talking to herself as she often did when working out a problem. "There's nothing in the ledgers or loan agreements that indicates anything wrong with the loan or payment amounts. And yet that man, what was his name? Mr Foster, that was it. His son thought something was wrong. If I could talk to him... but he seemed happy with what Mr Ransom told him, whatever that was. I wish I could have heard what he said. All right, so I can't talk to him, but there are other people who borrowed from the bank. Lots of them. If Mr Ransom is somehow cheating Mr Foster, then he must be cheating others, because why only cheat one person?" She clapped her hands together, coming to a halt in the centre of the room. "I need to speak to the other people who took out loans!" Her joy at discovering a course of action came to an abrupt halt. "But how am I going to do that? Why would any of them speak to me? They don't even know me." She resumed her pacing. "Somehow I need to get them to trust me. But how?"

A knock on the front door pulled her from her monologue. She walked through to the hallway, opened the door, and broke into a grin.

"Jo!" She grasped her friend's arm and pulled her inside. "Perfect timing."

"For what?" Jo said as she was dragged to the kitchen and pushed into a seat at the table.

"I need your help," Louisa said, going to the pantry. "Would you like a scone? Coffee?"

"Just water, thanks. It's too warm for coffee. And yes to the scone, as if you need to ask. Why do you need my help?"

Louisa gave her a glass of water and set about buttering two of the batch of raisin scones she'd baked the day before. "I have a problem and I need help to find a solution. Apricot preserve?"

"Please. So what's this problem?"

Louisa carried their scones to the table and sat opposite Jo. Her arrival had seemed the perfect solution, but now she wasn't sure how much to tell her. Jesse didn't mind Mrs Jones knowing, but he'd never even met Jo.

She took a bite of her scone and chewed slowly, considering what to say. "I need to get people I've never met to tell me something that's a bit... private."

Jo swallowed her first bite of scone. "I'm not sure you could be any more unspecific there if you tried. Did you make these? They're delicious." She took another bite.

"Thank you, I did. Mrs Jones made the preserve though." She put her scone down on the plate. "It's not that I don't trust you, but this is somewhat sensitive. If it got out... Not that I think you'd tell anyone." She sighed. She'd been raised to be more diplomatic than that.

Jo snorted a laugh. "Don't worry, I wouldn't trust me either. Look, I'll try to help you no matter what you want to tell me, but for what it's worth, I won't tell anyone a thing. I know how important secrets are to keep, believe me."

Louisa stared at her plate. Jo was her friend, one of the first real friends she'd had as an adult. If you couldn't trust friends, who could you trust? "All right, but please don't tell a soul."

"I promise. Now tell me what's going on because I'm dying to know."

165

"Jesse suspects a man he works with of cheating either the bank or its customers or both out of money. He deals with small loans and Jesse thinks it involves that, but he can't find out how he's doing it. I know he's worried and I want to help, but the only thing I can think of to do is go and talk to the individual people who've taken out loans in the past couple of months, see if anything doesn't seem right. But I don't know how to get them to speak to me. They don't know who I am so why would they talk to me?" She slumped back in her seat. Now she'd explained it to another person, it felt even more impossible.

A smile sidled onto Jo's face. "Now this just happens to be something I know a little about."

"Banks?"

"Getting people to do things they don't necessarily mean to." She finished her scone and sat forward, resting her elbows on the tabletop. "Right, what's your plan?"

"Um... I don't really have a *plan*. I just thought I'd go to their houses and ask them."

Jo heaved an exaggerated sigh and shook her head. "Louisa, you are very lucky I'm here. Now here's what we're going to do..."

~ ~ ~

Louisa looked down at her dress and smoothed a non-existent wrinkle in the material. Black was a terrible colour on her. "I look like I'm in mourning."

"That's the point," Jo said. "They'll think you're working because you're recently widowed and have no choice and they won't ask any questions because what would be more rude than questioning a young widow? It's a good thing Mrs Jones had this hideous thing."

"Hideous?!" Louisa looked at the dress again, horrified.

"It's meant to be hideous. You're in mourning for your tragically departed husband, not trying to attract a new one. Turn round, one of your arms is sagging."

Louisa turned her back, being careful to not twist her body at all. There were so many pins holding the too big garment in place that one wrong move and she'd become a pincushion. They hadn't found enough safety pins in the house to do even one sleeve.

Jo carefully removed Louisa's shawl, re-pinned the loose right arm, and replaced it to hide the excess material. She walked around to face Louisa again, running her eyes over the dress and nodding. "Good. It should be okay. Just don't, whatever you do, sit down."

Louisa rolled her eyes. "This is not going to work."

"Of course it's going to work," she replied, smiling happily. "I know what I'm doing."

"You're enjoying this far too much."

"That's because it's the most fun I've had all week." Jo grasped her hand and pulled her towards the door. "Come on, let's go save Jesse's bank."

~ ~ ~

They reached the first house on the list of addresses they'd taken from the loan agreements far too quickly for Louisa's liking. She'd spent the whole walk there torn between wanting to go as fast as possible in case she was recognised by someone on the streets and wanting to drag her feet to delay getting there.

They were starting with the places they could walk to in the town, her inability to sit affecting her ability to travel by buggy. If none of those worked Jo said they would rethink the dress. Louisa wanted to rethink the dress now, but Jo insisted and Louisa had to admit she seemed to know what

167

she was talking about. All she'd expected when she asked for Jo's help was someone to run ideas by, not a complicated, in depth plan with nuances within nuances. She couldn't help wondering how Jo knew to do it, but she didn't dare ask. It was certainly a good plan, if somewhat nerve-wracking.

"Right," Jo said, looking her dress over one last time, "who are you?"

"Mrs Clara Peterson," Louisa said immediately.

"And why are you here?"

"To make sure the bank's customers are happy."

She nodded and stepped back. "I wish you had some spectacles. Everyone trusts a person wearing spectacles. Well, can't be helped." She smiled. "Now go and lie like you mean it."

Louisa winced. "Must you?"

Jo took hold of her shoulders and rotated her in the direction of the small house behind the tall hedge. "Just keep telling yourself it's for a good cause. The man you love is depending on you."

Louisa spun back. "I don't... I mean, Jesse and I... it's just..."

Jo raised one eyebrow and smirked. "Yes?"

Huffing out a breath, Louisa turned back to the house. "Let's just get this over with."

She walked the short path through the unkempt garden to the front door and knocked. Seeing her hand trembling, she clamped it around the paper and pencil she'd brought and hugged them to her.

I can do this. For Jesse.

She glanced back at Jo standing at the gate. Jo gave her an encouraging smile that didn't encourage her at all. Then the door opened and Louisa's stomach dropped to her feet.

"Can I help you?" The woman at the door fixed Louisa with a suspicious look, sizing her up.

"Uh, yes." Louisa assumed her best fake smile, perfected from years of attending boring events to meet boring people. "Are you Mrs Fanshawe?"

The woman narrowed her eyes. "Might be."

"My name is Mrs Potterson..." *Wait, that's not right, is it?* "...and I work for the bank. I wonder if I could have a few moments of your time."

The woman frowned. "I've never seen you in the bank."

"Uh, no, I've just started work there. For Mr Vernon. He would like to..."

"That dress looks terrible on you. You in mourning or what?"

So much for no one questioning a widow. "Yes, ma'am. I've just moved here, after the death of my husband. As I said, I'm working for Mr Vernon and..."

Mrs Fanshawe opened her mouth to interrupt.

"...he would like to know if his customers are happy with the service they've received at the bank," Louisa said quickly. "So if you could just answer a few questions?"

Mrs Fanshawe stepped back. "You'll have to speak to my son. I don't deal with money and such. And I don't hold with a woman working neither, widow or no."

Before Louisa could say anything further, the door slammed in her face. She stared at the peeling paint for a few seconds before sticking her tongue out at it and turning away to return to Jo at the gate.

Jo was grinning.

"Why are you smiling?" Louisa said. "That was a disaster."

"But you were fantastic!" Jo took hold of her shoulders and rubbed them. "No one could have got anything out of that harpy, not even me. You're a natural! Let's go try the next one." She was practically jumping up and down.

"I'm so glad you're enjoying yourself," Louisa said,

169

checking her list of addresses. "Next one's this way."

The second person they visited was infinitely more pleasant than Mrs Fanshawe. Mr Weaver answered all her questions and confirmed he had taken out a loan. Sadly, however, it all correlated with the information she already had, and he even mentioned how helpful Mr Ransom had been. It wasn't what she was hoping for.

"Maybe there's nothing to find," she said to Jo as they walked away from Mr Weaver's house.

"Come on, we've only tried two. You can't give up yet. How many are on that list?"

"Twelve in the town. Another nine farther out."

"There you go. Ten more chances before we even have to get in my buggy."

Louisa suddenly realised she hadn't let Jo do whatever she'd come into town for. "Wait, why are you here?"

"Because I'm helping you?"

"No, I mean you never said why you came to see me."

"Oh. I just came into town to pick up some supplies and thought I'd visit. Gabriel is at his placer mine for a few days."

She sounded happy about that. If Jesse was gone, for even a few days, Louisa would miss him desperately.

"What's a placer mine?"

"Panning for gold, I think. I'm not clear on the specifics, or why he does it since he doesn't seem to get very much out of it."

They walked a few more steps before Louisa spoke again. "Are you happy with him?"

They walked even more steps before Jo answered. "Happy's not the word I'd choose, but we've only been here a week. Takes longer than that to fall in love." She glanced sideways at Louisa. "Unless you happen to have found a handsome accountant who makes you glow."

Louisa looked around them, partly to check no one was

close enough to overhear their conversation and partly so she didn't have to meet Jo's eyes. "I-I'm not glowing. And, and Jesse and I are just friends. I don't even know if I'm staying."

"Louisa, you're glowing," Jo stated. "Your eyes light up whenever you talk about him. And you're different. I adore you, you know I do, but on the train you wouldn't have said boo to a goose, much less do anything improper. Now look at you! Breaking into banks and lying like you were born to it. And you're having fun. Don't even try to deny it because I can see it all over your face. Jesse's good for you. I don't know how, but he's drawn you out of your shell and you're far happier for it."

Louisa was quiet for the remainder of the short walk to the third house on the list. Jo was right, she was happier than she ever remembered being, and there was no doubt it was at least partly thanks to Jesse. More than partly, if she was honest. Which would have made her decision whether or not to stay easy, if happiness was the only factor at play. But there was so much more to consider.

"Are you all right?" Jo said as they reached their next target.

Louisa stood tall, squared her shoulders, and said forcefully, "Yes!"

"That's the spirit," Jo said, clapping her on the back carefully so she didn't hit a pin. "Go get 'em."

It was a neat little house, with precisely planted flowerbeds in front of the porch and a spotless white picket fence. Louisa climbed the porch steps and knocked on the green painted door.

The woman who answered looked to be in her forties, with smiling eyes and a sprinkling of white amongst dark hair in a tidy bun.

"Good afternoon," Louisa said. "Are you Mrs Mackey?"

"I surely am," she replied with a warm smile.

Louisa liked her instantly which made her feel worse. She hated lying to people. "I'm from the Green Hill Creek Bank and I'm visiting a few valued customers to make sure we're providing the service you need. Would you have a moment to answer a few questions?"

Mrs Mackey's bright smile remained in place. "Of course! Come on in."

"Oh no, thank you," she said quickly, visions of being impaled on dozens of pins as she tried to sit swimming through her head. "It will only take a moment. I have quite a few people on my list to visit." She flashed a quick view of the list of names and addresses, too fast for any of them to be read.

Mrs Mackey's smile hadn't left her face. "Oh, I understand, dear. You go ahead and ask your questions."

"Thank you so much, that's very kind of you." Louisa touched her pencil to the paper she had for notes. "Are you happy with the service you've received from the bank?"

Mrs Mackey nodded enthusiastically. "Oh yes, very happy."

She made a note. "And have you found any staff you've dealt with to be friendly and polite?"

"They've all been a delight."

Another note. "Now, I understand you and your husband recently took out a loan of eighty dollars. How did you find that process?"

"Oh, very well done. We spoke to that lovely man, Mr Ransom. Mr Vernon's assistant, although I expect you know that, you working for the bank and all."

Louisa carefully didn't nod too eagerly.

"He was so helpful, explaining everything to us. I can't recommend him highly enough."

She forced a smile and wrote some more. "That's wonderful to hear, Mrs Mackey. And you were able to

172

borrow the full amount you needed?" She checked her list. "Eighty dollars was sufficient?"

"Oh yes. That helped with fixing the roof and building a bigger stable for our Strawberry. That's our horse. And improving the outhouse. And then there was the fee."

Louisa stopped writing. "Fee?"

~ ~ ~

Louisa walked back to the road, keeping her pace normal until she heard Mrs Mackey close the door behind her then rushing to where Jo waited across the street.

"How did it go?" Jo said. "You were there a while."

Louisa grabbed her hand, dragging her along the road and around a corner until they were out of sight of the house. Then she threw her arms around her.

"I found it! I found out what he's doing!"

"Ouch, pins."

Louisa let her go. "Sorry." She laughed, clapping her hands together. "I can't quite believe it! Thank you so much for helping."

"You're most welcome. Just please don't hug me again until you're out of that dress."

Chapter 16

Jesse was surprised to find Louisa waiting for him outside the bank when he finished work.

He would have liked to think the wide smile on her face was because she was pleased to see him, but he got the feeling something else was going on as soon as she greeted him.

"You look happy," he said as they started towards his home.

"Do I?" Her smile looked in danger of injuring her cheeks.

He couldn't help laughing. "Are you going to tell me now or torture me and make me wait until we get home?"

She glanced around them. "I can't tell you here."

He figured there were two possible reasons for her apparent joy, either she was going to tell him she was staying to marry him or she'd found out something about Ransom. He would have preferred it to be the former, but there was still another week to go until his probationary period was up.

"Is it about the mystery we've been working on the past few days? Rhymes with awesome? Kind of."

She looked confused. "Rhymes with awesome?"

"Okay, it doesn't rhyme with awesome," he conceded, "but you know what I mean."

"It's only a ten minute walk to your house. I'll tell you then."

It might as well have been ten hours. "I can't wait that long!"

She rolled her eyes. "Your ten-year-old sister has more patience than you. I'll explain when we get there. How was your day?"

"Frustrating. I wanted to shout at a certain someone the whole time. How was your day? Do anything interesting? Find out anything that could help with *my* day?"

She laughed and didn't answer. Oddly, it made him adore her even more. Being in love made no sense at all.

When they finally reached his home Louisa made as if to go into the kitchen. "Would you like me to make you some coffee after your long day of frustration?"

"Oh no," he said, wheeling around her and herding her into the parlour. "No coffee or tea or cake or anything else until you've told me what I know you've been waiting to tell me the entire walk home." He put on his best pleading expression. "Please?"

To his relief, she didn't take much persuading.

"Well, I so badly wanted to help you find out what Mr Ransom is doing so I thought, since you didn't find anything in the ledgers or loan agreements the only thing left to do was speak to the people who actually took out the loans. But I had no idea how to get them to talk to me." She smiled. "And then Jo arrived."

"Jo?"

"You know, my friend who married Gabriel Silversmith?"

"Yes, I know who she is. But how did her arrival help?"

She began to pace back and forth in front of him as she related her story. "Well, I have no idea how she knew to do all this, but she suggested I pretend to work for the bank and go to each of them saying I was checking on customer satisfaction. She gave me a fake name and a back story and everything. And I wore a black dress as if I was newly widowed. It was amazing!"

Now he was worried. "Um, I'm not sure if that was such a good idea. I mean, if it got back to Vernon that someone was pretending to work for the bank..."

She waved a hand. "Even if it did, no one would know who I am. None of them knew me and I had the fake name. It can't be worse than breaking into the bank."

She had a point there.

"And anyway, it worked!" she said, smiling widely. "I found out what Mr Ransom has been doing."

He stared at her in astonishment. "You did?"

"We came here and got the names and addresses from the loan agreements. You should really get a better lock for your shed, by the way. Jo got it open in hardly any time at all. Anyway, we got the details for people who'd taken out a loan and the first two I talked to didn't help at all, but then the third one, Mrs Mackey, she mentioned a fee and I hadn't seen anything in the agreements about a fee."

"There's no fee for taking out a loan," he said. "All the profit for the bank comes from the interest they charge."

"That's what I thought. At first she was horrified she'd even mentioned it. She thought she'd be getting Mr Ransom into trouble if she said anything else. But I managed to persuade her. I told her if charging a fee was a problem for people, Mr Vernon would want to know so he could change things. She was happy to tell me after that, as long as I promised to not specifically mention what Mr Ransom had done."

Jesse leaned forward in his chair, caught up in her tale. "And what had he done?"

She came to a halt in front of him. "He told her and her husband there was a fee for taking out the loan, and when they said they couldn't afford to pay it upfront he said he'd

176

add it onto the loan, but to not tell anyone because he wasn't supposed to do that. So it wasn't written in the agreement and the loan was down as being eighty dollars. But what actually happened was Mr and Mrs Mackey only got seventy-three dollars."

"And Ransom pocketed the rest," Jesse said, everything falling into place.

"And he made it sound like he was doing them a favour that he'd get into trouble for if they told anyone, so of course they wouldn't. Mrs Mackey thought he was wonderful. And that's just one small loan. I spoke to seven more after that and asked specifically about the 'fee' and he'd done the same thing to five of them, with varying amounts depending on how much the loan was for."

Jesse slumped back in his chair. "And that's just a few of the loans that have been granted in the past months. Who knows how long he's been doing this for? It could have been years. He could have taken hundreds, even thousands."

"But now you can do something about it, now you know it's happening."

He gazed up at her, awed. Every day she showed him more and more how amazing she was. "I never would have found this out without you."

She shrugged and lowered her eyes. "I just wanted to help. I don't like seeing you worried."

His chest filled with elation. He loved this woman. This extraordinary, resourceful, brilliant woman who cared about him enough to do all she could simply to make him feel better.

Leaning forward, he wrapped both hands around her waist and tugged her towards him, pulling her into his lap. It was a move he'd used plenty of times with Nancy and he was happy to find it worked just as well on Louisa. She landed with a yelp of surprise which turned to laughter.

Cupping her cheek, he gazed into her eyes. "Thank you. You have no idea what this means to me, that you would do this."

She touched her fingertips to his face and gave him a lingering kiss that set his pulse racing.

"I wouldn't have been able to do it without you," she said when their lips parted. "You make me feel like I can do anything."

He leaned his forehead against hers. "All I've done is shown you how amazing you are. The rest is all you."

Wrapping her arms around him, she nuzzled her face into his neck. Nothing had ever felt better.

More than ever he knew he had to convince her to stay, because he wouldn't survive if she left.

Chapter 17

Jesse wheeled along Green Hill Creek's main road, heading for the general store.

What with not having to work, he'd always liked Saturdays. But he was getting a whole new level of appreciation for the last day of the week since it had become the one day he got to spend the entire time with Louisa.

So far picnics had worked out extremely well for him so he was planning another for today. He needed just a couple more items for it to be perfect. This was going to be their day, just the two of them enjoying their time together. Hopefully there'd be kissing involved. And, of course, he'd be doing all he could to show her how good their life would be if she stayed and married him.

He figured he was doing well in that department. She still had doubts, he could tell, but every day they grew closer. And she seemed to be breaking away from her stifling upbringing. She was like a caged bird that had been set free and was learning to fly. Soon she'd be soaring with the sun shining on her wings, never to return to that cage again.

He smiled at the metaphor. Before Louisa he would never have been thinking in such flowery terms. She was turning him into a poet, albeit a terrible one.

His good mood evaporated abruptly when he saw Rotherford Ransom up ahead, standing outside the saloon. Jesse came to a halt, his anger rising at the sight of the man who was swindling so many good, hardworking people. Bad as he knew the idea was, he wanted to go up to him and demand Ransom tell him why he would do such a thing after having worked for so long at the bank. Had he been at it the entire seventeen years he'd been there? Surely he couldn't have got away with it for that long. Although Jesse had worked there for four years and he'd only just found out, and that completely by accident. Had he missed it all that time?

He wanted to go and ask him. Forcefully.

But he couldn't do anything until he'd told Vernon. He couldn't tip Ransom off and give him the chance to cover his tracks. If there were any.

He was about to cross to the other side of the road to avoid having to go anywhere near Ransom when he saw a man he hadn't noticed before, standing in the shadows between the saloon and the building beside it. He leaned casually against the wall of the saloon, smoke from the cheroot hanging loosely from his lips curling up across his face. His clothes were good quality but unkempt, as if he'd been riding for a while. Or as if he just didn't care what he looked like.

The two men were standing a good ten feet apart, not looking at each other, and to the casual observer they had no connection. But as Jesse watched the man's lips moved, then Ransom's did the same, back and forth between them. A conversation was undoubtedly going on.

To Jesse's frustration, he wasn't anywhere near enough to hear what they were saying. He wanted to sneak closer, but it was hard to be inconspicuous in a wheelchair. Instead, he moved behind a water trough and watched for fifteen more seconds as Ransom and the man spoke without acknowledging each other, until the man pushed away from the wall and walked out of sight towards the back of the saloon. Ransom looked around before heading in the opposite direction from Jesse, disappearing from sight around a corner.

Jesse resumed his journey to the general store, thinking about what he'd seen. He was probably reading too much into it. Now he knew Ransom was a thief, he was suspecting everything the man did. But something about the whole exchange between the two, if they had in fact been talking to each other, struck him as odd.

It didn't matter anyway. It wasn't like he could do anything about any of it. Right now he had more important things to deal with, like preparing the most perfect picnic ever made to woo the most perfect woman in the world.

Chapter 18

Louisa raised her hand to move a stray strand of hair into place then thought better of it. She'd opted for a softer style anyway and the errant curl suited it.

She gently prised a few more loose then turned her head from side to side to check the effect in the mirror. Satisfied, she went to fetch her shawl from the bed.

Her bonnet also lay on the bed and she stared at it for a few seconds before picking it up. Back home she would never have considered leaving the house without a hat, but now she was growing to hate the thing. She was far more comfortable without it, but it was Sunday and she was going to church. She couldn't go to the Lord's house without a bonnet.

Her thoughts strayed back to the previous day. She hadn't even taken a bonnet with her on the picnic and she hadn't missed it one bit. Neither had Jesse, if the way his gaze repeatedly strayed to her hair was anything to go by. She loved it when he looked at her like that. She probably shouldn't, but she did.

At a knock on the front door she grabbed her reticule and Bible and hurried through to the hallway. Her heart did its usual skip when she opened the door to Jesse's smile.

He cocked his head to one side, his eyes travelling slowly down to her feet. "I know I've seen the skirt, you wore it on Monday, but I'm not sure about the blouse."

She laughed. "Are you writing everything I wear

down?"

"Don't need to. Every day I look forward to seeing what new and wonderful outfit you have on. It's one of the highlights of my day."

That was going to be a problem. She'd worn just about everything she owned now. "I don't have that much more to wear that you haven't seen."

"In eight trunks? What's in the rest of them?"

She looked down. "I mean I don't have much more that I can reach. The trunks are all piled up in my bedroom. I can only get to a couple of them to open." That was more or less true.

He shrugged. "I can wait. And it's no hardship seeing things more than once. Just means I get to enjoy how beautiful you look in them all over again."

Her cheeks heated and she couldn't hide her smile. "You're going to make me conceited."

"That's a price I'll just have to pay. Are you ready to go?"

"Almost."

She glanced outside to check no one else was around then leaned down to kiss him, lingering against his lips for somewhat longer than she'd initially intended. When she straightened again, his mouth was hanging open.

"Shall we go?"

His jaw still slack, he nodded. "Uh huh. Where are we going again?"

~ ~ ~

Pastor Jones' sermon was on the prodigal son. It was a story Louisa had heard many times before so was one of the few parts of the Bible with which she was familiar, but with having only just begun getting to know her heavenly Father again, it resonated with her more than ever.

She couldn't help wondering if God had inspired the pastor to speak on that particular subject for her. The thought that He would do such a thing was both new and wondrous. God, the Maker of heaven and earth, who flung the stars into place and created enormous mountains and fathomless seas, was speaking to her. And even more amazingly, He was telling her that despite all the years she'd spent ignoring Him, He loved her and accepted her and was welcoming her home.

At one point she had to dab at her eyes with her handkerchief and Jesse reached over to touch her hand, looking worried. She smiled and turned her hand over to give his a reassuring squeeze. She wasn't sad, she was very happy indeed.

At the close of the service Mrs Jones came over and sat beside Louisa. "Simon and I have been invited to spend the afternoon with friends, so you'll have the house to yourself. I was thinking you could invite Sara, Amy, Lizzy and Jo to join you for lunch." She glanced over to where Sara and Amy were sitting near the back of the church. "It might be good for you to get together. Provide a bit of support for each other."

Louisa looked at Jesse. "I know your parents invited us to lunch again..."

He waved a dismissive hand and smiled. "They'll make do with just me. It's a great idea. I know I'm irresistible, but you'll just have to tear yourself away from me this once."

"However will you manage?" Mrs Jones said to Louisa with a smile. Standing, she patted her shoulder and ruffled Jesse's hair. "Have a good afternoon both of you."

Jesse smoothed his hair as she walked away into the crowd. "If any of your friends need help getting home, we can give them a ride in my pa's wagon."

Louisa dragged her eyes from the strands of golden-brown hair sliding through his fingers. "I'm sorry, what did you say?"

He lowered his hands, his lips curling into a knowing smile. "I can take Sara, Lizzy and Jo home, if they need a ride."

"Oh, thank you. That's very kind of you."

"And afterwards we could go somewhere, if you're not too tired."

She'd been thinking that very thing herself. "I'm sure I won't be."

~ ~ ~

Louisa tried to play hostess when they reached the house, but the others were having none of it.

"But it's my home, sort of," she protested as Amy, Jo, Sara and Lizzy swept into the kitchen and began opening cupboards and pulling out cooking utensils and pots and pans. "I should be serving you all."

"Nonsense," Sara said. "We're all in this together, even when it comes to getting lunch. Now where is the mixing bowl?"

Within twenty minutes the meal was cooking, including a cake for dessert made by Lizzy, and the five of them were gathered in the parlour. Louisa ached for each of her friends as they told their stories. It seemed very little was working out as they'd anticipated, for any of them. As she listened to Amy's reasons for coming and her confusion over what to do now, Sara's problems with Daniel since his accident, Lizzy's distress over the behaviour of her husband, and Jo's unhappiness with hers, Louisa came to realise something - of all of them, she was perhaps the happiest and most settled with Jesse. And yet she was one who was considering returning home.

When it came to her turn to tell the others about how

things had gone in the nine days since they'd arrived, she almost felt guilty at her situation not being worse. What right did she have to doubt her parents when Amy had grown up without a family? How could she be unhappy that the town wasn't larger when Jo was living so far away from it, more or less alone? What did she have to complain about when Jesse lavished her with attention while Lizzy's husband barely even spoke to her? Of what consequence was Jesse's disability that barely slowed him down when Sara's husband was coping so badly with his own? And yet, when she told them about it all they were as supportive and loving as if she'd been subjected to the worst of everything.

"I'm sorry," she said, wiping at a stray tear, "I feel like such a fool. Jesse's the most wonderful man and I adore him and I couldn't ask for anything more, but I'm still doubting."

Sara took hold of her hand. "You mustn't feel bad about that. We've been here nine days. I know a lot can happen in nine days, and it has, but we're not going to just forget about our lives before we came. I miss my family every day and I know we all do."

"Yes!" Lizzy nodded emphatically.

"It's completely understandable you'd be unsure of what to do," Amy said. "And I'm sure Jesse understands it too, seeing as, from what you've told us of him, he is the most handsome, caring, perfect man on the face of the earth."

Louisa smiled. "I may have got a little carried away. I didn't lie though. Does that sound like I'm boasting?"

Jo rolled her eyes. "If I had a gorgeous, loving, charming, funny, and all the other things you called him man enamoured with me, I'd be boasting too. Tell us again about when you saw him without his shirt on?"

Sara elbowed her side. "You're terrible."

"Actually," Lizzy said, leaning forward and resting her chin in both hands, "I wouldn't mind hearing that part again

186

either."

The sound of everyone's laughter filled Louisa's heart with gladness. This was what she'd always imagined having close friends would be like. "I love you all so much."

"Oh, stop," Lizzy said, fanning her face with her hand. "You'll make me cry again."

~ ~ ~

"Where should I go?" Jesse said as they approached Lizzy's house.

"Around to the back is good," she replied.

They'd already taken Sara home and Jo had brought her own buggy to church, so Lizzy was the last for Louisa and Jesse to drop off. The five friends had stayed at the Jones' house for a long time after lunch and it was now approaching five in the afternoon.

Jesse circled his father's wagon around the house, following Lizzy's directions and coming to a halt in the yard at the back.

Louisa gazed up at the white clapboard, two storey home, impressed. It was bigger than she was expecting, with a range of outbuildings and views to the distant mountains. "This is very nice."

Lizzy rose up onto her knees in the wagon bed and leaned her arms on the back of the seat between her and Jesse. "It's lovely inside, not that I've had anything to do with that. Mrs Lassiter takes care of everything, but it's her day off today. Would you like to come in and look around? I could make us something. Last week when I got the kitchen to myself I baked three different types of cake."

Louisa glanced at Jesse. It wasn't that she didn't want to spend more time with her friend, but she and Jesse hadn't had any time alone all day. She was itching to feel his arms around her.

Apparently her feelings showed because Lizzy said, "Or the two of you could leave now, which would give you a good two hours before dark for you to take a ride, see the countryside, talk." She looked down at her fingertip tracing a knot in the wood of the seat between them. "Kiss."

Louisa gasped in shock, partly at Lizzy's lack of subtlety, but mostly because she'd been thinking exactly that. "Lizzy!"

She raised her eyes, affecting a look of innocence. "Yes?"

Jesse snorted, covering his mouth to smother his laughter.

Louisa attempted to admonish him with a look, but the smile fighting to break onto her face made it extremely difficult.

"Well," Lizzy said, standing, "my work here is done."

Jesse took advantage of the time it took her to climb down from the back of the wagon and grabbed Louisa's hand, kissing the back quickly then releasing it as Lizzy walked around to the front.

Louisa had to stop herself from giggling.

"Have a good afternoon," Lizzy said, smiling. "Don't do anything I wouldn't do."

"What wouldn't you do?" Jesse said.

Louisa leaned over to nudge his shoulder with hers. "Don't encourage her."

A teasing look slid onto his face. "But I need to know where the boundaries are."

She lowered her chin and looked up at him, batting her eyelashes. "I'll let you know."

His smile faded, his eyes widening at her blatant flirting in front of another person. She loved being able to surprise him.

Lizzy exclaimed a loud "Ha!" which had May and June giving her a look. She reached out to pat May, the closer of the two horses. "Sorry."

Louisa waved to her as they pulled out of the yard, turning to the front when she was out of sight. "Do you know Richard Shand well?"

Jesse nudged the horses into a fast walk. "Only in passing. He hasn't been here long, about five years maybe. I don't think he spends much time in town. Why? Is everything all right between the two of them?"

"I don't know. Lizzy's having some difficulties. I just wondered what kind of man he is."

He glanced at her, looking worried. "Does she need help? Is she safe?"

"Oh yes, she's safe," she said quickly, not wanting him to get the wrong idea. "It's nothing like that. They just aren't really connecting."

"Well, I haven't heard anything bad about him, but that's about all I can say."

She shuffled along the seat closer to him and he wrapped his arm around her, turning his head to press a kiss to her temple.

She leaned her head against his shoulder and sighed in contentment. She wished Lizzy could feel this way with Richard. She wished every woman could find a man who gave her the kind of happiness she felt with Jesse.

A vision came to her of another woman taking her place in his arms after she left, experiencing the bliss with him that was now hers. Such intense jealousy welled up inside her that for a few moments she couldn't breathe.

At the sudden tension in her body, he dipped his head to look into her face. "You okay?"

She forced the image away and willed herself back to the present, where she was the one he held, the one he wanted to be with, the one he gave his kisses to. "I'm fine. Where are we going?"

He searched her eyes for a second more before brushing a soft kiss onto her forehead and looking back at the road in front of them. "I thought we'd go where we can watch the sunset. I think it's going to be a good one tonight."

She looked up into the sky where fluffy white clouds drifted beneath cotton-like wisps.

"I also thought it would be a good place to follow Lizzy's suggestion about the kissing," he said, "seeing as it's usually quiet there, no one else around."

Louisa settled her head back onto his shoulder. "Sounds like a good idea to me."

~ ~ ~

Louisa snuggled back into the pillows behind her and marvelled at the glowing pinks and oranges and purples blazing across the sky over the town below. It was the perfect place to watch the sunset.

"Comfortable?"

She rested her head against Jesse's chest and smiled. "Mm hmm."

For a while the only sounds around them on the hilltop were birds chattering in a stand of trees a little way away and the tearing of grass as May and June grazed.

They'd been there for around an hour, cuddled together in the back of the wagon on the blankets and pillows Jesse had thoughtfully brought. There'd been comfortable silences, easy conversation, and kissing. How Louisa loved the kissing. She was mystified as to how she'd survived twenty-three years never having been kissed, but then again, she was glad her first had been Jesse. Right now she couldn't imagine ever wanting to kiss anyone else.

"I'm going to tell Mr Vernon about Ransom tomorrow morning," he said into the silence.

She lifted her head to look into his face. "What do you think he'll do?"

He gave her a small smile, but it couldn't disguise the apprehension clouding his eyes. "I have no idea. I don't even know if he'll believe me without proof."

She huffed out a frustrated sigh. "I wish I could somehow have got something, but it was hard enough to get those people to admit to what Ransom had done. They all think he was being extra kind and risking his job for them."

"They trust him. He's official. He works for the bank and folks trust the bank. Apart from those who wouldn't go near one. I used to think people like that were being paranoid, but now I think maybe they have the right idea."

She hated seeing Jesse worried like this. It hurt her deep inside in a way that made her want to do anything to help him, no matter what it cost her. It was a little frightening, the way she cared about him, but it also made her happier than she'd ever dreamed possible.

"Is there anything I can do?"

He brushed an errant lock of hair back from her face, the touch of his fingertips sending warmth through her skin. "You've already done so much. I wouldn't even know any of this if it wasn't for you. You've been amazing, but only I can do this part."

She stretched up to kiss his lips then lay her head back down onto his chest, returning her gaze to the sunset. "I'm here if you need me. And I'll be praying for you."

He took her hand and entwined their fingers, tightening his arm around her. "Thank you. For everything."

Chapter 19

The knock took Jesse by surprise.

He didn't usually get visitors this early, not since Luke hit puberty and went from being exceptionally energetic in the mornings, wanting to spend time with his big brother before school started, to barely able to drag himself out of bed. Jesse didn't miss being woken at some terrible hour of the morning when the sun was barely up, but he did miss the time with his brother. But that was what happened when children grew up, he supposed. One day he'd have his own and the cycle would start over again. He was looking forward to that day.

He patted his face dry and grabbed his shirt, smiling at the thought of being woken by a little auburn-haired girl bouncing onto his bed.

Figuring it had to be one of his family at the door, he barely took the time to shrug his shirt onto his arms before opening it.

Louisa stood on his porch. Her eyes lowered to his bare chest and a smile tugged at her lips. "Exercising again?"

He grinned, wheeling back from the threshold to allow her in. "No, simply half-naked this time. It's early. I wasn't expecting anyone."

"I came to have breakfast with you and walk with you to work." She lifted the basket she held in her hands. "I brought cheese muffins. Although if you've already eaten, you can take them for lunch."

"No, I haven't eaten yet." He buttoned his shirt, watching her eyes follow the movement of his hands.

His chest covered, she raised her gaze and he lifted his eyebrows. She cleared her throat and turned away and he stifled a laugh as he followed her into the kitchen. She placed the basket on the table and went to fetch plates. He got the butter and knives.

They sat opposite each other and she reached out her hands. "May I say the blessing?"

It was the first time she'd wanted to in all the times they'd eaten together. He tried not to appear surprised as he took her hands. "Sure you can."

Looking a little nervous, she closed her eyes. "Dear Father, thank You for keeping Jesse and me since we were last together. Please bless this food and thank You for providing it. And, Father, You know Jesse is going to speak to Mr Vernon today. Please give him the words to say and take away any nervousness he may have. And give Mr Vernon wisdom and discernment, that he will see the truth of what Jesse tells him and do the right thing. Thank You. In the Name of Jesus, Amen."

"Amen," Jesse echoed. He opened his eyes but didn't release her hands. "You came here for me this morning, didn't you? Because you knew I'd be worrying."

She shrugged. "I didn't think you should be on your own."

He loved her so much it felt like his heart could burst in his chest. How was it possible to feel like this? He wanted so badly to tell her the whole truth about how he felt, but he was afraid that professing his love now, while she still had doubts, would scare her away. He'd promised not to pressure her and he wouldn't, but he needed her to know how much he appreciated all she'd done for him.

193

Bringing her hands to his lips, he pressed a kiss to each of them. "Thank you. This means so much to me. *You* mean so much to me."

Her eyes shimmered and she looked away.

He let go of one hand and touched her face, catching a tear as it trickled down her cheek. "Hey, don't cry. Everything will be all right."

She sniffed and wiped at her eyes. "I'm sorry. It's just that you mean so much to me too." She gave a teary laugh. "I'm supposed to be cheering you up and here I am getting all emotional." She pulled her hand from his and lifted the cloth from the top of the basket, releasing a mouth-watering cheesy aroma. "Let's eat, before these get cold."

Sharing breakfast with Louisa and then having her walk with him to work did wonders for Jesse's frame of mind. Yes, by the time they reached the bank he was nervous, but nowhere near as afraid as he would have been. Effective distraction as she was, while they were together he barely even thought of the upcoming meeting with Mr Vernon.

When they reached the bank she glanced at the others on the street then leaned down and whispered, "If there weren't so many people around, I'd kiss you."

His brain immediately began searching for ways to make that happen. Sadly, none of them were practical. "Would it really be so bad if I pulled you into my lap right here, in front of everyone?"

She laughed softly. "I'm not sure I'm ready for that quite yet. Maybe in a few days' time." She touched her hand to his shoulder briefly. "I'm going to be praying hard the whole morning. I'll see you this afternoon."

He watched her walking away for a few seconds before wheeling round to the entrance at the rear of the bank.

He hung his jacket on the coat stand in his office and placed his lunch of sandwiches and an apple into the drawer in his desk. He took a quick look into the lobby, but it was empty. Unsurprisingly as they didn't open for another twenty minutes or so and Adam hadn't arrived yet. He only worked mornings, at least for the next few days. Jesse was still hoping Mr Vernon would change his mind about firing him. He felt responsible, in a way. If he hadn't suggested Adam advertise for a bride... but he couldn't do anything about that now. One problem at a time.

He closed his eyes and raised his face. *Father, please guide me and give me the words to say to Mr Vernon. Open his mind to the truth. Please take control of this whole thing. In Your name, Lord Jesus. Amen.*

Opening his eyes, he took in a deep breath, blew it out slowly, and muttered, "Let's do this."

As always, Ransom was at his desk outside Mr Vernon's office. It had been too much to hope that he wouldn't be, but Jesse had hoped anyway.

"I need to speak to Mr Vernon," he said as he wheeled up to him.

Ransom withdrew his silver watch from the pocket of his waistcoat and flipped it open. "Opening time..."

"Is over fifteen minutes away," Jesse said. "I'll be done by then. Anyway, Adam can do that by himself."

Ransom narrowed his eyes. Jesse held his gaze. He didn't know if Ransom suspected he suspected him, but if he was cheating people he'd probably be paranoid about everyone.

After a few seconds, he pushed his chair back and stood. "Just make it quick. Mr Vernon's time is valuable."

Jesse couldn't help himself. "So is mine." Including all the time he'd spent the past week trying to work out what Ransom was doing. Time that would have been better spent thinking up new ways to convince Louisa to stay.

Ransom ignored the comment and went to Vernon's

office door, knocking and then opening it at the command to enter. "Sir, Mr Johnson would like to speak to you briefly."

Jesse rolled his eyes at Ransom's back.

"Send him in," Mr Vernon said from inside the office.

Ransom stepped aside to let Jesse past then pushed the door to behind him. Jesse looked back to see he'd left it ajar. He reached out to close it properly.

"What can I do for you, Mr Johnson?"

Jesse's boss could be an intimidating man. It wasn't his somewhat rotund frame or that he was a good thirty years older. It wasn't the huge oak desk he sat behind or even his clothing that probably cost more than everything Jesse owned in the world, combined. What made him intimidating was his complete and overwhelming air of confidence.

He didn't own Green Hill Creek but he did own some notable parts of it, including the bank and the hotel. He headed the council and, should the town ever decide to have a mayor, he would probably get the job. And he was undoubtedly the richest man for miles around.

From what Jesse could tell, he wasn't necessarily a bad man, but he also wasn't particularly moral. He made decisions based on two basic concerns, money and social standing, although Jesse suspected the social part was largely due to his wife. As such, it was sometimes difficult to predict how he would react. This was one of those times.

He rolled up to the desk, silently praying for strength. "Sir, I need to talk to you about Mr Ransom. There's no easy way to say this, so I'll just come out with it. In this past week I've discovered that he is using his position to cheat customers out of money."

Mr Vernon raised his hand. "I'm going to stop you before you go any further."

"Sir, I don't think you understand. Mr Ransom is..."

"He told me there was a chance you would do this."

Jesse frowned. "He what?"

"Mr Johnson, I like you. I'll admit, when you first came to me asking for a job I wasn't sure that someone with your condition could handle it, but you were qualified and there was no one else around. And I've never had cause to regret my decision. You're a hard worker and your work is always accurate and precise. I count you as an asset to the bank. But you are going to have to work out your issues with Mr Ransom for yourself. This kind of behaviour is beneath you."

Jesse gaped at him, his mind scrambling to recover from the derailment of his carefully prepared speech. "What has he told you?"

"He informed me some time ago of the disagreement you've been having and that you had threatened to resort to fabricating lies about him."

Some time ago? Before he'd even begun to suspect something was going on?

Jesse opened his mouth to speak, but Vernon stopped him.

"Mr Ransom has been working for me for seventeen years and in all that time he has been completely trustworthy in all matters. Did you really think I would believe these outlandish accusations?"

Jesse felt his control slipping away from him. "But... but he's lying to you! There hasn't been any disagreement between us. Sir, you have to believe me. He's stealing from customers and using the bank to do it."

"And do you have any proof of this?"

He frantically tried to think of something, *anything*. "Well, no, but..."

"I think you should go back to your desk, and for your sake we'll forget this ever happened." Vernon leaned forward over his desk, his voice tinged with warning. "But if you ever try this again, I will be forced to conclude that you are unable to uphold the professional conduct required to be an employee of this bank. Is that clear?"

How could this be happening? "But, sir..."

"Is that *clear*?"

In that moment Jesse knew nothing he said would make a difference. Vernon had made his decision, and once that happened nothing would budge him. Jesse's cause was lost even before he'd wheeled into his office.

"Yes, sir."

"Good. Now I suggest you get to work. We're about to open."

Jesse turned away, barely feeling his arms as he propelled his chair towards the door.

"And Mr Johnson?"

He stopped but didn't look back.

"I think you should apologise to Mr Ransom."

His knuckles turned white on the push rims of his wheels. Clamping his teeth together before he said anything he'd regret, he continued to the door. Ransom looked up from his desk as he exited the office. Had he been listening at the door? Did he know that Jesse knew?

Did it matter?

Without a word, Jesse wheeled back to his office. When he got there Adam was hanging his jacket next to Jesse's.

"What's wrong?" Adam glanced at the door beyond him. "You weren't talking to Vernon about me, were you? I told you, I don't want you risking your job over me."

Jesse wheeled in behind his desk. "No, I wasn't talking to Vernon about you." He'd already tried that, more than once. It seemed his boss wasn't inclined to listen to him about anything.

Adam planted his hands on his hips. "Why not?! Call yourself my friend?"

Not many people could have made Jesse laugh at that

moment, but Adam was one of them. "I can't win with you, can I?"

He smiled and wandered over to sit on the edge of Jesse's desk. There was a permanently clear space there just for him. Jesse had learned soon after Adam began working at the bank two years previously that anything he put there would just be shoved out of the way the next time he sat anyway.

"What's wrong though?" he said. "Is it Louisa?"

Jesse considered telling him the truth, but Adam had enough worries of his own. When all this was over and everything had worked out, one way or another, he'd tell him then. And probably get berated for not telling him sooner.

"I still don't know if she's going to stay. Two weeks seemed like enough time when I started this, but it turns out it's no time at all."

"She'll stay," Adam stated firmly. "I've seen the way that girl looks at you. I may not know much about how women think, or anything about them really, but even I can see she's crazy about you. I wish Amy looked at me like that."

Jesse sighed, shaking his head. His friend truly was clueless. "You really have no idea, do you?"

Chapter 20

When Jesse got out of work that afternoon he half expected Louisa to be there waiting for him. He was sorry that she wasn't.

He considered going to the smithy and seeing if his father had time to talk but decided to go home first. He had a deep urge to get out of his work clothes and wash away all trace of his day at the bank. If he'd had a choice, he would have quit and never gone back. He'd had enough, of Ransom, of Vernon, of everything to do with the place.

Once home he wheeled into the kitchen. His foul mood drained away when he looked out the window into his back yard.

Louisa sat at the small table outside, reading. She had on the same dress she'd worn the first Sunday after she arrived, the cream coloured one with lace cuffs and collar that had taken his breath away.

She'd changed a lot in the week since then. When she'd arrived, her hair was always perfectly fixed with not a single strand awry, her bonnet always properly in place, and she always sat demurely, like he imagined some high class lady would. She was stunning but like a porcelain doll; perfect, brittle, untouchable.

Now her hair was pinned into a more relaxed style, several loose strands framing her face as she focused on the book on the table in front of her. He hadn't seen her bonnet in days, other than in church, and then she'd removed it the moment she got out. Her whole demeanour was softer, more relaxed, and she seemed happier. It made her even more beautiful, if that was possible.

He liked to think her transformation was due largely to his influence, although it was more likely a combination of being away from home, her new friends, and the Joneses. And him. He had to be in there somewhere.

He unlocked the back door and wheeled outside, adoring the way her face lit up when she saw him.

"I'm going to have to get you a key."

"I would have come to meet you at the bank," she said, closing her book, "but I wasn't sure if you'd want me to or if you'd want to be alone for a while."

He wheeled to the table, took her hand and kissed the back. "There will never be a time when I don't want to be with you."

The way her eyes shone when he said things like that gave him hope for their future. It made him think that one day she could love him the way he loved her.

She took his hand in both of hers. "How did it go with Mr Vernon? Did he believe you? I brought cherry scones, just in case."

He looked at her hands wrapped around his and sighed. "I didn't stand a chance." He related the brief conversation with Vernon from that morning. "I don't know what Ransom told him, but it was obviously something he was prepared to believe over anything I could say."

Louisa sat back, lips pressed together and eyes sparking with anger. Jesse had never seen her so furious.

"Why that... that... *scoundrel!*" Letting go of his hand, she leaped to her feet and began to pace back and forth, gesticulating as she spoke. "How dare he tell Mr Vernon such things?! How could anyone believe you are anything less than completely trustworthy? You're one of the most caring, thoughtful, honest people I know! How in the world did Mr Vernon get to own a bank being such an appalling judge of character? What is *wrong* with him? And that Mr Ransom, I'd like to find him and give him a piece of my mind. If he was here right now I do believe I might even slap him!" She rushed back to her seat and leaned forward to grasp Jesse's hand again. "So what's next? What are we going to do?"

"I... I don't know," he said, taken aback by her vehemence when he was on the verge of giving up.

"There must be something. We can't let him get away with this. He's attacked your good name now. He has to be stopped!"

The last thing Jesse wanted was to let her down, but he was at a loss. With no proof and not even a shred of evidence, how could he possibly do anything to stop Ransom?

"Let's go over this logically," she said when he didn't answer. "We know what he's doing and how he's doing it, but we have no proof. Without proof no one will believe us. So what we need to do is find some proof."

No one will believe us. What we need to do.

Us.

We.

This was his problem and yet she spoke as if it was hers as well. He wasn't alone. And with God and Louisa on his side, how could he fail?

"All right," he said, encouraged. "So how are we going to do that?"

At his change of mood, she smiled. "Can we go back to the people who took out the loans? Tell them what Mr Ransom has done and get them to speak to Mr Vernon?"

Much as he didn't want to point out the obvious, he felt he ought to. "You mean the people you told you worked for the bank and were conducting a customer satisfaction survey?"

Her face fell. "Oh."

"And Ransom must have done something to ensure that couldn't happen. He's too meticulous to leave anything to chance." He hated being the one to dampen her hopes, but there it was.

She stared at their entwined hands for a moment. "Then we just have to find something he can't control. Something that, even if he'd thought of it, he couldn't do anything about."

They both lapsed into silence as they considered the problem.

"What about that man you saw Mr Ransom talking to on Saturday?" she said after a while.

"I don't know who he was. Or even if they were really talking."

"But you think they were?"

"Yes." He thought back to two days before and the strange sight of Ransom talking to the man outside the saloon without actually looking at him. "He had to have been. There was no one else nearby and I'm pretty sure he's not given to talking to himself."

She sat back. "So let's go find him."

"Without knowing who he is? Or where he is?"

She smiled, standing up. "It's a small town. Won't take us long to look."

He had to admit he had no other ideas and it was better than doing nothing. And he didn't want to do anything more to discourage her drive to help him.

He wheeled himself back from the table. "We just need to do one thing before we go."

"What's that?"

He smiled and patted his lap.

Her cheeks turning the most delicious shade of pink, she

sat and wrapped her arms around his neck. He took his time with the kiss.

"All right," he said when it was over. "*Now* I'm ready."

~ ~ ~

"I'm afraid it's not very good."

Louisa held out the sketch, wishing she'd practised her art more. At the time, she hadn't seen the point.

"No, this looks like him," Jesse said, studying the drawing. "It's far better than I could have done. Which isn't saying much, but it's still real good."

"You're just being nice. Mother thinks sketching and painting are very ladylike pastimes so she made me do it for years. I never was very good though. And you don't want to see what happens when I get my hands on a paintbrush."

He laughed, handing the sketch back to her. "I mean it, it's good. Could you just make the nose a bit narrower at the top?"

"It's a pity Jo doesn't live closer to town," she said as she added some shading. "She loves drawing and she's very talented." She showed him the sketch again. "Better?"

He nodded. "This'll make it much easier to find him."

Taking the sketch with them, they spent some time walking around the town showing it to people they knew, but most didn't recognise him. Mr Lamb in the general store said he looked familiar but he didn't know who he was and so he couldn't be a regular customer. Zach Parsons was working reception in the hotel and told them the man wasn't staying there.

Finally they ended up on the other side of the street from the saloon, where Jesse had seen him in the first place. It was a large, slightly shabby building with a balcony on the first floor where two women reclined in rocking chairs. They wore low cut dresses, the hems of which barely covered their knees. Advertising the wares inside, no doubt. One of them was painting her nails. The other was reading a thick book.

Louisa lowered her gaze to the door. "We need to go in there and ask," she said, trying hard to keep her voice steady.

She'd never been anywhere near a saloon before, where women brazenly lounged with so much skin showing. And as for the men who frequented such places... She watched a seedy-looking man slouched on the stairs leading to the front door spit a wad of chewing tobacco onto the ground and flinched in disgust. The men were the kind she'd cross the street to avoid.

"I'd never get up those stairs," Jesse said. "They don't design buildings for people like me. I go to the restaurant in the hotel sometimes, but I have to go around the back through the kitchen to get in."

She moved her eyes to him. "That's terrible! You're a paying customer, the least they could do is install a ramp so you can get your chair in."

"They could, but they won't. Such is my life."

She looked back at the saloon. "I could go in." She didn't want to, but for Jesse she'd do just about anything.

"No, absolutely not," he said firmly.

"But..."

"It's not safe in there for a woman. You're not going in there and that's final."

She looked down at him and he huffed out a breath.

"Okay, I know I can't stop you, but please promise me you won't ever go in there. Please."

She sighed. "I promise. But what can we do?"

He pursed his lips, watching the spitting man climb unsteadily to his feet and slouch back inside. "Maybe I could ask Will."

"Will? You mean Sara's brother in law?"

His eyes snapped back to her. "Never mind, I was just thinking out loud."

She looked across the street, studying the building. "I think I have an idea. Come on."

Before he had a chance to object, she hurried across the street, looked around to make sure no one was paying her any attention, and slipped quickly into the shadows along the side of the saloon.

Jesse joined her a few seconds later. "What are you...?"

She raised her hand to stop him and moved to where the balcony attached to the building. "Pardon me?" she whisper-shouted upwards. "Up on the balcony, could I have a moment of your time?"

A few seconds later a blonde woman appeared, the one who had been painting her nails. She leaned over the wooden railing as she looked down, causing her ample chest to almost spill from her indecently low cut dress.

From the corner of her eye, Louisa saw Jesse look away and she suddenly regretted bringing him.

The book reading woman joined the first. Although her dress had no sleeves and was almost as low cut, she stood more carefully, leaning her hands on the rail.

Louisa waved up at them. "Good afternoon, my name's Miss Wood and this is Mr Johnson and I wonder if you could help us."

The blonde woman smiled. "Sure, sweetie. What's it worth to ya?"

The other woman nudged her arm. "Be nice, Peg." She smiled down at Louisa. Under all the makeup, she was very pretty. "I'm Rebecca. What do you need?"

Jesse handed Louisa her sketch of the man they were searching for and she stretched up to give it to Rebecca. "We're looking for this man. We don't think he's local, but he has been seen around the saloon. Do you know him?"

The two women studied the drawing.

"Hey, that's Lem," Peg said. "He's been in a few times the past couple of weeks. Has a few drinks, sometimes gets in on one of the games. Always has a bath and... you know. If we're lucky, in that order." She leaned down to return the sketch, her dress appearing on the verge of giving up the struggle.

Louisa glanced at Jesse. To her relief, he was fastidiously studying the wall. By his expression, he couldn't decide whether to be embarrassed or amused.

"Do you know his last name?" she asked Peg. "Is he from around here?"

"Don't remember him ever mentioning his last name. He's not much of a talker. Oh, once he mentioned something about having to get back before they did something stupid. Don't know who *they* were or what he thought they were going to do though."

"I think there's a group of them," Rebecca said. "I've seen them in the bar. None of them are local and they don't sit together or anything, but I just get the feeling they know each other. They all started coming in around the same time. You know, Peg? There's Cyrus and Jeb and Luther and Ralph and that other one with the scratchy beard and yellow teeth."

Peg grimaced. "Yeah. Hate that beard."

Louisa suddenly felt immensely sorry for Rebecca and Peg. She couldn't imagine what it must be like for them to have to go through what they did every day, in addition to having everyone else look down on them as soiled doves.

She smiled up at them. "Well, thank you so much. You've been very helpful."

"Our pleasure," Rebecca said, returning her smile.

Peg's eyes went to Jesse. Now she was standing more or less upright, he was looking up again.

"I've seen you around," she said, leaning one elbow onto

207

the railing and curling a strand of blonde hair around her finger. "Never kept company with someone in a wheelchair before, specially not as good looking as you. You know, if you was to come on inside, I bet I could get Rufus to give you a discount. If you'd like."

The smile dropped from Louisa's face. "He wouldn't," she said as firmly as she could, so as to leave no doubt. "At all. Ever."

She glanced at Jesse. His lips were pressed together, eyes sparkling with suppressed laughter.

"Peg!" Rebecca exclaimed. "She's standing right there."

"What?" Peg looked between Louisa and Jesse. "They ain't married."

Rebecca rolled her eyes. "Sorry."

"Thanks for the offer, ma'am," Jesse said, "but I'm afraid I'll have to decline. And we're obliged for the help, ladies. It's been a pleasure meeting you."

"Pleasure's all mine," Peg called after them as they made their way back to the street.

"What are you smiling at?" Louisa huffed as they walked away from the saloon.

Jesse's attempt to straighten his face was entirely unsuccessful. "Oh, just the way you were so eager to make sure Peg knew I wouldn't be needing her services now or ever as long as I live and possibly as long as the earth exists."

She looked at the dusty road in front of her. "Well, you wouldn't... would you?"

He reached out to briefly touch her hand. "Don't worry, there's only one woman holds any appeal for me."

The way her heart felt, it must have been doing a dance of joy around her chest. "So what do you think of what Rebecca said about there being more than one of them?"

He shrugged. "To be honest, I have no idea. Let's go home and think about it over those scones you brought."

Chapter 21

They hadn't come up with any new ideas about the Ransom situation by the time Jesse took Louisa home that evening so the following morning he decided he was ready for a break from the whole debacle.

He wasn't giving up, simply having a rest and concentrating on more important things, the most important thing in his life at that moment being Louisa. She was out with Mrs Jones when he stopped at their house so he gave Pastor Jones the invitation he'd written to pass on to her and carried on to work.

That afternoon, when he was done with another excruciating day at the bank, he went to the general store for supplies and then hurried home. He didn't have much time to get everything ready.

~ ~ ~

An hour and a half later there was a knock at the door.

Jesse grabbed the matches to light the candles on the table then went to let Louisa in. He should have been used to having all the breath leave his body whenever he saw her, but her beauty still overwhelmed him. Especially today.

"I was wondering if the dress you wore yesterday is my favourite or this one," he said as she walked in, "but I think I'll go with this one."

She lifted the skirt of the midnight blue dress she'd last worn to break into the bank and twirled in a circle. "And look, it doesn't drag on the ground anymore. I decided to get rid of that awful bustle once and for all and sew the excess material at the back. Bustles may be the very latest fashion, but I find I truly don't care anymore."

He took the opportunity to drink in all of her, from her lustrous auburn hair to her exquisite, he assumed as he'd never seen them, feet. "Well, I don't know about fashion, as Nancy often tells me, but for what it's worth I think you're the perfect shape without any help."

It occurred to him that commenting on her figure might come across as overly intimate, but if her delighted smile was anything to go by she didn't mind.

"I think blue suits you very well," she said, touching his shirt. "It makes you look even more handsome."

"Thank you." He held her gaze, not caring that his admiration must be written all over his face. Surely by now she must know the depth of his feelings for her.

After a few seconds her eyes lowered, a slight flush to her cheeks and a smile playing on her perfect lips. He considered pulling her into his lap, a move she was becoming familiar with and seemed to have no objections to at all, but then remembered the food he had cooking. If he became lost in her kiss now all they'd have to eat would be charcoal.

"May I take your shawl?" he said, hoping for an uninterrupted view of her bare arms and shoulders for the evening.

She allowed the green article to slip free and he hung it on one of the pegs by the door, waving her through to the kitchen.

Once there she took in a deep breath. "Something smells delicious."

He lifted the lid on the bread sauce, gave it a stir, and

removed it from the heat. "I hope you like gammon. One of Mrs Goodwin's recipes with a few tweaks of my own."

"I like gammon very much. Can I help?"

"Nope. You're my guest and I plan on spoiling you. Go on outside and I'll bring you a drink."

She stepped through the back door and came to a halt, her hands going to her mouth. "Oh!"

It was exactly the reaction he'd hoped for. He wheeled out behind her and stopped at her side. "Do you like it?"

"It's so beautiful," she breathed, looking around her.

Candles and lanterns adorned the table and walls and raised flowerbeds and, even though sunset was still two hours away, they created a twinkling patchwork of light. Multi-coloured ribbons wreathed the trunk of the tree in the centre of the garden and draped from its branches. The table was covered with a white, lace-edged tablecloth, courtesy of Malinda, and the chairs adorned with ribbons and cushions. The whole effect had an enchanting, fairytale quality to it.

He'd asked Malinda and Nancy to help him and they'd outdone themselves in the short amount of time they'd had. Nancy had been thrilled with the finished effect and now wanted all her birthday parties, and everyone else's, to look exactly the same.

Jesse couldn't help thinking, though, that it all paled in comparison to the woman it was all for.

He reached out to take Louisa's hand and brought it to his lips, pressing a soft kiss to the back. "Have a seat. I'll get that drink."

It was so easy with Louisa. He didn't have to behave differently, didn't have to constantly guess what she wanted or what would make her happy. The connection between them felt simple and easy, and yet at the same time deep and profound.

Jesse had thought he'd found her, but he knew he

couldn't have made such a perfect choice on his own. He had no doubt God had picked her out especially for him. The years of frustration and loneliness when the disease he was born with drove every other woman away made sense now. Louisa was worth every moment of the wait.

They talked over the meal, laughed, relaxed in the simple pleasure of being together. Afterwards, with the lowering sun just beginning to taint the clouds with orange, they moved to one of the benches which Jesse had covered with blankets and pillows in anticipation of this part of the evening. He wrapped his arm around her without having to worry if she'd want him to and she leaned into his side, resting her head on his shoulder.

She'll stay, he thought as he pressed a kiss to her forehead and she smiled. There was no way she would leave him, not with their relationship growing the way it was. Not when they so clearly belonged together.

"Was it difficult for you, growing up?" she said, taking his hand and knitting their fingers together.

"Sometimes." His thumb traced slow circles on the back of her hand. "There were times when I got frustrated, especially when I hit puberty, but I had some real good friends and people like Pastor and Mrs Jones and Adam's folks and George who helped make my life as normal as it could be. Though I wouldn't have got the chance at any kind of life if it hadn't been for my pa."

She nodded against his shoulder. "It's easy to see how much he loves you. I imagine he did everything he could to take care of you."

"Not just that. He saved my life, in more ways than one."

She raised her head to look at him. "He did?"

"When my mother died giving birth to me, there were people who told him he ought to give me up for someone else to raise, that a man on his own couldn't take care of a baby, but he refused. Then when it became obvious I wouldn't ever be able to walk, the doctors said he should put me in one of those institutions, but he refused again. He told me I was his son and a part of my ma, and there wasn't anything or anyone on earth who could take me from him."

Louisa blinked glistening eyes. "I'm so glad you have him."

"Truth is, I may not have still been alive if I'd been in one of those places. I've heard they don't take care of children real well. And people with Little's Disease don't always live to be adults anyway."

Worry clouded her face. "Are you all right? Could you..."

"No. At least, I'm pretty sure not. Doctor Wilson, when he took over the practice here sixteen years back, he studied up on it so he'd be ready if I needed anything." He smiled. "It helps when the town doctor's sister is married to your father. But I've always been all right. Some who have it have trouble with their breathing, but I never did. And my pa always made sure I was healthy. At the first sign of a sniffle he'd rush me to the doctor when I was small. He encouraged me to be active and get strong and do everything I could." He leaned forward to whisper in her ear. "And he made me the dumbbells you like so much."

She giggled, her cheeks flushing.

"So, all things considered, I've had a pretty good life." He brought her hand to his lips and kissed the back. "And just lately it's become even better."

She smiled and lay her head back against his shoulder.

"How about you?" he said. "What was your life like growing up in New York?"

"Not so bad, I suppose. We didn't have much. My father works on the docks and I don't think they pay very well.

Although my parents didn't ever tell me and my sisters about money, but I always knew. My mother takes in sewing when she can get it."

Jesse frowned in confusion. "But I thought, from your letters and the way you carry yourself, I thought your family was wealthy."

"That's what my mother and father wanted you to think. And I did too, at first." She tightened her hold on his hand, as if afraid what she said would make him pull away. "All my life it has been instilled in me that my sisters and I had to improve our social station by marrying well. My mother has always wanted better for us than she had, so we were taught manners and bearing and to behave like proper ladies, and we weren't allowed to associate with what she thought of as the lower classes, even though they were our neighbours. But it didn't work because people still knew who we were. I've had plenty of suitors, briefly, until their families discovered I wasn't who they thought I was. Not that it bothered me overly. Most of them were either louts or bores, just with money. So my mother finally came to the conclusion that to find a suitable husband we would have to look elsewhere, where no one knew who we were."

That explained a lot. "So an accountant in a railroad town on the opposite side of the country..."

"Was the best of the bunch," she said. "Among all the farmers and miners, you were a prince in my mother's eyes."

He couldn't help smiling. "So it was really your mother who chose me?"

"Oh no. I mean yes, she thought you were suitable, but I liked your advertisement very much. And then your letters were so interesting. I thought you were wonderful, so much better than any of the stuck up, boorish, conceited men I met in New York who thought coming from good families and having money meant they were irresistible no matter how they behaved. You sounded caring and funny and intelligent. I couldn't wait to meet you."

"And then I ruined your perfect view of me by not being able to walk."

He'd meant it as a joke, but she lifted her face immediately, looking worried. "No! I was shocked, I admit, but... but..." She glanced away, the corners of her mouth twitching with a smile.

Now this he had to know. "But what?"

Her eyes returned to him then lowered to his chest. "I thought you were so incredibly handsome and you had the most delicious voice. That's why I left so quickly after we first met in your parlour. I wanted to make a logical decision about whether or not to stay, but I had trouble thinking straight around you, right from the start."

He touched his fingers to her chin, raising her face and lowering his voice. "Oh you did, did you?"

"Mm hmm." Her gaze went to his lips. "Still do."

He caught her smiling mouth in a lingering kiss that made his head swirl and his heart thud and sucked every thought from his mind, just as every touch of her lips did. And the best thing was, by the way she returned his kiss he knew she had to feel the same way.

"What about now?" he said softly when they parted, resting his forehead against hers. "Do you think you made the right decision to stay?"

"Yes," she replied, without hesitation. "Being here with you has been the happiest time of my life."

Her answer gave him the courage to ask the one question to which he so desperately wanted the answer. "Does that mean that you'll stay and marry me?"

His heart dropped when she didn't answer immediately. His stomach went with it when she drew back, her expression filled with pain.

"I... I don't know."

She looked away and his arms slid from around her. Everything had been going so well. What had just happened?

"How can you not know?"

Her lips pressed together and she shook her head.

"Look at us, Louisa." His voice rose in frustration. "Don't you see how close we've become? We spend every moment we can together, but it's still not enough. I've never felt anything like this before. You can't tell me you don't feel something for me too."

She shook her head again. "I do feel it, every bit of it, but it's not that simple."

"Why? Why isn't it simple? I want you to be my wife. If you want it too, why isn't that enough?"

"They're my parents, Jesse! They matter to me. What they want matters. They've worked hard so I can have a better life. I can't just ignore what they want for me after I've been following their lead my entire life."

"And I'm not what they'd want." He didn't bother hiding his bitterness. "I can't walk so I'm not good enough for them. And I guess I'm not good enough for you either."

Her eyes widened. "That's not true! I've never ever thought that, not even once."

"Then what? Because I'll likely never leave this backwoods town? Because my pa's just a blacksmith and not an earl? What about me wouldn't meet your high and mighty parents' approval?"

He regretted the words as soon as they'd left his mouth.

Louisa gasped, staring at him in disbelief.

"Louisa..."

She stood and backed away from him, tears shining in her eyes.

"I didn't mean that..."

Before he could say anything more, she fled inside. A

216

few seconds later he heard the front door slam.

Cursing his legs and wishing he could run after her, he rammed his fist into a pillow beside him. Then he dropped his head into his hands.

What had he just done?

~ ~ ~

Louisa clamped her lips together as she hurried along the street. Her head ached from the effort of fighting her tears, but she was determined to reach the sanctuary of her bedroom before her emotions released in the torrent she knew they would.

She entered the house as quietly as she could, hoping neither of her hosts would be there, and rushed straight to her bedroom, closing the door behind her.

For a few seconds she stood still, back pressed to the door, and then the pain erupted in her chest and she threw herself onto the bed, muffling her sobs in the pillow.

Why couldn't Jesse understand how difficult it was for her? She'd had a lifetime of being instilled with her parents' ambitions for her. Never once could she remember doubting how her life would be.

She *would* marry a man with good prospects.

She *would* rise in society.

She *would* surpass the humble circumstances of her birth.

She *would* fulfil all her parents' dreams for her.

That was how things would be, and it had all made perfect sense to her. She had never doubted any of it.

Until Jesse made her doubt everything.

He made her want to forget all that her parents had taught her, shake off their chains, and throw herself into his arms forever.

Chains.

217

She'd never even thought of them as chains until she met him.

But it wasn't that easy. It wasn't like she could simply forget her upbringing. Honouring your father and mother was one of the Ten Commandments. How could she disobey God, just when she was truly getting to know Him?

"What do I do, Lord?" she whispered into her pillow.

Her tears faded as Jesse's face came into her mind, how betrayed he'd looked when she told him she couldn't disregard her parents' wishes. She hadn't been fair to him, getting angry as she had. All he'd done was care about her enough to want her to feel the same way about him. And she did feel the same. The last thing she wanted was to hurt him, but that's just what she'd done.

Sitting up, she dug into her pocket for a handkerchief and wiped at her eyes. She had to go back and tell him how sorry she was.

She jumped from the bed and rushed to the washbasin. The mirror above it revealed puffy eyelids and a red nose, but there was nothing for that but to hope her skin had settled by the time she got back to his house. She rinsed her face with the cold water in the bowl and hurried out into the hallway.

Mrs Jones was walking from the kitchen. "Oh, Louisa, I didn't realise you were back."

"Sorry, Mrs Jones," she called as she breezed past, "I'm just on my way out again. I'll be back later."

She took the quiet back roads as far as possible to Jesse's house, picking up her skirts and running when no one else was around. The thought of Jesse unhappy because of her ignited an urgency that transcended decorum. She just wanted to get to him as fast as possible.

Arriving at his door, she smoothed her hair and knocked, taking in deep gulps of oxygen to calm her breathing as she waited.

And waited.

When a second knock also went unanswered she tried the door and found it locked. She made her way round the side of the house to the back yard, but Jesse wasn't there and the back door was locked too. All the candles and lanterns had been extinguished. Seeing her fairytale garden no longer sparkling with light made her want to burst into tears again.

Returning to the front, she looked down at the porch. It looked clean, but it couldn't be completely devoid of dirt. But there was nowhere else to sit and she didn't feel like hauling a chair from the back, tired out after her unaccustomed run as she was. So she sat down at the top of the ramp and settled in to wait, watching a few early moths flit across the wisteria and hoping Jesse wouldn't be long.

She'd leaned her head against the railing beside her and closed her eyes by the time his voice roused her from a semi-doze.

"Louisa?"

She started awake, her eyes snapping open to see Jesse at the foot of the ramp. He wheeled up to the porch and she climbed to her feet and brushed off the back of her dress.

"I came back, but you weren't here." She flinched at the ridiculously obvious statement.

"I went to find you but Mrs Jones said you'd been and gone," he replied. "We must have missed each other."

She nodded and tried to think of something else to say. Why did apologising feel so awkward?

"Would you like to come in?" he said, moving to the door and unlocking it.

She nodded again and walked inside ahead of him, turning to face him when she was in the parlour. "I'm sorry I overreacted. I feel just terrible about all this. You have every right to be angry with me."

He wheeled over to the settee, moved onto it, and patted

the seat beside him. When she sat he wrapped his arms around her and she buried her face gratefully into his shoulder.

"You don't have anything to be sorry for," he said softly, resting his head against hers. "I'm the one who needs to apologise. I'm not angry at you. I have no right to expect anything. What you do is your decision, not mine, and you should follow your own conscience and heart."

Except her conscience and her heart were telling her two entirely different things. "My parents aren't bad people. They just want what they think is right for me."

"I know and I'm real sorry for what I said. I didn't mean it."

She sighed against his chest. "I shouldn't have led you on. All the kissing and everything. I don't blame you for being frustrated with me."

He drew back and lifted her face to look at him. "Are you saying you'd rather all the kissing and everything hadn't happened?"

She lowered her eyes, lips twitching with a smile. "No, I'm not saying *that*."

He grinned and pulled her closer and she snuggled into his embrace. There was no better feeling on earth than having his arms around her.

"But if all we have together is these two weeks," she said, "wouldn't it have been easier on you if we hadn't become so close?"

He pressed a kiss to her forehead. "Louisa, if all I get with you is two weeks, the memories will stay with me for a lifetime. I wouldn't change one single moment of the time we've had together."

"Neither would I." She was quiet for a while, her head resting against his chest, listening to his steady heartbeat. "I wish I was strong, like you. You know what you want and you don't let anything stop you. I wish I could be like that."

He turned his head so his breath brushed her forehead when he spoke. "Do you know why I'm like that?"

She shook her head.

"It wasn't me, it was my pa. If he hadn't fought for me, I would have spent my life locked away in an institution. He was always there for me. He was strong when I couldn't be and he taught me to not let anything stand in my way. Like when I decided I wanted to study to be an accountant, none of the universities I contacted would allow me to attend. I was ready to give up, but he convinced one of them to allow me to study by correspondence. He gave me that drive and determination. And when things get tough, he's still always right there with me. If it wasn't for him, I don't know what I'd be."

She considered her own upbringing. "My parents instilled in me a drive to become more than what I was born into, but I don't remember them ever asking if that was what I wanted. I thought I did, but I'm beginning to wonder if I only wanted it because they did. I'm not sure if I know how to make my own decisions. I don't know if I'm strong enough to do that."

He touched his fingers to her chin and raised her face to look at him. "You're strong, I don't have any doubts about that. Look at everything you've done since you've been here. You got the ledgers from the bank, you found out what Ransom was doing when I hadn't got any idea what to do, you've supported me all the way. Do you have any idea how much that means to me, that you believe in me? I couldn't have done any of it without you."

"But I did all that because of you," she said. "I do believe in you. You're the strong one."

He brushed the backs of his fingers down her cheek and smiled. "Then maybe it's time you believed in yourself, because I do. I believe in you, Louisa. I know you can do anything you set your mind to, not because of me or anyone else, but because of you. You are strong and smart and amazing, and I'm real proud of you. You don't need to change one bit. You're perfect just as you are."

She didn't want him to know how the conflict inside her was tearing her apart, but tears rose unbidden to her eyes and, pressing her face into his shoulder, she began to cry. He held her close, not saying anything, simply offering his comfort, and his tenderness cut to her heart. She wanted to stay with this amazing man who made her happier than she could ever remember being. She couldn't think of a better life than one spent at his side.

She may have been unsure of everything else, but she was certain of one thing. She knew she wanted to be Jesse's wife.

~ ~ ~

Jesse accompanied Louisa home and stayed when Mrs Jones invited him in for coffee and cake. Louisa was glad. With the two week deadline up only two days later, she wanted to spend every moment she could with him.

When he'd left, she slumped into a chair in the parlour and leaned her head on her arms. Every evening when they said goodbye she wanted to stay with him. How was she going to say goodbye forever? How could she bear to never see his smile again, never hear his laugh, never feel his fingers entwine with hers, his arms hold her, his kiss?

Am I in love, she wondered to herself. Was this what love felt like? And would she ever be able to feel it with another man?

She brushed absently at the tears in her eyes. She couldn't imagine wanting to love any man other than Jesse.

"Is there anything I can do to help?" Mrs Jones said.

Louisa hadn't heard her come in. "I don't know."

"Well, if you want to talk, perhaps we can find out," she said, walking over to sit on the settee.

Pastor Jones was in his study so they were alone. Maybe talking would be a good thing. And Mrs Jones was a pastor's wife so she would know more about the Bible than Louisa did.

"Do we always have to keep all of the Ten Commandments all of the time?" Better to just come out with it.

Mrs Jones smiled. "Ideally, yes."

Louisa sighed, her shoulders drooping. The answer wasn't a surprise, but she'd been hoping there was a loophole somewhere.

"Which of the commandments are you having trouble with?"

Should she tell her? Louisa didn't want the Joneses to think badly of her. She knew how close they were to Jesse and how much they wanted him to be happy. But time was running out and, without her own parents to advise her, and her now doubting their advice even if they'd been there, she needed help.

She wound her hands together on her lap. "Honouring your father and mother."

She told Mrs Jones all about how her parents wanted her to marry a certain type of man, how their dreams for her had shaped her entire life, how she was almost certain they wouldn't approve of Jesse.

Through it all Mrs Jones sat and listened, her expression unreadable. When Louisa finished, she said, "So you don't know for sure how your parents would feel about Jesse?"

"Well, no." Although she had a very good idea.

"Then it seems to me that the best thing for you to do

would be to wait for your mother and father's reply to the letter you sent them after arriving. It could be that they would have no objections to Jesse and you're fretting for no reason."

Louisa sighed. "Fretting is my speciality, reason or no."

Mrs Jones leaned forward and took her hand. "Louisa, you're a lovely girl with a bright future ahead of you and you shouldn't have to worry like this. Life has enough difficulties as it is without adding to them." She released her hand and sat back. "But as far as God's commandment to honour your father and mother goes, honouring doesn't mean obeying, especially when you're grown. It's a credit to you that you care so much about what they want, but I'd say you're old enough to make your own decisions. You're a sensible young woman. Trust God to guide you, and trust yourself to know what it is you want for your own life."

Mrs Jones was right, Louisa knew that, and it was a relief to hear that disobeying her parents wouldn't be wrong in God's eyes.

The problem was, with a lifetime of following their instruction in everything, did she have it in her to stop now?

Chapter 22

Following breakfast the next morning, Louisa made her customary visit to the post office.

It had become something of a routine for her to go after finishing the dishes. Adam had told her that on most days either the train or the stagecoach brought in a mail delivery, so the letter from her parents could arrive at any time. She couldn't help feeling relieved every time he told her there was nothing for her.

"Good morning, Louisa," he said when she walked in, smiling at her from behind the counter.

"Good morning, Adam. How are you and Amy?"

"Amy and I are well, thanks. How are you and Jesse?"

"Jesse and I are also well, thank you."

It was their usual exchange. Despite the fact that neither he and Amy nor she and Jesse were married, there was always the unspoken possibility that one day they might be. She liked being an *and* with Jesse.

Adam turned to the wall of cubby holes behind him. "I have a couple of letters for Pastor Jones, if you wouldn't mind taking them." He placed two envelopes on the counter. Another envelope joined them. "And I also have this. I'm guessing this is the one you've been waiting for?"

Louisa's heart dropped at the sight of her name in her mother's flowing script.

Adam's smile faded. "Is this not what you've been

hoping for?"

"Uh, yes, this is it. Thank you."

He ducked his head to look into her eyes. "Is everything all right?"

She picked up the letter from her parents and stared at it. "I don't know yet."

~ ~ ~

When she got back to the house Louisa left the mail for Pastor Jones on the kitchen table and went straight to her bedroom, closing the door.

Sitting on the bed, she placed the letter on the cover in front of her and stared at it. And stared at it. And stared at it.

She didn't know how long she sat like that, drumming up the courage to open it. One question kept playing over and over in her mind – what would she do if they told her to return to New York?

"I'm old enough to make my own decisions," she murmured to herself, echoing Mrs Jones' words from the night before.

She knew the truth of it, and yet that knowledge didn't reach her heart. She didn't feel old enough. She felt like a child lost in a sea of indecision, not knowing which way to turn. Leaving the safety of her mother and father's will was a terrifying prospect. Could she truly make it on her own?

"What do I do, Lord?"

I will never leave thee nor forsake thee.

The verse came into her mind which was strange because, even though she'd been reading her Bible more over the past two weeks, she still barely knew it and couldn't remember reading that one anyway. Was it confirmation that she should follow her own desires? But how did she know her desires were God's will? How could she know what to do

226

if she wanted one thing, her parents wanted another, and she had no idea what God wanted?

Shaking her head, she thumped both fists into the bed at her sides, a squeak of frustration escaping. All this second guessing and uncertainty was ridiculous.

Grabbing up the envelope, she tore it open, pulled out the letter inside, and unfolded the sheet of paper.

Dearest Louisa,

Your father and I are very glad to hear you have arrived safely. Both of us are well, as are your sisters.

I was shocked to hear of your experience with Mr Johnson. How awful of him to deliberately conceal his infirmity from you until you arrived. And what a relief that he didn't expect you to marry him straight away. I hope it hasn't been too much of a chore to spend all this time there.

Your description of the town of Green Hill Creek is also troubling. You are correct, it is most certainly not what we had imagined when we selected him as a suitable husband. I understand that you do not wish to cause him any further hardship and I'm proud of you for being so thoughtful and kind. But your future is at stake and no one could blame you for putting your needs first. Mr Johnson, through no fault of his own, is clearly not a man who will suit you well.

By the time you receive this letter you should have fulfilled your obligation to stay for two weeks and can ask him to provide you with passage home without concern for not having done what he asked. I have started searching for a more suitable candidate and have already found a lawyer in Denver who seems far more promising. It is a pity we didn't find him before you left for California.

I look forward to having you home, Louisa. Your sisters and I have missed having you here. We will have a wonderful window shopping trip on your return!

Love,
Mother.

Louisa lowered the letter to the bed, staring numbly at the pile of travel trunks heaped in the corner of the room.

When the pain in her heart finally became too much, she collapsed onto the pillows and burst into tears.

Chapter 23

Louisa was outside the bank when Jesse finished work that afternoon.

She was watching a woman with two small children talking to Mr Graves, the owner of the greengrocer across the street, and it seemed that sadness clouded her face. But then she saw him and smiled and he wasn't sure if he'd imagined her melancholy.

He wheeled up to her. "After a long day of doing my best to avoid Ransom, seeing you waiting for me is like the sun coming out of the clouds after a thunderstorm. That's assuming you are waiting for me."

She craned her neck as if searching for something along the street. "Well, I was waiting for my other beau, but he's late so I'll go with you instead."

Smiling, he took a quick look around to check no one was watching them then grasped her hand and kissed the back. What he really wanted to do was pull her into his lap and greet her properly, but that would have to wait until they got back to his house.

"Could we go to the general store on the way home?" she said as they began walking. "I didn't want to miss you and I didn't have time before. Lizzy and Sara and I went to visit Jo today and I only got back just now."

"Sure we can. How's Jo?"

"Still adjusting to being here, I think. It doesn't help that she's so far out of town and that Gabriel spends so much time at his placer mine. Although she didn't seem bothered by that. She didn't say as much, but I think she's relieved."

"Relieved that he's not around?"

She nodded slowly. "I don't think she likes him much. I'm worried about her."

"Do you think he's mistreating her?"

"Oh no, I don't think Jo would put up with that. She's very independent and tough. It's just..." She sighed and shrugged. "I suppose I want all my friends to be as happy with their husbands as I am with you."

He didn't say anything for a few moments, carefully formulating his reply. "You're happy with me?"

She turned her gaze to him. "Very. I know I'm having trouble with what my parents want me to do, but it's not because I'm unhappy with you. That couldn't be further from the truth."

"I'm glad to hear that." He was extremely glad. He'd have been more glad to hear her say she was staying, but after the previous day he knew better than to press the issue. She would work through it at her own pace. All he could do was wait and pray.

Looking at the street ahead of them, he stopped abruptly.

Louisa walked a couple more paces before she realised he was no longer at her side. "What's wrong?"

"That's him."

She followed his gaze along the road. "That's who?"

"Those two men in front of the feed store, see them?"

She nodded.

"The one with dark hair is Lem, the man I saw talking to Ransom." He wheeled back a little so he was hidden from their view by the corner of a building. The two men were a good fifty feet away and not looking in their direction, but it was hard to blend in when he was the only one around in a wheelchair.

Louisa moved back to join him. "That must be the man Rebecca and Peg talked about, the one with the scraggly beard?" She frowned, biting her lip. "Wait, he could be..."

"What?"

"Remember I told you about the man that turned up at Sara's farm last week? The one who scared her?"

"I remember. You think that's him?"

"It could be. I can't be sure, but he looks just like she described him." She stepped forward. "I'm going to get closer, see if I can hear what they're talking about."

Jesse's heart hit his throat. "What?! No! What if they see you? They could be dangerous."

"It won't matter if they see me, they don't know who I am. Don't worry, I'll be careful."

Before he could say anything to stop her, she was gone. Not that he thought anything he said would have stopped her. Her courage and determination were part of the reason he loved her, and he especially loved that she was doing it all for him. But that didn't assuage his fear as she walked along the street towards the potentially dangerous men.

"It's a good thing I'm young," he muttered to himself, "because she's going to take years off my life."

The closer she got to Lem and the man with the scraggly brown hair and beard, the higher Jesse's heart rate rose. What if Ransom had told them about her? What if they were looking out for a beautiful, blue-eyed, auburn-haired woman who might be spying on them?

He tensed as she neared the two men, hands gripping his push rims, ready to explode from his hiding place and fly to her rescue if either of them so much as gestured in her direction.

She stopped within six feet of them, pretending to look

231

in the window of the bakery. Neither man appeared to notice her. After a minute or so during which Jesse relaxed just enough that his knuckles returned to their natural colour, the bearded man glanced in her direction.

Jesse tensed again.

Leering disgustingly, scraggly beard spoke to her and Louisa spun around, her eyes wide. Glaring at him, she said something in return and marched into the bakery.

Jesse breathed out.

Lem burst into laughter, clapped scraggly beard on the shoulder, and strolled in the direction of the saloon.

Scraggly beard gave the bakery door a look, shook his head, and marched along the road in Jesse's direction.

He immediately backed into the alley he was using for cover, waiting for the man to pass before coming out again. When the man was out of sight, he wheeled in the direction of the bakery. Louisa emerged as he reached the door and his eyes went to the paper bag she was holding.

"I needed an excuse to be in there," she said. "Apple tart seemed an excellent excuse."

He fell in beside her as she started in the direction of the general store. "Are you all right? What did he say to you?"

"Oh, just something I wouldn't repeat in polite company. Or any company, for that matter."

A flash of anger twisted Jesse's gut. "I should have run him over and punched him."

"Ooh, I would have liked to see that," she said, smiling.

"What did you say to him? He didn't seem too pleased, although Lem thought it was funny."

"I told him that until he learned what soap is he would do better propositioning something he had a chance with, such as a mule with extremely low standards."

Despite his lingering outrage, he smiled. "That's my girl. Could you hear what they were talking about?"

"Ely, that's what Lem called the other one, he said it was taking too long and he was sick of hanging around here. Lem said they almost had him where they wanted him and it wouldn't be much longer before the big score came in. Ely said he wasn't convinced it would work and Lem got annoyed and said he was welcome to leave. Ely backed down after that. I think Lem is in charge. Lem said he was going to have a talk with him tonight. Ely said it probably wouldn't work and he was going to get a horse to replace his old nag, just in case he needed to run. That's when he saw me."

Jesse thought over the conversation she'd related. "Sounds like something's going on, but without any names or specifics we don't even know if Ransom's involved."

"He could be the 'him' they were talking about."

"Could be, but right now that's just a theory."

She was quiet for a few more paces. "I have an idea."

The way she said it made him nervous. "You do?"

"If Mr Ransom is who they were talking about, Lem said he was going to talk to him tonight. I think we should watch his house and see if Lem turns up."

Jesse nodded slowly, thinking about it. "That's a good idea. But you don't have to come, I can do that by myself."

She smiled as she looked at the ground in front of her. "I don't have to, but I'm going to."

"And I'm guessing there's nothing I can do to persuade you otherwise?"

"Nope."

He had to admit, sitting outside Ransom's house in the dark would be a lot more pleasant if Louisa was there with him. "You just want to sneak out again, don't you?"

"Oh, I do," she said, her eyes shining with excitement. "But won't we have to be there early, to make sure we don't miss him?"

"I figure he won't turn up before nine, at the earliest, if

he doesn't want to be seen."

"Hmm. Pastor and Mrs Jones don't usually go to bed before ten, but I could always say I'm tired and go earlier so I can sneak out while they're still up." She grinned. "That would be even more thrilling than sneaking out while they're asleep. So much more danger of being caught."

Attempting to look distressed, Jesse came to a halt at the door to Lamb's General Store. "I've created a monster."

She laughed and skirted around him. "By the way, what's your favourite colour?"

"Uh, green, I guess. Why?"

She smiled back at him as she walked inside. "Because I'm going to pick out some material for a new dress. In green."

He followed her in, pretty sure his heart had melted a little bit.

Chapter 24

Climbing through the bedroom window turned out to be a lot easier with Louisa's dress not trailing on the ground behind her.

She dropped silently to the ground outside, pulled the window closed, and listened for any sign she'd been heard. Hearing nothing, she smiled and tiptoed around the side of the house.

It occurred to her that her love of doing something forbidden was somewhat childish, but she'd had a whole childhood of studiously not being childish. She had some catching up to do.

She saw Jesse's silhouette as soon as she reached the front garden and hurried to join him on the street.

"All clear?" he whispered.

She glanced back. The parlour window curtains were lit from within where Mrs Jones was working on some needlepoint and Pastor Jones was reading. At least, that was what they'd been doing when she'd feigned tiredness and excused herself for bed. Or maybe, she suddenly thought, as soon as she'd left they had moved to the settee together and taken advantage of the time alone to get closer. Perhaps they were even in there kissing.

Did couples do that after thirty years of marriage? Louisa's own parents had been married for twenty-four years and were on occasion affectionate, but she'd never seen them indulge in anything more than a brief kiss. But perhaps they saved that for private moments. If she had been married to Jesse for thirty years, would she be any less eager to spend time in his arms? Looking into his beautiful face shadowed in the darkness of a cloudy night, she couldn't imagine so.

"All clear," she whispered back.

They started along the road.

"You're getting good at this sneaking out business," he said.

"I know. Isn't it wonderful?"

Rotherford Ransom's house was close to the railroad station, on a quiet street near the edge of town. From Jesse's description of the man, it was much as Louisa imagined it would be. Flagstones formed a narrow yard between the fence and the building, with no porch and not an inch of greenery in sight. Jesse had told her that Mr Ransom had never been married. From the austere appearance of his home, Louisa could have guessed it even without knowing.

They found a spot hidden by a stand of bushes and trees a little along the street from where they'd have a good view of the house and she looked around for a suitable patch of grass on which to settle.

"Louisa?"

She glanced back at Jesse's whisper.

He patted his thighs and held out both hands.

"Won't your legs get uncomfortable?"

"We'll deal with that problem when it happens," he replied, beckoning her in with his fingers.

She looked around. "But what if someone sees us?"

"I think the whole point of us being here is that no one can."

She couldn't fault his logic, nor could she deny that his lap was a far more comfortable prospect than the ground.

Shrugging off her awkwardness, she settled onto his lap,

smiling when he wrapped his arms around her and kissed her temple.

Definitely a better place to sit than the ground.

They sat in silence, watching the house along the street and enjoying the simple pleasure of being close.

"Jesse?" she whispered after a while.

"Hmm?"

"Thank you for letting me do this with you."

The curving of his lips was just visible in the darkness. "Pretty sure I didn't have much of a choice."

She smiled, resting her head on his shoulder. "You could have stopped me coming but you didn't, and you've let me help you even when you were afraid for my safety. You've given me the freedom to make my own decisions and I'm truly grateful for that."

"You're a smart, capable, strong human being. Even if we were married, I wouldn't have the right to tell you what to do. All I want is for you to be just who you are."

She considered his words. "You really mean that, don't you? About wanting me just as I am?"

"Why would I want you to change? You're perfect."

She smiled against his shoulder. "I'm far from perfect."

"That depends on your point of view," he whispered into her hair. "To me, you are."

She lifted her head to look into his face shadowed in the darkness and touched her palm to his cheek. "I think you're perfect too."

There was a long pause before he answered. "Even my legs?"

She didn't hesitate. "Every part. I wouldn't change a thing about you. Not one."

He stared at her for a moment, then leaned forward and caught her lips in a kiss that stole her breath with its intensity. Her eyes fluttered closed and she pushed her fingers into his hair, her passion blossoming to match his. By the time they parted she was gasping for air and her heart was pounding so hard she felt sure it would betray their hiding place to anyone passing.

"Uh... we should... um..." Jesse took a deep breath, "...probably concentrate on watching the house."

She swallowed and managed a shaky nod. "Uh huh."

They waited another half hour, as near as Louisa could guess. After twenty minutes Jesse sheepishly asked her to leave his lap because his legs were going numb. She was amazed he'd lasted so long. Pulling her cloak around her, she settled on the ground at his feet and leaned against his legs.

She was just beginning to doze when he shifted behind her, leaning forward to stare intently into the darkness. Louisa followed his gaze, wondering what had his attention. At first she saw nothing but the vague shapes of the fences and occasional shrub and tree along the street. And then one of the shapes moved.

Jesse touched her shoulder and she took his hand, not taking her eyes from the dark shadow making its way to Mr Ransom's house.

Reaching his door, the shadow paused and looked around. Louisa immediately looked down, hiding her pale face in the folds of her cloak and holding her breath, trusting Jesse was doing the same.

After a few seconds she carefully raised her head, saying a silent *thank You* to God when she saw the man at the door raise his hand to knock, apparently still oblivious to their presence.

After twenty seconds or so a window lit up and the door opened, the light that spilled from inside illuminating Lem's face.

Mr Ransom, clearly visible from where they were hiding, frowned and looked past him to the street. "What are you doing here? I told you never to come to either my home or the bank. What if someone sees you?"

"There's no one out here." Lem stepped onto the doorstep. "We need to have a talk."

Mr Ransom huffed an agitated breath and stepped aside to let him in, closing the door behind him.

"Now we know it's him," Jesse whispered.

"We need to know what they're talking about in there," Louisa said, looking up at him. "Jesse..."

"Yes, I know, you're going over there." He gently cupped her jaw. "Just please, be careful."

She climbed to her feet and kissed his cheek. "I will, I promise."

Lifting her skirt, she ran on silent feet to the gate into Mr Ransom's front yard and slipped in. The light had moved from the window at the front of the house and she crept around a path to the side where another stood out bright in the darkness. At least there were no plants to grab at her as she passed. Although there were no trees or bushes to provide her with cover either.

Being careful to stay out of the light, she took a brief peek into the room. Mr Ransom stood by a polished dining table, gesticulating at Lem. Neither of them looked happy.

Muffled voices filtered through the glass, but she couldn't make out the words. Ducking back into the shadows, she crept up to the window and pressed herself against the wall to one side, hoping to hear more clearly. It didn't help.

After several minutes of straining to hear anything, she was about to give up and leave when the voices suddenly grew louder.

"...getting as much as I can!" Mr Ransom shouted.

Lem's reply was too soft to hear.

"We had an agreement! You said you'd wait. I need time

239

to prepare. I don't want to lose my job."

Again, Lem didn't speak loudly enough to make out.

"Well that's not my problem, is it? He's *your* man. Don't you trust him?"

"Of course I don't trust him!" Lem yelled.

"Keep your voice down! We'll be heard."

Their voices quietened again and the remainder of the conversation was frustratingly lost in the wall between her and the two men. A handful of minutes later she heard the front door open and close.

Louisa pressed herself into the shadows, listening to Lem's footsteps walk away. She waited until he was long gone and the light in the house had been extinguished, then she crept from her hiding place and rejoined Jesse amongst the trees along the road.

"Oh, thank goodness," he said as she approached, reaching out to take her hand. "I don't know how much more of seeing you in danger I can take."

"I wasn't in any real danger," she said, smiling, "but I don't mind you being worried about me."

"Did you hear anything?"

"Mostly not. The window was closed and they were speaking too softly, but I did hear a bit when they started shouting." She related the few lines she'd heard.

Jesse stared at the ground, absently rubbing his thumb over the back of her hand in the most distracting fashion. "So we know for sure that Ransom is working with, or for, Lem. And that Lem and his cronies may be planning something more than cheating the bank's customers."

Louisa dragged her attention from his touch on her hand. "Is that enough?"

"It'll have to be." He looked up at her. "I'm going to Marshal Cade before work tomorrow. Maybe Lem and whoever else is with him are wanted men. Then I'll talk to

Vernon when I get into the bank."

"I'll go with you," she said immediately. "I can tell the marshal everything I heard."

He smiled. "I wouldn't have it any other way."

Chapter 25

"What're we having for breakfast today?" Jesse said, moving back to allow Louisa inside.

She leaned down to kiss him, and walked into the kitchen, setting her basket on the table. "Freshly baked cornbread and butter with ham. Would you like it warmed up?"

"Cold is just fine." He wheeled to the table and lifted the cloth, taking in a deep breath of the delicious aromas that wafted from inside. "You baked this this morning? When did you sleep?"

She went to the cupboard to fetch plates. "I haven't been sleeping so well the past couple of nights. Thought I might as well make use of the time rather than tossing and turning in bed."

He caught hold of her hand. "Is it because of this whole business with the bank? I don't want you to be so worried you're losing sleep. You should have told me."

She smiled and touched her fingertips to his cheek. "It's not because of the bank."

He stared up into her blue eyes, searching for the truth. "Is it because you don't know what to do about me?"

She sighed. "It's because I don't know what to do about myself. Please don't worry about me. I'll work it out."

He wished he could think of some way to ease her mind. "I'm praying for you, that God will guide you to the right decision."

She gave him a small smile. "Not that He'll guide me to stay?"

"All the time, but I know He won't if it's not His will. But I still pray it. Can't help myself."

Her smile grew. "Glad to hear it."

When breakfast was over they went together to the marshal's office. Marshal Lee Cade was at his desk, chair tilted back against the wall, the local newspaper in his hands.

He dropped the chair forward onto all four legs with a thud as they walked in. "Good morning, Mr Johnson, Miss Wood. What brings you to my door at this ridiculous time of the day?"

"Not a morning person, Marshal?" Jesse said, wheeling up to the desk.

"Never have been, never will be. And yet I still manage to get myself into jobs that mean I have to get up early. What can I do for you?"

Louisa took a seat beside Jesse. "We may have uncovered a conspiracy. Or possibly a plot. We're not sure."

Marshal Cade's eyebrows rose. "Sounds like I'm going to need to write this down. Hold on." He opened a drawer in his desk and pulled out several sheets of paper and a pen. "Okay, go ahead."

Together, they told him the whole story, from Jesse's initial suspicions about Ransom to seeing Lem at his house the night before. When they'd finished, Marshal Cade looked over the pages of notes he'd taken.

"This is interesting," he said, tapping the end of the pen on the paper. "You know what happened yesterday with Miss Watts, and that I've got Ely locked up?" He jerked his head towards the closed door in the back wall of the office that led to the cells.

Jesse nodded.

"Now I know he's wanted for more than one crime, so it's highly likely this Lem person is also a criminal, if he's associating with Ely. I know the men the two girls at the saloon were talking about. I pay attention if anyone's new in town. But I didn't know for sure they were together. I'm going to have a talk with Ely again." He pushed his chair back from the desk. "I'm not going to say I entirely condone your methods, especially breaking into the bank, even if you work there. And watching Ransom's meeting with Lem could have been dangerous. But this is good work. You leave it with me and I'll let you know what I find out. I'll also need to talk to Mr Vernon, which should be fun since he and I rarely, and by rarely I mean never, see eye to eye. Take my advice, never become a town marshal."

"That was my second choice after accountant," Jesse said, rolling back to let Louisa out of her seat. "Sounds like I made the right choice."

From the marshal's office they went straight to the bank, it being time for Jesse to be at work anyway. He took Louisa in through the back door and to his office.

Ransom walked into the room as they arrived.

"This area of the bank is for employees only, Mr Johnson," he said, frowning at Louisa.

"I don't believe we've been introduced," she said, holding out her hand. "I'm Miss Wood."

He took her hand briefly. "It's a pleasure to meet you, Miss Wood," he said, sounding like it was anything but. "However, you are not meant to be here. So if you would kindly..."

"What's going on out here?" Mr Vernon strode into the room, his pocket watch in his hand. "Miss Wood?"

Jesse wheeled towards him. "Sir, I need to talk to you again."

Vernon heaved a longsuffering sigh. "If it's regarding

the same nonsense you talked to me about on Monday, I don't have the time. I still haven't found anyone to replace Mr Emerson so Mr Ransom will be manning the lobby this morning, which means I will have to deal with his duties. So..."

Jesse had had enough. "Mr Vernon, I'm only here telling you this as a courtesy. We've already been to the marshal and he'll be by to talk to you later. So if you want to know what's happening in your own bank, you should listen. Sir."

A flash of irritation crossed Vernon's face. He wasn't used to his employees contradicting him. "The marshal? What would he get involved with? This, whatever it is, is purely a bank matter."

"No, sir, it isn't. There are other factors involved." Jesse didn't want to say too much in front of Ransom, but he didn't seem to be getting anywhere with Vernon.

He glanced back at Louisa, wondering if it had been a good idea to bring her. She'd wanted to come and he'd wanted the support, but now the situation was becoming contentious he didn't want her caught up in it.

Mr Vernon huffed out an annoyed breath. "This is ridiculous. All right, I'll hear you out, but right now it's opening time. Mr Ransom, please open the doors. I'll be in to stock the drawers in a few minutes."

Ransom cast a nervous glance between him and Jesse. "Sir, I don't think..."

"It's one minute to nine, Mr Ransom," Vernon said, pointedly flicking open his watch. "We never open late."

Ransom narrowed his eyes at Jesse as if trying to read his mind. "Yes, sir."

He walked through to the lobby, casting Jesse a scowl as he left and leaving the door open.

"This had better be good, Mr Johnson," Vernon said. "I don't appreciate flippant interruptions of the bank's time."

Before Jesse could reply, Louisa stepped forward, her eyes flashing with anger. "Mr Vernon, you appear to care about your bank, and yet you dismiss everything Mr Johnson says even though he is a valued employee. Has he ever given you reason to doubt his word or his intelligence in the whole time he has worked for you?"

Mr Vernon blinked at her, appearing as taken aback as Jesse felt. "Well, no, but..."

"Exactly. And yet you treat him as if he's an annoyance. Is it because he can't walk? Is it your prejudice that's blinding you?"

"I..."

"Because he has spent the past week in turmoil because of what he's discovered. He cares about this bank and its customers and he has spent many hours of his own time investigating this. So the very least you can do is be civil to him and listen to him with an open mind."

"Uh, I, uh, yes." Mr Vernon cleared his throat and pushed his watch back into his waistcoat pocket. "You're right, Miss Wood."

Jesse couldn't tell if he really thought she was right or if he was simply embarrassed.

Seeming to suddenly realise what she'd done, Louisa nodded and stepped back to Jesse's side, her eyes dropping to the floor. He wanted to reach up and hug her.

Mr Vernon cleared his throat again. "Well, let's go to my office and you can tell me what you've found, Mr Johnson. Miss Wood, if you'd like to..."

He was interrupted by angry voices from the lobby.

"What are you..."

"Close that door and lock it."

"You can't do this!"

Frowning, Vernon strode to the door. "What's going on in here?"

He came to an abrupt halt and backed up, his hands rising. Lem followed him into the room, a revolver pressed almost casually into Vernon's belly.

Behind him a huge man with curly brown hair and beard wrestled a struggling Ransom through the door and threw him away from him with a curse. Ransom spun round to glare at him.

"Jeb, go and watch the street," Lem ordered, turning his attention to Jesse and Louisa.

Jesse pushed his chair forward, moving to where he could roll in front of her if he needed to. His hands felt slick on the rims and he wiped them on his trousers.

"Well now, seems to me I've seen you before, miss. I never forget a pretty face." Lem's eyes travelled down Louisa's body. "Or other things." He glanced around the room. "Anyone else in the building?"

"What is the meaning of this?" Vernon growled, with more bravado than Jesse would have credited him with.

"This here is a bank robbery," Lem said, grinning. He raised his voice. "Get in here, West."

A swarthy man wearing a black bowler strolled in from the lobby. His dark eyes immediately went to Louisa, his mouth twisting into a leer.

Jesse moved forward a few more inches. West didn't even glance at him.

"Check the rest of the building," Lem said. "If there's anyone else here, bring 'em out."

West gave a sharp nod and headed for the door leading to the back of the building, twisting his neck to keep his eyes on Louisa until he'd left the room.

She moved closer to Jesse and placed her hand on his shoulder.

He wrapped it in his own, looking up into her scared eyes. "It's going to be okay."

"Right, this is how things are going to go," Lem said, gesturing with his gun. "There will be no screaming or doing anything stupid like trying to escape. Do as you're told, stay quiet, and you'll all get to go home without any holes in you. Sound good?"

"You'll never get away with this," Vernon said. "The marshal's office is just down the road."

His seemingly relaxed demeanour vanishing in an instant, Lem rounded on him and shoved the gun beneath his jaw. Vernon stumbled back against the filing cabinets.

"Did I say you could speak?" Lem hissed, his face inches away, twisting the barrel of the revolver against Vernon's skin.

"N-no."

"Then don't..." he moved the gun and tapped it against the side of Vernon's face, "speak."

Vernon shook his head. Lem stepped back and he slumped against the cabinets, rubbing his neck.

West walked back into the room. "Rest of the place is empty."

"Good," Lem said. "You keep an eye on this lot while Ransom and I take a walk." He looked at Ransom. "Where's the safe?"

Ransom's eyes darted to Vernon. "Uh... I don't..."

A knock from the lobby interrupted him.

Jeb appeared at the door and hissed, "There's a woman outside."

Lem puffed a sharp breath through his nose and gestured at Ransom with the revolver. "Get rid of her."

His jaw dropped. "How am I supposed to do that?"

"I don't care," Lem said through gritted teeth, "just get rid of her."

Shaking his head, Ransom followed Jeb back out to the lobby and Lem closed the door behind him.

Before Jesse could react, he strode to Louisa and grabbed her around the waist, pulling her back against him and pressing the gun to her temple. "Anyone makes a sound, I mess up this pretty face."

Jesse's heart hit his throat. He started towards them.

"That includes you, wheels," Lem growled. "It may have escaped your notice, but I'm not above killing women or cripples."

Jesse stopped, his jaw clenching. "If you hurt her..."

"Shhh," Lem hissed as the sound of the front door opening filtered from the lobby.

Louisa's terrified gaze found Jesse's and icy fear clutched at his spine. He couldn't let anything happen to her.

It's all right, he mouthed, hoping she understood. *I won't let him hurt you.* He had no idea how he was going to keep that promise, but he knew he would. He would do anything to protect her, even if it meant losing his own life.

Muffled voices came from the lobby, too soft to make out the words.

Please, Jesse prayed, *make whoever it is see something is wrong. Please, Lord.*

For what seemed like an age they waited until finally he heard the main door close again. Jesse didn't know whether to be relieved or disappointed.

The door opened and Ransom walked in. "She's gone."

Lem released Louisa and she flew into Jesse's lap, clutching onto him and pressing her face into his neck. He wrapped his arms around her trembling body and glared up at Lem.

"She suspect anything?" Lem said, ignoring them both.

"No, she did not suspect anything." Ransom fixed him with a stare, as if daring him to disagree.

West scowled like he'd tasted something bad. "Let's just get this done, Lem, and we won't ever have to deal with this

249

slimy rat again. Which can't happen soon enough, far as I'm concerned."

The colour drained from Ransom's face. "I-I don't know what you're talking about. I don't know who you are."

"Give it up, Ransom," West snapped. "We don't have time to coddle you anymore. Ely's gone and got himself locked up and he could be blabbing to the marshal about us right now, for all we know. We're leaving and we're taking the contents of that safe with us."

Ransom's pale face turned red, a vein throbbing in his neck. "You promised I wouldn't be suspected of involvement. Now everyone knows."

Vernon's mouth dropped open. "Mr Johnson was right?"

Ransom ignored him. "This wasn't the deal. I told you to wait and..."

Lem darted forward, shoving him against the wall and wrapping one hand around his throat. The revolver jammed into his cheek. "Up to now I've let you think you had a say in all this because having someone on the inside of a bank ain't something that comes along every day. But you got yourself into this. Man can't hold his tongue when he's got some liquor in him shouldn't be drinking at all. Maybe this'll teach you to keep your mouth shut about how you're using the bank to scam people. Now you're going to do what I say, when I say it." He released Ransom and shoved him in the direction of the door to the back. "Get going."

Ransom caught the edge of Jesse's desk to stop himself from falling and coughed for air, rubbing at his neck.

"I said *get!*" Lem shouted.

Ransom flashed him a look of utter hatred before turning in the direction of the door.

"Watch them," Lem said to West as he pushed Ransom out the room.

"With pleasure," West said, settling his leer on Louisa again.

Seeing the danger, Jesse whispered in her ear. "Get behind me."

She raised her face to look at him then turned her gaze on West. Seeing his approach, she climbed from Jesse's lap and moved to stand behind him, gripping the back of his chair.

Jesse fixed West with a stare. "Stay away from her."

West gave a derisive snort. "Or what?"

He didn't answer, but when West moved to go around him, he moved into his path. The thug changed direction. Jesse went with him.

"Get out of my way, cripple," West snarled.

"No." Jesse's heart pounded, his mouth felt like a desert, and his stomach sat somewhere around his ankles, but he would die before he let the monster in front of him anywhere near Louisa.

West raised his revolver and cocked the hammer. "All right then."

"No, please don't!" Louisa ran around Jesse, stopping between him and West and raising her hands. "I'll... I'll do what you want. Just don't hurt him."

Jesse reached for her frantically. "Louisa, no!"

West's leer returned. "Now that's more like it."

"There's no need for this," Vernon said from where he stood in one corner of the room. His hands shot up when West's revolver swung round to point at him. "I just mean, you can take whatever you want from the bank."

"Already getting all the money," West said, returning his attention to Louisa. "Only one thing here I want."

Jesse grasped his push rims and tensed to move. He didn't know what he was going to do, but West wasn't going to lay one finger on her.

West took a step towards her, his eyes sliding disgustingly down her body.

The door to the front room burst open and Jeb rushed in. "Where's Lem?"

"Out back getting the money," West said, frowning in annoyance. "Shouldn't you be watching the street?"

The back door opened and Lem and Ransom entered, each carrying bulging leather bags.

"Lem, something's wrong," Jeb said. "Street out front just got real empty. And I can't see Ralph and Luther no more."

Lem dropped his heavy bag onto the floor. "There's a door at the back. Go see if it's clear outside."

Jeb nodded and headed for the back.

"West, check the street out front again."

Clenching his jaw, West cast a glance at Louisa and strode into the front room.

Jesse wheeled up to her and took her hand.

"Please don't do that again," he said when she looked down at him.

Her eyes shimmered with moisture. "I couldn't let him hurt you."

"I'll see you in jail for this, Rotherford," Mr Vernon growled, his eyes on the bags of money. "After all I've done for you."

Ransom gaped at him. "All you've done for me? What have you ever done for me? Seventeen years I've worked for you and I barely even get a pay rise once in a blue moon. I..."

"Yeah yeah, no one cares," Lem snapped. He raised his voice. "What's going on out there, West?"

"Road's empty," West called back.

There was a crash from the rear of the bank.

A voice shouted, "Come out here with your hands up."

A door slammed shut.

Jeb ran into the room. "Deputy's out there. Might be more."

Lem grabbed both bags of money and handed one to him. "Everybody, out front."

They crowded into the lobby and Jeb and his revolver shepherded Jesse, Louisa and Vernon against a wall.

Lem went to the front door and opened it a crack.

"You're surrounded, Lemuel Carver," Marshal Cade shouted from outside. "Throw your guns out and come out with your hands in the air and you might walk out of this alive."

"We've got hostages, Marshal," Lem yelled back. "You try anything and people start dying."

"You want to add murder to robbery?"

"Don't matter, long as I don't go to jail."

Jesse touched Louisa's arm to get her attention and beckoned her closer. When she leaned down he whispered, "If they start shooting, get down behind my chair."

She stared at him in horror. "No! I can't use you as a shield."

He cupped his hand to the side of her face. "*Please,* Louisa. If you were hurt..." He stopped as his voice trembled.

She closed her eyes and rested her forehead onto his shoulder. "Dear God, please keep us both safe."

He wrapped his arms around her and buried his face in her hair. "Amen."

The sound of the front door slamming startled them apart.

"What are we gonna do, Lem?" Jeb said.

Lem looked at the floor.

"Lem..."

"Shut up and let me think!"

Jeb lapsed into silence, glancing nervously out the window.

Half a minute later, Lem lifted his head. "Jeb, you see the horses across the street?"

"Yeah, they're still there. Marshal probably doesn't know they're ours."

"Good." He gestured at Jesse with his revolver. "Get him out of that chair. I don't want him doing anything rash."

Jeb eyed Jesse uncertainly. "But, Lem, he's a cripple."

Jesse ground his teeth. If one more person called him a cripple...

Lem rolled his eyes. "Sometimes I can't believe we came out of the same woman. Just put him on a chair, or throw him on the floor, I don't care. Just anywhere he can't move!"

Puffing out a breath, Jeb grabbed a chair, planted it beside Jesse, and walked around behind him.

Belatedly, Jesse realised what he was going to do. "Don't you dare..."

Jeb's hands thrust beneath his arms and he was hoisted into the air and dumped onto the chair. He let out a frustrated growl as Jeb pushed his wheelchair across the room, leaving it well out of reach.

Louisa rushed to his side. "Are you all right?"

He swallowed his anger and took her hand. "I'm fine." He noticed Jeb wouldn't meet his gaze.

"Right." Lem hefted the bag of money over his shoulder and grabbed Ransom, wrapping his left arm around his neck and holding the gun to his head with his right.

Ransom yelped. "What on earth are you doing?"

"Grab yourselves a shield," Lem said. "We're getting out of here."

"A shield?!" Ransom exclaimed, struggling.

Lem tightened his arm until he started to choke. "Do you want me to shoot you right here? Or do you want to stay out of jail?"

West strode to Louisa and grasped her wrist, forcing her

hand from Jesse's and pulling her roughly against him.

She cried out. "Jesse!"

"Let her go!" He reached forward, freezing when the barrel of West's gun swung round to push into his forehead.

"Can I shoot him, Lem?" West said. "Just let me shoot him before we go. He's useless anyway."

"No shooting. We fire a shot in here the marshal will come in, guns blazing. We need to do this smart."

"You are a lucky man," West said. Then his eyes went to Jesse's legs and he smirked. "Or maybe not."

Jeb grasped Vernon, propelling him to join Lem and Ransom at the door. West dragged Louisa to follow.

She twisted round to look back at Jesse, her eyes wide with fear.

"We go out together," Lem said. "Keep your hostages in front of you, guns at heads, fingers on triggers." He sounded as if he'd done it before.

Jesse looked around desperately for some way to save Louisa.

At Lem's bidding, Ransom opened the door a fraction.

"We're coming out," Lem shouted. "We've got hostages with us. You try and shoot us, they're the ones get shot."

Jesse's eyes landed on a pole leaning against the wall in the corner by the door. It had a hook on one end and was used to open the tall, high windows that faced the street. It was usually kept behind the counter. Ransom must have been using it before the robbers came in.

"Go on," Lem said to Ransom.

Jesse glanced at them, checking if he was being watched, but as usual he might as well have been invisible. That was finally a good thing.

Ransom pulled the door wide and Lem manoeuvred him out onto the boardwalk outside.

The pole was several feet beyond Jesse's reach. It would

take a miracle, but it was his only chance.

He shuffled himself to the edge of the chair and gripped the armrests.

Jeb followed Lem out, Vernon clutched in front of him. West was behind them, his arm around Louisa's chest, forcing her back against him.

Jesse had only seconds before he lost her.

Help me, Lord. Make my legs work.

West pushed Louisa into the doorway.

"Louisa! Get down!"

She obeyed Jesse's command without hesitation, softening her knees and sagging in West's grasp.

Commanding his legs to obey him for once in his life, Jesse launched himself from the chair.

West spun round, raising his gun.

Jesse's feet took two impossible strides. He grabbed the pole and swung it with all his strength. The end hit the side of West's head.

Jesse's legs gave way beneath him and he crashed to the floor.

The room echoed with a gunshot. Somebody screamed.

Shouting and gunfire erupted outside.

Jesse looked up to see West lying several feet away, unmoving, Louisa on the floor beside him.

A window shattered. Vernon plummeted through the doorway and rolled into a ball against the wall.

Louisa raised her head. "*Jesse!*" She scrambled to her hands and feet and threw herself down beside him.

He wrapped himself around her, shielding her with his body as chaos rained down around them. Squeezing his eyes shut, he held the woman he loved tight against his chest and begged God for her protection.

Bullets ricocheted off the walls above. Shouts came from the street. Somewhere behind Jesse, Mr Vernon whimpered.

A volley of gunfire shattered another window. Someone cried out.

And then silence, so abrupt it echoed in Jesse's head.

When nothing happened for at least ten seconds, he opened his eyes. The sounds of running feet and then shouts of "Hands in the air!" came from outside.

"Louisa?" he whispered into her hair. "Are you all right?"

Gasping in terrified breaths, she moved her face from his chest and lifted her eyes to his.

"Are you hurt?"

She shook her head. "Are you?"

He searched his body for pain. "No."

A vision of West holding the gun to her head came to him. What if he'd lost her? The thought of spending the rest of his days without her sent a shock of pain through his chest worse than any bullet could have. He needed her. She held his life in her hands.

"Don't leave," he whispered, staring intently into her beautiful face. "Please stay with me."

Her breathing stilled and for a few seconds she didn't say anything. Then she raised a trembling hand to his cheek. "Jesse..."

"Everyone all right in here?"

Her gaze moved beyond him and he looked back to see Marshal Cade standing in the doorway.

"Is it over?" Mr Vernon said from the corner where he was huddled.

"Yes, it's over." The marshal's boots crunched on broken glass as he walked inside. "We've got the gang in custody, including the two they had outside. Well, most of them."

Mr Vernon's gaze shot to the door. "*Most* of them?"

"All those who are still in my jurisdiction." He walked over to Jesse and Louisa as they sat up. "You two okay?" He offered Louisa his hand.

She swayed a little when she stood and Jesse reached up to steady her. Cade brushed a few shards of window glass from the seat of Jesse's wheelchair and pushed it over to him then went to West's still form and bent to press two fingers beneath his jaw.

"Is he alive?" Jesse said, pulling himself up into his chair.

"Yup." He straightened. "Which one of you laid him out?"

"I did." Jesse silently thanked the Lord he hadn't killed the man. A death, even West's, was something he didn't want on his conscience.

"Nicely done," the marshal said, moving the unconscious man's hands behind him and slapping on a pair of handcuffs. West groaned.

Jesse took Louisa's hand and was surprised at how cold it felt. The usual rosy glow of her complexion was missing, her skin pale.

"Louisa?"

Her gaze moved slowly from the man on the floor to him.

"Marshal," he said, not taking his eyes from her, "would you mind getting Miss Wood a chair?"

Cade took one look at Louisa and rushed to fetch the chair Jesse had been dumped into earlier. He placed it behind her and gently took her elbow.

"Miss Wood, would you like to sit?"

He helped her onto the seat and Jesse moved to her side. He wrapped his arms around her trembling body and she leaned her head against his shoulder. If they'd been alone, he would have drawn her into his lap where he could hold her as close as humanly possible.

"What do you mean you have *most* of them in custody?"

Mr Vernon said again. He hadn't moved from the corner.

A grim look shadowed the marshal's face. "I mean one of them isn't going to be bothering anyone in this life again."

Understanding dawned on Vernon's face. "Oh. I see. What about my secretary?"

"Mr Ransom is a mite the worse for wear, but he's alive. Bullet grazed his shoulder. From the way he's carrying on you'd have thought he was dying."

Mr Vernon pushed to his feet as rapidly as his out of shape form would allow. "You must arrest him immediately! He's been taking money from my customers. He was helping them rob the bank!"

"Already got him in a cell," the marshal said. "He tried to pretend he was an innocent hostage, but the men in the gang didn't take too kindly to that."

West groaned again, raising his head to look around blearily.

Deputy Fred Filbert appeared at the door. "Everything all right in here, Marshal?"

"Got another one for you, Fred," Cade said, indicating West.

Fred walked over to him and hauled him roughly to his feet. As they passed Louisa, she turned her face away and pressed it into Jesse's shoulder. Not caring who saw, he tightened his arms around her, whispering words of comfort he hoped would help.

"I need to get back to the office," Marshal Cade said, "but I can send someone to fetch Pastor Jones if you want?"

Jesse nodded. He wanted to keep Louisa with him, but he saw the sense in getting her home as soon as possible.

Mr Vernon approached from across the room, brushing off his clothing. "Well, it appears I owe you an apology, Mr Johnson. I should have believed you from the start. Miss Wood, if there's anything I can do, please don't hesitate to

259

ask."

She lifted her head and gave him a small nod.

Running footsteps approached outside and Jesse's father burst through the front door. "Oh, thank goodness." He crossed the room in two long strides and sank to his knees in front of them, reaching out his hand to cup Jesse's face. "When I heard the shooting and then someone said there was a robbery at the bank, I thought..." He blinked the sheen of moisture from his eyes.

Jesse took his hand. "I'm all right, Pa. We both are."

Peter wrapped his free hand around Louisa's and bent his head. "Thank You, Father, for protecting my boy and Louisa."

Jesse blinked his suddenly burning eyes and added his silent thanks to his father's.

Chapter 26

The following hour passed in something of a haze.

Pastor and Mrs Jones arrived at the bank and took Louisa home. Jesse went with them, unwilling to let her out of his sight, while his father returned home to reassure the rest of his family that he and Louisa were safe and unharmed.

Marshal Cade arrived soon after to get their accounts of events in the bank.

"It's a good thing you came and told me about your suspicions beforehand," he said when Jesse had finished relating all that had happened. "When I overheard Mrs Ogilvy telling her husband how Mr Ransom had made some strange excuse for the bank being closed, I knew something had to be up. Though I admit, I wasn't expecting it to be a full blown bank robbery. First one since I've been here. Mr Vernon's nigh on apoplectic right now."

Jesse was almost sure he saw the marshal's lips twitch.

"Anyway," he said, closing his notebook, "how are the two of you doing?"

Jesse looked at Louisa, but she didn't answer. She'd barely said a word since they left the bank.

"Just a bit shaken up," he said. "A few cuts and bruises. We'll be okay."

After Marshal Cade left, Pastor and Mrs Jones left Jesse and Louisa alone.

Neither of them spoke. Usually that wasn't a problem.

They had become close enough that silences were never awkward. Until now.

With all his heart Jesse wanted to comfort her, but for the first time since they'd met he had no idea what to say to her. He was responsible for what she'd been through that morning. If he hadn't confided in her, if he'd never involved her in any of it, she wouldn't have been in the bank when the gang came. She wouldn't have been manhandled and groped and had a gun pressed to her head while he sat terrified and helpless to do anything.

He wanted to tell her he was sorry and beg her forgiveness. He wanted to wrap his arms around her and take away all her fear and hurt. And yet all he did was sit and watch her stare at her lap, feeling more useless than he ever had in his life.

Lying on that floor in the bank, unable to think of anything other than how he couldn't live without her, he'd asked her to stay. But now all he could think was that he didn't have what it took to be a husband.

For the first time in his life, he doubted his ability to do something.

Mrs Jones walked into the room, taking a moment to look at the two of them, and Jesse raised his eyes to hers, silently begging for help.

She sat beside Louisa and took her hand. "Can I get you anything, Louisa?"

"No, thank you." Her voice was barely above a whisper.

Tell me what to do, Jesse wanted to beg her. *Tell me how to make it better. Please.*

Mrs Jones glanced at him, shrugging slightly. "Would you like to go to bed and rest?"

There were a few seconds of silence before Louisa answered. "I think so."

His heart sank. She wanted to get away from him.

"All right," Mrs Jones said gently, standing.

Louisa stood with her, her face devoid of emotion, as if she wasn't thinking about her movements, only following instructions.

Jesse reached out to take her hand. Not caring that Mrs Jones was there, he brought it to his lips and pressed a kiss to the back, closing his eyes against gathering tears. He needed her to know how much he cared. How sorry he was.

When he looked up she was watching him. She touched her free hand to his cheek, cradling his face for one blissful moment.

And then she turned away, pulling her hand from his grasp, and left the room.

~ ~ ~

Jesse wheeled slowly along the road away from the Jones' house, each yard he moved taking a mile's worth of effort.

He couldn't banish the events in the bank from his mind, Louisa's look of terror when West held the gun pressed to her head, her body trembling in his arms as gunshots exploded around them, the paleness of her face when it all caught up with her, the quietness he didn't know how to fix in the Jones' parlour.

And it was all his fault.

The knowledge made him feel sick to his stomach. She could have been killed and it would have been as much his doing as if he'd pulled the trigger himself. And Louisa knew it. She could barely even meet his eyes back in the parlour.

There was no way she'd stay with him now.

Emotion clogged his throat and he had to stop to gasp in a breath. What would he do without her?

He looked around him. He'd been heading in the direction of his house with barely a thought, but that wasn't where he wanted to go.

Turning his chair, he started in the other direction.

~

Jesse wheeled into the smithy, stopping just inside the open door.

The stifling heat of the forge, the constant pounding of metal on metal, the caustic smell of burning wood and molten iron, the fiery sparks that could singe skin - to most people it was a place in which to spend as little time as possible.

Not to Jesse though. For him, it was home.

As a baby he'd lain in his crib in the corner while his father worked, ears plugged with cloth to protect them from the noise, lulled to sleep by the sound of hammer on metal. As a small child he'd eventually learned how to stay safe around the heat and fire, after a handful of burns he still carried the scars from and a period of being looked after during the day by Mrs Jones until he was old enough to understand. As a young man in his teens he'd helped his father in his work with anything that could conceivably be done sitting down, even though he'd never felt a calling to take it up as a profession. Not like his younger brother did. But Jesse could still shape a horseshoe and fix a broken knife blade and forge an axe head.

For him, the blacksmith's workshop was a place of security and peace. It was where his father was, the one constant of his entire life.

Peter Johnson stood at the large anvil, pounding at the rough beginnings of what would become, in his skilled hands, the rim of a wagon wheel. The brand new wooden wheel itself stood off to one side, ready to be fitted with the circle of metal that would hold it together.

Jesse watched his father in silence, absorbing the

calming effect of the familiar sight. It was a couple of minutes before Peter turned to pick up some tongs and noticed his son by the door.

"Jesse?"

He swallowed and looked away, the emotion of the day suddenly threatening to overwhelm him.

His father pulled off his thick leather gloves and walked over to him. "Son, you all right?"

Jesse pressed his lips together and shook his head.

"Come on, let's go inside."

Jesse's childhood home sat behind the smithy, across a wide, packed earth yard. It was bigger now than it had been when he was born. Back then it had just been two rooms, an open parlour and kitchen, and a bedroom. When his father married Malinda, Peter built another room, giving ten-year-old Jesse his own bedroom for the first time. Another bedroom had followed when Luke came along, then one more four years later when Nancy was born. After Jesse moved into his own house, his old room became a new kitchen. With Peter's building skills and Malinda's good taste, it was a beautiful and happy home. Jesse loved it.

He wheeled into the parlour and moved onto the settee, focusing on his hands in his lap as his father sat beside him. "Is Malinda in?"

"I took her to see her sister. She was a bit shaken up by what happened to you so we went by the school on the way, part to make sure Luke and Nan knew you were safe in case they heard about the robbery but mostly to check on them. We both needed to know you were all safe."

Jesse nodded silently.

After a further few seconds of quiet, Peter said, "Is Louisa all right?"

He nodded again then shook his head, squeezing his eyes shut. "I don't know." When he opened his eyes again they stung with tears. "I think she's going to leave me."

His voice broke on the final word and Peter wrapped his arms around him as he dissolved into sobs.

It had been years since Jesse cried in front of his father. Not that he was embarrassed. Having been just the two of them for the first ten years of his life, they were as close as any parent and child could be. Peter held him silently as the emotions of the day, of the previous two weeks, drained from him in tears. Being strong when Jesse couldn't be.

When the sorrow had finally wrenched all it could from him, Jesse sat up and wiped at his eyes.

Peter dug in his pocket for a handkerchief and handed it to him. "Did Louisa tell you she's going to leave?"

"Not in so many words, but I know she is." He stared, unseeing, at the red patterned rug beneath his feet. "She couldn't even look at me when we got back to the Jones' house. I'm sure she blames me for what happened, and she's right."

"Why on earth would she blame you for a bank robbery?"

Releasing a deep sigh, Jesse hugged his arms around himself. "There's something I haven't told you."

"Why didn't you tell me about this before?" Peter said when Jesse had finished telling him the whole convoluted story of Ransom and the bank.

"I didn't want you to get involved. My job is my responsibility. I thought I could handle it. I thought it was just Ransom trying to scam extra money."

"So why did you tell Louisa?"

"She guessed something was wrong. I could have lied and told her it was all fine, but she'd have known." He looked at his father. "She knows me, Pa. I don't know how, but it's like she sees inside me. I never thought..." He shook his head, moisture burning at his eyes again. "That man had his hands on her. He threatened her. He held a gun to her head."

"Son..."

"She could have died and it would have been my fault. I got her into it. I accepted her help because I wanted to be with her and I liked it when she took risks to help me. I *liked* it. What kind of man does that?"

"Jesse..."

"She did it all for me and it almost got her killed. Why would she stay now? Why would she possibly want to stay with someone who put her at risk like that?" Leaning forward, he dropped his head into his hands, squeezing his eyes shut against the tears that threatened to fall again.

His father's hand rested on his shoulder. "Jesse, I don't know what's going to happen, although I'd guess if Louisa cares about you enough to do everything she did, it'll take more than what happened today to scare her away. But I can tell you this – if she does leave, you will get through it."

Jesse shook his head, wiping at his eyes. "I love her. How do you get over love?"

"I didn't say you'd get over her, I said you'd get through losing her. I do know what it's like to lose the woman you love."

Jesse raised his head to look at him.

"It took me a long time to recover from losing your mother, and there were times when the only thing keeping me going was that you needed me. But with God's help I got through it. And then I met Malinda and I learned that, even though I will always love your ma, it was possible for me to love another woman just as much." He wrapped his arm around Jesse's shoulders, tugged him closer, and kissed the side of his head. "Don't give up, Jess. God will give you all the happiness in the world. I have no doubt of that."

Jesse leaned his head against his father's shoulder. "How

can you be so sure?"

"Because I've been praying for it since the day you were born."

Chapter 27

Louisa woke with a start, the sound of a gunshot echoing in her ears.

It took her a few disoriented moments to realise where she was. Sitting up in her bed, she rubbed both hands across her face and groaned softly. She wasn't used to resting during the day.

Despite all the restless, late nights she'd had recently, sleep had only come in fits and starts, accompanied by barely recalled yet disturbing dreams. In more than one of them, Jesse had been shot. That scared her most of all.

Checking her watch, she was unsurprised to find it not yet noon. She rose and walked to the window, sinking into the chair there with a sigh.

She wished she'd asked Jesse to stay, but she'd been afraid to talk about any of what had happened. Afraid she'd burst into tears and never stop if she even looked at him.

He could have died in the bank today. Her chest twisted in pain at just the thought.

Releasing a long breath, she closed her eyes. "Father," she whispered, "I know You're here with me and I know You looked after Jesse and me at the bank. Thank You for keeping him safe. I don't know what I'd do if anything happened to him."

Her thoughts returned to lying on the floor in the bank, Jesse's arms around her secure as bullets punctured the walls and windows above them. For the first time, she didn't think of the terror she'd felt, she thought about the way Jesse had launched the attack on the man holding her hostage and then covered her with his own body, shielding her from harm the only way he could. He'd saved her life, she was sure of it.

"I want to stay with him, Lord. I love him so much. Just the thought of leaving him makes my heart feel like it's being crushed to nothing."

So stay.

She heard the words in her head in her voice, and yet she had the strangest notion they weren't her own.

"But... Mother and Father..."

They want you to be happy.

She watched a bumblebee buzz past the window and land on a penstemon, crawling into one purple trumpet.

"Jesse makes me happy."

Was it that simple? Could she really just stay?

There was no answer.

But then perhaps she already knew the answer. Perhaps she'd known it all along.

She leaped from the chair, pulled on her shoes, and checked her hair in the mirror. It was a mess, but she was in too much of a rush to do anything about it now. Raking her fingers through the worst of the tangles, she shrugged and turned away.

She paused for a moment with her hand on the doorknob and closed her eyes. "Thank You, Lord. I love You."

Then with a smile on her face, she carried on out the door.

Mrs Jones was in the kitchen preparing lunch and Louisa walked straight up to her and hugged her.

Mrs Jones stiffened in surprise before returning the embrace. "Well now, what's this for?" She drew back and held Louisa out by her shoulders, studying her face.

"I just wanted to thank you for everything you've done. You've been such a wonderful friend and so generous with your home and your time. You've truly helped me a lot. I'm so glad I've got to know you and Pastor Jones."

A small frown creased Mrs Jones' brow. "It was entirely my pleasure, but are you all right? You talk like you're leaving or something."

Louisa shook her head and smiled. "I've just made a decision. I know now what I'm going to do." She drew in a deep breath. "And now I have to go see Jesse."

Mrs Jones' frown deepened. "Are you sure you're all right? After what happened this morning, don't you need more time to recover? I can walk you to Jesse's house if you'd like."

She leaned forward to kiss Mrs Jones on the cheek. "Thank you for caring, but I'm fine to go by myself. It won't do me any good to start being afraid of walking along the street in broad daylight. It's not far anyway."

"But you seem... nervous."

Louisa gave a small laugh. "I am, but not because of the walk. Don't worry, I'm sure I'll be just fine." She turned and headed for the door.

"Will you be back for lunch?" Mrs Jones called after her.

"If everything goes as I hope it will, no."

The walk to Jesse's house seemed longer than usual yet at the same time far too short. Despite her assurances to Mrs Jones, Louisa found herself staying away from blind corners and peering down shaded alleys as she passed. She scolded herself for being so jumpy. The men who had robbed the bank were all in jail, as was Mr Ransom. She had nothing to fear. And yet there was a feeling in the pit of her stomach she couldn't shake. But maybe that was more to do with her intentions once she reached Jesse than anything else.

271

After a minute of walking she began to pray, not stopping until she reached Jesse's front yard. On a whim, she bypassed the front door and skirted around the outside of the house. As she'd suspected, Jesse was in the garden, sipping from a steaming cup as he watched a cloud of butterflies flitting around the purple flowers of a lilac bush. It felt as though those butterflies were passing through her stomach on their way to the nectar.

She paused for a moment to admire him. From the moment she'd first seen him she'd been captured by his good looks, but he was so much more than that. He was strong and determined, intelligent and funny, charming, thoughtful, caring. He never let anything hold him back. He had saved her life with no thought for his own. He was everything she'd never let herself dream she wanted.

It was time to break free of her parents' well-intentioned but misguided wishes and make her own decisions. And this decision was clear.

Her heart pounding, she left the cover of the house.

Jesse looked round at her approach and his face took on a smile that seemed to hold a hint of sadness. "How are you feeling?"

"I'm... I'm all right. Better than I was."

"Did you get any rest?"

"Not much. I kept dreaming you... I had bad dreams. I don't think sleep is what I need at the moment."

He looked down at the ground between them, his shoulders rising and falling in a deep sigh. "I think I know why you're here."

"You do?" Were her intentions that obvious?

He raised his eyes to hers. "After what happened today, I don't blame you. And it's not like you didn't warn me." He smiled a little. "More than once. I want you to know, although I wish with all my heart that things could be different, I understand. And I wouldn't have missed the past two weeks with you for the world."

Louisa suddenly realised what he was saying. He thought she'd come to tell him she wanted to return to New York. Her legs began to tremble and she considered sitting down, but instead she plunged into what she had to say while she could still stand upright.

"Do you love me?"

His eyes widened at the question. "Do I... are you asking if I'm in love with you?" When she nodded he placed the cup onto the table beside him and pushed his chair forward until he was close enough to take her hand. "Louisa, I thank God every minute of every day for bringing you into my life. You're the best thing that's ever happened to me. You're everything I could ever want. You are the most beautiful, wonderful, fun, smart, brave woman on this earth. Yes, I'm in love with you. I love you so much that sometimes I can barely breathe when you're near me."

It was all she needed to hear. Breathing out, she sank to her knees beside him, not caring at all that she would likely get dirty, and took both his hands in hers. "Then will you marry me?"

His mouth dropped open. "I thought you..." His eyes flicked between hers and she watched his astonishment turn to wonder and then happiness. "Isn't that my line?"

She smiled. "Is that a yes?"

Eyes sparkling, he pressed his lips together and looked up at the sky. "Hmm, I may have to think about it."

Gasping in mock outrage, she rose to her feet and turned as if to go. "Well, if that's your answer..."

He grabbed her waist, just as she knew he would, and pulled her, laughing, into his lap.

His beautiful green eyes gazing into hers, he whispered with a smile, "Yes. Yes yes yes. With every part of me, yes."

His expression sobered. "But what if your parents say no?"

She lowered her eyes to his chest. "They already did. Their letter arrived yesterday morning."

"And... you still asked me to marry you?"

She raised her eyes to his again and brushed her fingers down his cheek. "They don't know you. They don't know what an amazing, wonderful, strong, courageous, incredible man you are. And they also don't know how completely and utterly and absolutely I am in love with you. If they did, I think they'd understand why I want more than anything in the world to be your wife."

She wasn't entirely sure about that, but it didn't matter. She was a grown woman who could make her own choices. And for the rest of her life, she would choose Jesse.

His mouth was hanging open. "Could you repeat the part about being in love with me?"

Instead of saying the words, she slid her fingers into his silky hair, pulled him to her, and kissed him with the force of all the love in her full heart.

What did it matter that the town was small or that Jesse couldn't walk or that she wouldn't be the social butterfly her mother wanted her to be? God had given her everything she could possibly want, and that was more important than anything.

When their lips parted a very long, blissful time later, Jesse kissed the tip of her nose. "How about today?"

"How about today what?" she murmured, contemplating the beautiful golden flecks in his eyes. She wondered if, fifty years from now, she'd be tired of gazing into those remarkable eyes. She decided she wouldn't.

They crinkled in a smile. "How about today we get married?"

They were just the perfect shade of green and... "Wait, what did you say?"

"Let's get married today. I don't want to spend another day without you as my wife." His smile widened. "Or night." He waggled his eyebrows.

She ignored the tingly feeling that blossomed in her stomach. "We can't get married today, there's too much to do! There's the dress and flowers and inviting the guests and arranging the church and food and..."

She stopped abruptly when he placed one finger onto her lips.

"Do you love me?" he said.

"With all my heart," she replied around his finger.

He lowered his hand. "And do you want to marry me?"

"Yes."

"And is there any reason, other than all those easily taken care of things you just listed, why you don't want to marry me as soon as humanly possible, meaning today?"

She pressed her lips together to stop her smile and looked out over the garden, pretending to consider it. The truth was, when she really thought about it she knew she would marry him that second if Pastor Jones had been there.

Except all those things mattered. They were what was done. You couldn't ignore them and just get married.

Could you?

Letting go of the final repressive piece of her upbringing, she let the smile through. "No, there isn't any real reason why we can't get married today. If Pastor Jones is free."

He kissed her again and, smiling against her lips, said, "Then let's go find out if the pastor's free."

Chapter 28

As it happened, getting married right away turned out to be more difficult than either of them had anticipated.

Pastor Jones was out visiting far flung members of the congregation and didn't return until late, and what with everything that happened to Louisa and Jesse's friends the next day and over the weekend, it was the following Wednesday before they were able to finally get everyone to the church.

Jesse endured the delay with good natured exasperation, but Louisa knew he would never have got married without Adam at his side. The two of them were about as close as two friends could be. And Louisa didn't want Amy or Lizzy to miss the occasion either.

The extra few days also gave Jesse time to help sort out the mess Rotherford Ransom had left. Mr Vernon made a start on the enormous task of meeting with each customer who'd taken out a loan from the bank to find out the exact details of what had happened. He'd had no choice, Jesse told Louisa. Word was getting round. Jesse said he'd be going through old ledgers for weeks to check if Mr Ransom had done anything else in the seventeen years he'd worked at the bank.

Mr Ransom himself wasn't talking, and the day after the robbery he and the gang were fetched by the federal marshals to be taken to the prison in Sacramento for trial. Lem's body was buried in a corner of the town's cemetery with little ceremony and marked with a simple wooden cross.

Louisa had wondered if maybe the delay would weaken her resolve to marry Jesse against her parents' wishes, but to her delight every day that passed made her want to marry him more, her love growing stronger with each moment they spent together. He was going to be her life from now on and she had not one single doubt it was exactly what she wanted. She'd had it all wrong before. Now she knew the only thing that truly mattered was love, and she had enough of that to last her a lifetime. A lifetime she would spend blissfully in Jesse's strong arms.

On the Saturday morning she wrote to her parents. Despite her unshakable resolve, it still took her several attempts to produce a letter she was happy with. Or if not happy, at least something she didn't want to tear into pieces.

Dearest Mother and Father,

I hope you both are well, and Jemima and Isabella too. How is the weather there in the east? It seems to be constantly sunny here, with only sporadic cloudy days, although Jesse assures me there will be rain in the fall and winter.

I received your letter. Thank you for your advice and thoughts on the matter of me staying to marry Jesse. I understand your reasoning and I know you only want what is best for me, but the truth is, I've come to realise in the two weeks since I arrived that what's best for me isn't what I thought it was. I thought having the life you want for me, marriage to a man who could improve my social prospects, was what I needed, but it isn't.

These past two weeks I have been happier than I ever remember being. That isn't to say I was unhappy with you. You gave me a good life and I'm thankful for all you've done for me, and for all your sacrifices. But here, with Jesse, I've found true contentment, something I never had before. I've come to understand that God doesn't look on outward appearances and He doesn't care about status.

Jesse is a good, wonderful man. He's kind and strong and capable and loving and generous and everything I could want. He truly loves me, and I love him too, with all my heart. I never even knew it was possible to feel this way. God has blessed me so much.

I know you will be unhappy about my decision to stay and marry Jesse, but please know that I am very, very happy. This is what I want and I hope you can be happy for me.

Give Jem and Belle my love.

All my love to both of you,

Louisa

She prayed that they would understand her decision. It wouldn't change her mind if they didn't, but she wanted their approval. Despite everything, she loved them. They'd raised her the best way they knew how.

When it finally came to the evening before the wedding, Louisa and Jesse were sitting in his back yard. He'd moved onto the bench so they could cuddle together while watching the sky change colour as the sun touched the horizon.

"You know, tonight will be the last time I have to say goodbye to you when the sun goes down," Jesse said, his voice low and soft against her forehead in the hush of the evening.

"I know." She'd been thinking about it all day.

"Are you all right about that?"

A smile tugged at her lips. "Very all right."

"Then can we agree I won our wager?"

She tried to think what he was talking about. "What wager?"

"The day after you arrived, remember? We were sitting at the table and I bet you that in two weeks I'd be seeing the real you. I'm pretty sure I am."

278

"You are." And she was more than grateful for it. "But we didn't agree on what you'd get if you won."

He pressed a soft kiss to her forehead. "You. My prize is you. I don't want anything else."

Chapter 29

"You look so pretty!"

Louisa smiled at her soon to be sister-in-law where she sat on her bed. Rather, her former bed since she'd no longer be using it after today. "Do you like the dress? My friends and I made it together."

Mr Lamb hadn't had any suitable white fabric in his general store so Louisa had opted for pale blue instead from which she, Jo, Amy, Sara and Lizzy had created a simple, fitted gown accented with cream coloured lace and a matching ribbon tied at the waist. She loved it, not just because of how it looked, but because so much love and laughter had gone into its making.

"It's beautiful." Nancy jumped from the bed and walked up to her. She touched her fingers to the lace edging the square neckline almost reverently. "Ma, don't you think it's the most beautiful dress you've ever seen?"

"I think Louisa is the most beautiful bride I've ever seen," Malinda said. "And I couldn't be happier that she's about to become my daughter-in-law."

Louisa fanned her face with her hand, blinking back sudden tears. "Stop or I'm going to cry and have to get married with red, puffy eyes."

"Could I try the dress on sometime?" Nancy said, fingering the ribbon. "I promise I'll be careful with it."

Louisa walked over to the wardrobe. "I think I can do

better than that." She reached in and withdrew a similar dress, this one in peach and sized for a ten-year-old girl. "Because we made you one too."

Nancy's eyes opened wide. "For me?"

Louisa handed it to her. "Just for you."

Nancy held the dress against herself and looked down at it. "It's the prettiest thing I've ever seen." Her eyes shimmering with tears, she threw herself into Louisa's arms. "Thank you. You're the best sister-in-law in the whole world."

Louisa looked at Malinda to see her smiling and wiping at her eyes. She mouthed *Thank you* and Louisa smiled back, her own eyes burning. Having been raised to be pragmatic in everything, she certainly was turning out to be an emotional soul. Not that that was a bad thing.

"Can I try it on now, Ma?" Nancy said, bouncing from Louisa's embrace and twirling round with the dress held against her.

"As long as you're careful if you eat before the service," Malinda replied. "You don't want to get anything on it."

Nancy squealed and rushed to the bed, laying the dress out carefully before starting to undress.

Malinda walked over to Louisa. "How about your hair? Do you need any help with it?"

She turned to look in the mirror and imagined Jesse's reaction when he saw her. "I think I'll leave it down."

~ ~ ~

She was surrounded by friends and loved ones and she adored them all, but the moment Louisa walked into the church her gaze was only for Jesse.

Sitting in his wheelchair on the platform at the front of the church with Pastor Jones, his eyes widened when she

281

stepped through the door and didn't leave her for the entire walk along the aisle to join him. As she stepped up beside him, his gaze went to her hair and he gave her the smile that sparkled in his eyes. She had the sudden urge to laugh. She'd known he would like it.

He took her hand and they faced the pastor together.

"Friends," Pastor Jones began, "we're gathered here to celebrate the joining in marriage of two very special people who my wife and I couldn't be happier have chosen to spend their lives together. Watching their love for each other blossom and grow over the past weeks has been a joy and a privilege I know many of you have shared. And had a hand in." He winked at Nancy and she giggled.

The ceremony was perfect and would only have been better if her parents had been there to share her joy. But she was certain they would be happy for her if they could see her now, the assurance so strong she knew it was from God.

She said her vows with conviction, meaning every word, and she could see it was the same for Jesse. There were no more doubts. She was exactly where she wanted to be. Where she was meant to be.

"I now pronounce you man and wife," Pastor Jones finally said.

Adam and Peter immediately rose from their seats and stepped up onto the platform. Standing to either side of Jesse they slid their arms beneath his, and Louisa gasped as they pulled him to his feet in front of her and held him upright.

She gazed up at him. And up.

All she could think to say was, "You're so tall."

"Told you I was," he whispered with a smile.

"Jesse," Pastor Jones said, "you may kiss your bride."

Stepping closer, she placed her hands on his chest and pushed up onto her toes, he tilted his head down, and their lips met in a soft kiss, sealing their promises to each other.

When Peter and Adam had lowered Jesse back into his chair, Pastor Jones began, "Ladies and gentlemen..."

Jesse raised his hand, his eyes fixed on Louisa. "Just a moment there, Pastor. We're not quite done."

Only realising his intentions at the last second, she squeaked in surprise when he grasped her waist and pulled her into his lap.

Then he pushed his fingers into her hair and kissed her.

It was a kiss filled with adoration.

A kiss that promised a lifetime of love and laughter and joy.

A kiss that flooded her with warmth and left her gasping for breath.

Right there in front of everyone.

And Louisa didn't mind one single bit.

~ ~ ~

Following a celebration held in the Jones' garden filled with music and dancing and delicious food, Louisa and Jesse returned to his home.

Their home, he reminded himself. He'd never be alone here again.

He led the way into the bedroom and swept his hand to encompass the array of travel trunks his father and brother had moved while the rest of them enjoyed the festivities.

"My pa and Luke brought them over. I want you to know this is your home now and you can do whatever you want in it, including putting anything you've brought with you wherever you'd like." He wheeled over to the closest trunk. "Would you like some help unpacking? I don't know if we'll have space for everything, but if we don't I can get some more furniture. Anything you want. What do you have in all these anyway?"

Louisa walked over to stand beside him and he looked up at her. She was stunning with her hair cascading loose and free over her shoulders and down her back. He'd barely been able to take his eyes from her since she had stepped into the church. Other men may have had full use of their legs but only he had Louisa, and that made him the most blessed man in the world.

"They were so kind to bring them all here," she said, looking uncertain. "If I'd known they were going to, I would have said something first."

"Said something about what?"

She unfastened the trunk and opened the lid to reveal a scrunched up hessian sack. She pulled it out and he leaned forward to see inside.

"Bricks?" Jesse stared at the blocks fixed to the bottom of the trunk. "Um..."

"Mother said I should appear as though I had lots of possessions and we were wealthy, even though we weren't. To make a good impression. The bricks are to make them heavy, like there's something inside."

He looked over the pile of trunks. "So how many of these have your actual clothes and such in them?"

She drew her lower lip between her teeth. "Three."

He glanced at her then back at the eight trunks. "*Three*?"

"I feel so guilty that Peter moved them all," she counted on her fingers, "four times."

He stared at the trunks for a couple more seconds. Then he burst into laughter.

"Why are you laughing?" she said, giggling.

"Just, the idea of Pa carrying a load of bricks back and forth. I shouldn't laugh, I know, but it is funny. I can't wait to tell him."

Her smile vanished. "Oh no, please don't do that."

He sighed in mock resignation. "All right, although I

promise he'd think it was funny too. Can I at least tell Malinda? She'd probably laugh for a full day."

She swatted his shoulder playfully. "You're terrible."

He caught hold of her hand and pressed a slow kiss to the back, his heartbeat speeding up at the feel of her soft skin against his lips. "So would you like help with unpacking your bricks? Or could we put it off until tomorrow?"

He waggled his eyebrows and the most adorable blush grew on her cheeks, making him want to do so many things other than unpacking the trunks.

She looked at her luggage, a small smile on her lips. "I think I can do without my bricks for now."

He didn't need any more encouragement. Grasping her waist, he pulled her into his lap and gazed into her beautiful blue eyes. "I love you so much."

She wrapped her arms around his neck. "I love you more."

"Not possible," he murmured as his lips touched hers.

She melted into his kiss in the way that made him want to never let her go and, their lips firmly joined and her fingers tangling in his hair, he wheeled them away from the trunks and towards the bed.

Chapter 30

"Don't let go."

"I won't."

"You're letting go!"

"I'm not letting go." Jesse rubbed his hand against Louisa's back beneath the water. "See? My hand's right here."

She nodded a little, just a tiny movement of her head as if she was afraid anything more would send her sinking into the depths.

"It would work better if you relaxed," he suggested.

"All right."

He waited for her to relax. She didn't in the slightest. "You know, I can think of a good way to get you to relax."

Her lips pressed together, her eyes fixed on the trees overhead crinkling at the corners as she tried not to giggle.

He moved closer so that his bare chest brushed against her hand floating on the surface of the water. "No one ever comes here apart from us. If you'd just get rid of this ridiculous bathing suit..."

She burst into laughter, curling in on herself then squeaking when she began to sink.

He grasped her waist and held her up until her feet were firmly on the bottom of the lake.

She flicked a splash into his chest. "How am I supposed to learn to swim if you're not concentrating?"

He drifted closer, looping one arm around her waist and

pulling her against him. "We have plenty of time."

Eyes dropping to her lips, he tilted his head and leaned in... and found himself kissing the palm of her hand when she inserted it between them.

"Focus," she ordered, stepping back. "I want to learn to swim. I can't even float by myself yet."

He grabbed her hand and kissed it, while he had the chance. "You can float by yourself, you just don't have the confidence to do it."

She heaved a sigh, a movement that caused her body to move at the surface of the water in the most enticing way. He dragged his eyes back to her face. She was right, it wasn't helping her at all when he was so distracted. But it was nigh on impossible to not get distracted by the most beautiful, wonderful, incredible woman on the face of the earth. Especially now she was all his.

He leaned forward to kiss her forehead then looked into her eyes. "You can do this. You can do anything."

A smile touched her lips. "I know."

He laughed and kissed her again. Her newfound self-belief, buoyed by the letter she'd received that morning from her parents telling her they approved of their marriage, filled him with pride. He would have loved her even more for it, but he was pretty sure that wasn't possible. He already loved her so much he often thought he must be glowing.

"You know, you'd be lighter if you were wearing less," he said, running his hand down her side over the bathing suit she'd insisted on buying.

He hated the ugly thing. She might as well have been wearing a dress in the water, a hideous black dress with even more hideous voluminous pantaloons beneath, gathered at the ankles. Even the dress she'd been wearing the first time they kissed, in this very spot, would have been better. Whenever he went swimming, he simply stripped off and

287

plunged in. He was determined to one day convince her to do the same.

She splashed him a second time. "Stop it."

"All right, let's try it again," he said. "And this time, try to remember three things. One, the lake is only four feet deep here. Two, you are lighter than the water. Three, I won't let anything happen to you."

She nodded, took a deep breath, and slowly lay back in the water.

He kept one hand beneath her back supporting her while he steadied himself with the other on the rock beside him. "Can you feel how the water is holding you up?"

"I don't know."

"Concentrate on your arms, how they're floating. I'm not holding them up, the water is. Feel it?"

She was silent for a few moments. "I think so. Yes, I do."

"Okay, now your legs. Feel the way the water keeps them on the surface. How you'd actually have to push them down if you wanted them to go under."

To his surprise, she moved one of her legs down a little then let it spring back up.

A tiny smile blossomed on her face. "I did! I had to force it down."

"That's real good. Now feel your body, how the water is pushing up beneath you, keeping you on the surface." As he spoke, he gradually lowered his hand, moving it away from her back. "It doesn't want to let you sink. Your natural state is to stay on the surface. Can you feel it?"

"I... I think I can."

He waited for ten seconds then lifted his hand from the water and held it up, waggling his fingers. "Louisa?"

Her eyes swivelled towards him, widening when she saw his hand. "Am I floating? By myself?"

"You sure are."

Her smile grew. "I'm floating. I'm floating!" She lowered her feet and threw her arms around his neck, laughing. "I did it!"

He hugged her to him, laughing with her. "I'm so proud of you."

She moved back. "Now teach me to swim."

He contrived to look hurt. "What, I don't even get a kiss for helping you to float?"

Smiling, she drifted back to him, wrapped her arms around his waist, and gave him a kiss that left him panting for air and barely able to remember his own name.

"I love you," she whispered, resting her forehead against his.

"I love you too." He'd never imagined such all-consuming, overwhelming love was possible. Until Louisa became his wife.

She gave him another brief kiss then stepped back. "Now teach me how to swim."

He laughed and pushed away from the rock wall. "Anything you want, Mrs Johnson. For the rest of our lives, anything you want."

THE END

Dear Reader

Thank you for reading An Unexpected Groom and I hope you've enjoyed Louisa and Jesse's story. If you have a moment, please consider leaving a review on Amazon, even just a few words. Reviews are very important for independent authors like me and they really do help others find my books. I will be extremely grateful when you do!

A reminder, all spellings in my books are British English and are provided free of charge for your enjoyment and delight, and because I honestly can't spell any other way! If you'd like to contact me about anything, please do get in touch via my Facebook page or website or at nerys@nerysleigh.com. I love hearing from readers. You can also sign up there for my newsletter and never miss a new release.

Jesse suffers from Little's Disease, which was the name at the time for what is now known as spastic diplegia, or diplegic cerebral palsy. This is a condition with a multitude of causes including a difficult birth, as in Jesse's case, and is characterised by chronically tense muscles and spasms, particularly in the legs. It affects everyone who has it differently and many can walk with it, even though Jesse can't. During my research for this book I was shocked by the accounts of how appallingly those with both physical and mental disabilities were treated historically, but even worse is the fact that this inhuman treatment still goes on today. Please join with me in praying that such cruelty and prejudice comes to an end and that those like Jesse are seen as the valuable, worthwhile members of society they are.

Thank you for your support in reading my books and I

hope you are enjoying them so far. Next up is Jo who has a rocky road ahead of her. And a devoted man to help!

nerysleigh.com
facebook.com/nerysleigh

Bible Verses

The following are the verses quoted, or referred to, in An Unexpected Groom, this time from the New International Version (NIV) translation.

Chapter 3 – Honour your father and mother, so that you may live long in the land the Lord your God is giving you. Exodus 20:12

Chapter 7 - I keep asking that the God of our Lord Jesus Christ, the glorious Father, may give you the Spirit of wisdom and revelation, so that you may know Him better. I pray that the eyes of your heart may be enlightened in order that you may know the hope to which He has called you, the riches of His glorious inheritance in His holy people, and His incomparably great power for us who believe. Ephesians 1:17-18

Chapter 10 - And I pray that you, being rooted and established in love, may have power, together with all the Lord's holy people, to grasp how wide and long and high and deep is the love of Christ, and to know this love that surpasses knowledge—that you may be filled to the measure of all the fullness of God. Ephesians 3:17-19

Chapter 14 - 'And why do you worry about clothes? See how the flowers of the field grow. They do not labour or spin. Yet I tell you that not even Solomon in all his splendour was dressed like one of these.' Matthew 6:28-29

Chapter 23 - Keep your lives free from the love of money and be content with what you have, because God has said, 'Never will I leave you; never will I forsake you.' So we say with confidence, 'The Lord is my helper; I will not be afraid. What can mere mortals do to me?' Hebrews 13:5-6, a quote from Deuteronomy 31:6 which says, Be strong and courageous. Do not be afraid or terrified because of them, for the LORD your God goes with you; He will never leave you nor forsake you.

Made in the USA
San Bernardino, CA
08 October 2017